The Lonely Poet
And
Other Stories

Books
by
Branka Čubrilo

The Mosaic of the Broken Soul
Fiume – The Lost River
Dethroned

The Lonely Poet
And
Other Stories

Branka Čubrilo

SPEAKING VOLUMES, LLC
NAPLES, FLORIDA
2016

The Lonely Poet And Other Stories

Edited by Irina Dimitric (University of Zagreb B.A. English and French, Dip.Ed Sydney Teachers College) and Althea Kuzman (University of Technology Sydney)

ISBN 978-1-62815-352-1

Prologue

The collection has two parts. Part One, Scattered Vignettes from Otto's Life, was written during my stay in Cadiz, Andalucia, in 2002. Some of those stories were published in various literary publications in print and online. Otto is a lonely poet, a sad figure with a bitter-sweet outlook on life, who knocked at the door of my, almost equally lonely, room blown by levante, one windy and mysterious evening. I was keen to listen to his narrations and eager to introduce him to the world.

Part Two presents stories that were written more recently, and just as Otto's stories, some were published in literary journals whilst others have never been shown, except to my daughter Althea and my friend Irina who are always my first audience, critics and editors.

I pick my characters mainly from my own experiences but hide them skillfully without the need to glorify or displease in any way. But, I wouldn't recommend anyone to flatter themselves, for it might, or it might not, be them as we humans are alike and share similar experiences, emotions and habits.

The last two stories were written with a broken heart as a tribute to my own family when my dearest father, Milan Cubrilo, a very proper and kind gentleman, quietly left this world on 26 November 2014.

Branka Čubrilo

Part One

Scattered Vignettes
from
Otto's Life

Otto the Poet

It's morning. Nothing special about it. Just one of those mornings when I wake up tired, yet I can't sleep any longer. Some thoughts keep on haunting me. The tree under my window is still snoozing, I can see by its leaves that are lazily and listlessly swaying in the wind. What should I do today? Go to the office? Or write a poem? Go to the office? No, no, I can't stand seeing those faces any more. Dull, deadpan, chairborne. Not a spark of desire left in their eyes, not a single dream, nothing, simply nothing at all. Those boring conversations, the drinking of morning coffee and stringing out of those droning dreams that they, supposedly, dreamt. No, no, I won't take it any more. I'll hand in my notice today, and as for the rent, I'll cope with it somehow. But, what will Vivienne say? Miss Vivienne. What will she say? She might even fail to observe that the *muddle-head* is no longer present. I'm sure she calls me *'Muddle-head'*. Because I am indeed muddle-headed in her company. A real fool! Why?

I won't write a poem (dedicated to Miss Vivienne again, which she of course wouldn't read anyway), nor will I go to the office today (on second thought, I won't quit the job, I'll just call to tell them I'm sick, which I am, very sick: sleepless nights, nightmares and nebulousness), but I could write a story. There's a story I've been wanting to tell. I heard it from one of my father's relatives, back when I still communicated and mingled with relatives, and only later I saw how twisted and greedy, petty and spiteful they were, and so I broke away from them; yes, I really apostatised myself and from then on they have been calling me weird, peevish, a hermit and what not; but that pleased me, and tickled me pink. Let them call me names, as long as I don't have relations with them, and don't have to have any, since I no longer belong. I didn't want to belong. Especially not to my relatives, and least of all to the relatives of my ex-wife. What a bunch of oddballs they were, not to say chumps, not to say pests and what not! But, come what may, I decided to break the chains and get the hell out of that jail. Indeed a jail, a dungeon, a prison. Fortunately, the confinement did not last long, only several months, not even a year, when I said, *"Ta-ta, I'm leaving."* I plainly didn't fit in. My mother used to say, *"Otto, you are a monster! Who would cope with you?"* Nobody! And it's best that way. I don't feel like doing time any more, no, not me, especially not in any institutions. Would you believe it- matrimony! How would I be able to function, actually how did I manage to endure even those several months, and then her mother came, the mother of my ex-wife, to put us in line. First to command her, then me... so okay, for wanting to have power over her, after all, she's her mother and anyway her daughter is of weak character, I mean, too weak to resist, to stand firm, to say anything... at least a word, but no! The mother wanted to order me around, too. As if we were in the army, she'd come up to us like some commissar, commander-in-chief, general, whatever. I couldn't bear it, that raising of the voice, those orders, especially coming from a woman; and not some old woman deluded by age. But deluded nevertheless, because growing old did not bring her wisdom, the calm modesty that comes with the aging of honourable folks. Age simply distorted her. Turned her into a shrew. She was mad at life, at growing old, and that it should, of all people, happen to her! Oh no, no, not with me, thank you, I was there, tried it, and left, walked away. That's not for me.

But I seem to have lost track of my story. I didn't want to talk about that woman-general. That's water under the bridge, and I've completely forgotten it. Yes, completely. Erased it, in fact.

As I said earlier, there's a story that one of my relatives told me. I'll tell it to you, not with the aim of entertaining you or spellbinding you with it, but merely because of an inner need, because the story upsets my system. Like a thorn stuck somewhere in the vicinity of my heart, or lower, so that every time I recall parts of that story I feel a blunt pain, sometimes a stinging prick; sometimes even the shortest sentence from his story can put me into a complete state of chaos. That's why I have to tell it, and maybe that's

4

how I'll get it out of my system, that thorn, with which my malevolent relative pierced me (actually whom I no longer call a relative, since I've renounced them completely, and therefore I allow myself the liberty to say - *'The story that The Malevolent man told me'*).

But before I begin The Malevolent man's story I'd better go wash my face. Stand by the window and inhale the fresh air. In essence, so many things drive me crazy. I said, fresh air. The air is polluted; this city is too big, voracious and full of exhaust gases, factory smokestacks, stench and poor people. Actually, I loathe this city; it has no soul for a poet. But I unquestionably must wash my face, make myself a coffee and light a cigarette. I'm addicted! How many times have I decided to stop smoking! How much effort I've put into it, and willpower! I have an iron will, but that damn cigarette, every time I give in and light a cigarette my enemy wins. In point of fact, it's an evil, worldwide evil, and what should be done? All cigarette factories should be shut down! Send them to court. How many lives have they ruined! Polluted. Take me: I get up in the morning still dizzy from last night's smoking. Countless cigarettes. And how costly they are; it's as if I'm working just to pay my rent and cigarettes. That's a shame! What a standard of living! And was *that* what was in store for me! A destiny of *that* kind! The fate of the miserable! Look down there at that parvenu, two houses away from here, in his shiny suit, white shirt, tie, shoes gleaming as if he had been shining them all night; and you should see that face of his, shaved smooth as a baby's bottom, one wonders how he manages not to cut himself, and then that hair, slicked down with some kind of gel, and perhaps he sprinkles it with *eau de Cologne* because the whole street smells after him. Then he sits down in - a *Mercedes*. And for me? It's public transport. You think he's better than I am? In what respect is he better? If you could only see the look on his face. That satisfied look; but when he gazes at the bus stop crowded with people, his face manifests disgust. Ah, how some people deserve to have … ah, it's better I skip that subject and instead get back to the story I wanted to tell; as I said, when I inhale this polluted air, overused by people and automobiles, and when I make coffee and light a cigarette, right, then I'll begin to tell the story. But there's one more thing to do first. I ought to phone the office to tell them that I'm sick. I detest the voice of Mister Big Boss. What a fusspot! What a cynic! Every time I call to say I'm sick, and that I can't come, he replies:

"You're sick? Yet again?"

Yet again? Yes, again! I'm sick, what can I do, my health is frail, I'm of a gentle constitution and my nervous system is hypersensitive. What does that lumberjack expect? A healthy peasant child? That's not me. He calls me *'Poet'*. I won't forget that. Never. I published a collection of poems; just imagine what success! It isn't like anyone can publish a collection of poems, but he, with that cynical twisted smile on his lips, says *"So…Mister Poet,"* and I turned my head, in fact I looked down at his shoes and not into his eyes. He has that agent provocateur stare, and I'm in no need of the likes of him. I only mingle with sophisticated persons, or am at least on the lookout for them. Even if, I may say, life has not endowed me with a lot of them; as I said earlier, my first wife and her relatives were totally low-level folks. They had no desire to do anything that was above average. And there I was, creating poetry that was well above average; believe me, well above average! My poem collection did not sell, that's true. Who knows the reason why, but the newspaper published a very nice appraisal of my book. I had the article framed and hung it on my wall above my desk. I almost knew where every comma was by heart. But, it just didn't sell. Do people even know what poetry really is? And who reads poetry today? Everything is just a continual scramble to make money, and money is a measure of success. Bah, I don't want to belong to such a world! It's disgusting! I must hurry and call the office, beat him to it. He will not have arrived there yet, and so I'll leave him a message. I can't stand his voice, especially not on the telephone.

"Aurora, is that you? Yes, it's me Otto. Listen, tell the boss that I'm ill. Oh, he's there? Well yes, okay, put him on."

I'm waiting for him to answer the phone. I thought he wasn't in yet.
But that guy is always first. Just to see when the rest of us will arrive. Like,
he came earlier; he's got a lot of work. The hell he has; it's just snooping,
controlling, looking over one's shoulder, criticising, smiling cynically ...

"Good morning mister Boss. No, I'm not. I am not well, as a matter of fact ...
I'm sick. What do you mean- yet again? But I wasn't sick for a long time. What's
wrong with me? It seems I have an inflammation of a sinus. Yes. What did you say?
You didn't know that I also suffer from sinusitis? Well, uh, yes. Actually, no! So far
I've never had any sinus trouble. But now, this morning I woke up, you see, and my
nose is completely clogged, my head is aching, actually, I'm having a dizzy spell, my
knees are buckling when I get up, I have to go to the doctor's right away. Truly, I found
it hard to call you, to tell you that I can't come, but I'm really feeling very bad ... I hope
you understand? Understand? Hello, hello, can you hear me sir, hello ... hello. Oh, you
do hear me; I thought we were cut off. So, you say you were listening, and I had the
feeling we were cut off, but anyway, as I said, today I'll go to the doctor, and hope to be
in the office tomorrow. Yes, yes, I'll get well in a day, I hope so, in fact I have to, I can't
be absent, I don't like being absent; you know that I'm a hard working employee. Ha,
ha, and a good poet you say! Well thank you, if you really think so. Good, good, I'll
call you. Thank you, thank you very much, so long ..."

The pig. The repulsive, cynical pig! He thinks I'm lying. I know he
thinks I'm lying. He says *'yet again'*, and I haven't been sick for a long time
now. I can't recall the last time I phoned to say I could not come to work.
I've been in the same job for ten years already, I've used all the vacations
that I'm entitled to regularly; I'm not going to yield them to him, and as
for sick-leave during the ten years, not even ten times, which means that
I've been on the disabled list once a year. And people do get ill, at least
catch a cold, have the sniffles, catch a virus. He says *'yet again?'* What about
him? Untouchable! Untouchable by disease as well. Never took a vacation,
never on sick-leave, never a free day, never a free minute, no other interests, no hobby; and he is to tell me that I'm ... a good poet, he says to *me*
—'*... and a good poet'*. And what is he? What is he talented for except to

snoop over the shoulders of his employees? Especially women-employees! You ought to see how he looks at a person full in the face, how he grins at the ladies, how the tone of his voice changes when he speaks to Miss Vivienne. He chews the fat, prattles, tells some stupid jokes at which she laughs only because he is the person telling them, because he is her boss, because she wants to carry favour with him. But she really doesn't find him funny, neither him nor his jokes, and I think she finds him disgusting, like most of us do.

But no matter. Now I got a free day. But I'll really have to see the doctor. He'll ask me about what my doctor said. And you ought to see what a character my doctor is! He's another oddball who chose the wrong profession. He is not at all interested in people or their health. He is interested in soccer; he should have been a coach, or a soccer player, and then he wouldn't have needed to go to school. This way, he lost a lot of time studying medicine to no purpose, because he isn't a good doctor, and medicine does not interest him at all, and as I rightly said before - he chose the wrong profession. I go to him and he says:

"Oh, it's you again, Mister Otto."

What's that *'you again'* supposed to mean? I'd like to ask him, although I don't. Why ask, anyhow, when he will insist on doing things his own way. I'll have to change doctors; there probably are better ones than this bloke. I told the other one at the office that it was sinuses; should I say the same to this doctor? But regardless, no matter how disinterested he is, he'll see that the sinuses are in order. I could say that I have a headache; that's what I'll say, and when he scribbles something I'll go back home and spend the day writing. The thoughts, the contemplations … it's not easy to repeatedly turn over all those ideas in one's head, arranging them, understanding them and disclosing their deeper meanings, turning them into the symbolism of pictures that transpire in the skull. If I leave for the doctor's earlier, a good part of the day will remain to let me sit down and dedicate myself to writing. I'll write a poem …

But forget it! I said I'd narrate the story that I got from that so-called relative of mine. I'll start that story today. Today is a new day, the best for beginning such a story; in fact I've been waiting for Monday to begin it; that's the best day for all beginnings. But I really hate to think of the underground, full of bums to boot; full of busy and tense people, running, rushing, all of them in the race for money, more and more money, the most gluttonous and greedy people, without dignity; nobody walks slowly, in measured movements like a real gentleman; it's all rushing, pushing and cursing. The train is packed with viruses: people sniffling, sneezing, shoving newspapers into your face, stepping on each other's toes without apologising, yawning; some of them don't even cover their mouths; one sees their decayed teeth, larynxes, the white layers on the surface of their tongues, phooey! Still, I have to go, I have to see the doctor today or otherwise the Fat Pig won't believe me. He doesn't believe anybody, probably because he himself never speaks the truth. He says, *'Yet again'* to me, and *'It's you again?'* When do I ever call him? Not even in the office when I need him. I solve everything myself, whether its good or not; let him check, because I'm not going to call him for help or advice! He pretends as if he knows everything anyway! And he doesn't have more school than I do. *L-e-s-s!* That's right, mister Fat Pig, you have *less* school than I do. I wonder who's standing behind him? Somebody must be, because he has less school than I do, and I haven't had a promotion in ten years; always in the same job from the first day.

Bugger! It looks like rain. Damn, I never get a lucky break! Now that I've decided to go to the doctor's, it will rain, meaning I'll have to ride three stops in the underground railway and I'll have to be carrying an umbrella. There couldn't be a worse combination. I don't have enough money to take a taxi and the local bus does not run frequently. Nor regularly, I must say! I've quarrelled with the bus drivers so many times! The timetable at the bus stop lists the time of arrival, yet they sometimes come with up to ten minutes delay- and who cares? Wait! It's written all over their faces.

Wait! Who's to blame that you have to ride the city bus? The number of times I asked, *"Who do you think we are, monkeys?"* Everybody is silent, everyone is afraid to utter a word; but I have to protect our rights, the rights of us citizens, people, people who are waiting. They all calmly stand there; they are late, but not a word! That's when I opted for the underground railway. It stinks and is always crowded, a permanent stampede; but trains are not late. Choose the lesser evil of the two that are almost equal. That's why I travel on trains, inhaling their heavy and foul-smelling air, the sweat of overweight women overloaded with shopping bags, cheap men's lotions; I don't want to be a part of all that, I don't … but … often I simply can't grasp what my reality is, or to put it more fatally, my destiny. Why all this rush on underground trains, these crowds, the unbearable boss, the shallow and irresponsible doctor, the dim-witted relatives, the unreliable and insincere friends, the ridiculously low salary in spite of my university degree … why is all that befalling *me?* Well, it's good that I'm sick today; to have a break from all that; to sit down in front of my typewriter and start that story that has been eating away at my insides, completely upsetting my system like some perilous foreign body that threatens to destroy it.

Not a trace of satisfaction. Trivial, everything so trivial! I got stuck in a marriage that I actually didn't want. I comprehended that right after the wedding, but by then it was too late to do anything about it, at least not right away. Frankly speaking, I pondered that things might yet change; she might begin to see things differently, to realise what her mother is like and become aware that her mother was poisoning our relationship … but no, not her, that wasn't poisoning her! Actually, it nourished her. That's probably known as motherly love! Hence that other woman thinks she is entitled to meddle in my life, to hand out advice to *me* about how I should find a better job, get a better salary, how I should do this and that … well, I've had it up to here, fed up to my back teeth! And anyway it wasn't the kind of marriage I desired. I was tricked there too. Deceived by my, as I said,

Malevolent relative. He was behind all that, he knew the story I didn't know and told it to me *'at the right time'*, to poison me, to totally poison me with hatred; and after that I got married, because I thought I needed a woman to help me weather the crisis somehow. And that's how I met that wretch, namely ... I thought it would be good, but the devil it was, and it turned out to be hell. I'm not for that kind of marriage. I'm a sensitive, poetic soul. I needed a woman who would understand me; I needed a Muse. And she was not that ... Yes, she was an ordinary woman, doing a common job; she conducted herself and behaved in a common way; why, she wasn't even below average and I would have forgiven her for that, as long as she wasn't the typical run of the mill. But, okay, it's water under the bridge now. Forget it and may it not be repeated, which of course it won't, nevermore, I'm sure. I'd just like to add that she was agreeable when I met her. Therefore, I honestly thought she would be an adequate substitute for *Her.* She was agreeable, nice, didn't talk much, wasn't a prattler (and I had not yet met her mother, but had I, then I would have given it some thought; I know what genetics are, and would have considered the matter).

Well, I met her after several mournful months had gone by since my Malevolent ex-relative confronted me with the truth. About the woman I loved. Those were infernal months indeed. I cried for days and nights and didn't know how or could I ever forgive; nor did I see any reason to find forgiveness, especially not for the person who confronted me with the truth. My mental state was undermined completely. At the time, I still maintained certain unsteady relations with my mother. She advised me to go see a doctor, ask for help, comfort, pills, whatever ... and I did get them, the pills, but no comfort whatsoever. I was given treatment that was not adequate, but I became indifferent to everything around me, or I could say, I became more objective. Now, that was actually the first time in these ten years of service that I was absent from work, an absence of several months, which was needed to cure me of my relative's truth, of my lost love. I went back to work because I had to work again; I could not rely on my medicaments alone; lying there, waiting for things to get better; I was healing satisfactorily, and I had to *fit into life'* again.

Her name was Carla. As I already said, she was agreeable and well built. I thought, *"If she were mine, I'd have her put on some more weight."* I liked women with a fuller figure, but that was no impediment. My wanting her fatter was just pure thought. A thought can easily be rejected, replaced with another, more adequate at a given moment. Politicians do that all the time, changing their thoughts whenever a certain idea wears out or when it is no longer to their liking. They come out with some other thought, at the top of their voice, but never with full conviction that they won't replace it tomorrow with some other that is more suitable for the moment. So why couldn't I? Am I not the master of my own thoughts?

I mean, her physical appearance did not suit her character at all. That's precisely what fooled me. I thought she was different, that she was in harmony with her appearance; but hell no, that was the trap, the bait to catch me. She was pale and I thought she was not of a sanguine temperament. She had big eyes that looked somewhat sleepy, like the eyes of a faithful dog and so I expected her to be obedient and loyal. But hell no, it turned out that something quite different lay behind that peaceful façade. She had a fine-looking straight nose that gave her face elegance. Often her lips would stretch into a seemingly kind-hearted smile, but I know that this also was faked, learned somewhere, and did not come from the heart. It was not sincere. But, being so pretty and, I might say, disguised by that façade of hers, she seemed a promising replacement for *Her*, ah; I even hesitate to utter *Her* name. That's why I write poems for Miss Vivienne, because the two are almost the same, almost identical, save for Miss Vivienne having a different temperament, the kind I would not like; but if I could come close to her, if she could really get to know me, there might be a possibility for me to change her in some way, to make her better, more to my taste. No, I wouldn't meddle with her looks; it's more a matter of getting her to keep both feet on the ground; she seems a bit bluff-mannered and superficial on top of that; but let's get it straight: she's a typist and what more can one expect of a typist, ha, ha, not intelligence! But okay, her looks make her acceptable. I'd teach her as much as necessary: to behave in a more civilised way; I'd take her to the opera, to the theatre by all means; I'd recommend the proper books to read and that would suffice.

But to get back to Carla. If I saw her at the station (we would wait for the same train) I would always try to get the same compartment and grab a seat across from her to study the features of her face, her gestures and movements, in order to learn more of what I could expect from her. That's a skill that I practise on the train and I think that I have developed it quite well. I observe people as they enter, sit down, I look them straight in the face and it is then they start looking around at other passengers, then through the window, then at their own hands; some bite their nails while others immediately reach for a book or newspaper. These are usually worthless, cheap books, since that is probably the structure of people that ride the train. Every morning when I saw her, I watchfully calculated where she intended to enter, by which door, and I'd be right on her tail. That was precisely the period when I was never, really never, late for work; nor ever took a day off, not a day off, not a day of sick leave! (but the Fat Pig doesn't remember that period. No, not him!). I would observe her, and she would contritely lower her eyes when they met mine. Sometimes she would readjust her blouse, do up the button located between her breasts, redress her hair or make some other comparable gesture that spoke of her confusion. I fancied her. I was really keen on her. I am fond of shy girls, the ones that lower their eyes when a man looks at them! Properly brought up, I thought, but damn, that's where I fell for the trick, like some simpleton, somebody who had no life experience, as innocent as a strawberry. That's how it was.

The weather was frightful, a drizzling, monotonous rain. However, that dreadful weather seemed to be in my favour, as if the bad weather was on my side. I always carry an umbrella. I can't stand my hair getting wet. It then gets curly, turns into ringlets, like an old lady's bad hairdo. I would smooth it (my hair) out. In the evening I'd wet my hair, mixing gel in an equal quantity of water, rubbing it between my hands until I got a smooth mass, which I would distribute evenly throughout my hair. While the hair was still moist and pressed close to my head, I would put on a bandana and cover it with a cap. The next morning when I got up, my hair would be perfectly straight. Nobody would ever guess that I had naturally curly hair (I can't bear the sight of men with curly hair!). But my only enemy was dampness. Especially rain. Therefore whenever I suspect a weather change, I carry an umbrella. I listen to the weather forecast carefully every night so that the morning does not surprise me, or God forbid, the afternoon with sudden showers.

And so it was on the day I met Carla, I took my umbrella; I looked out of the window, it wasn't raining, but the sky was completely grey and I was aware of the kind of rain that falls from such a sky. It's the kind of sky from which showers never fall, but drizzly and fine drops of monotonous and ceaseless rain do. My hair is particularly affected by that kind of rain. It's the type of weather with the highest percentage of humidity, which is, as I said, a disaster for my hairstyle.

We got off at the same station and I of course noticed that she had no umbrella, not even a raincoat, so I hurried to catch up with her. We came up from the underground station and she looked up at the sky and sighed. I was watching her from the corner of my eye; the expression on her face was one of indecision or worry. Then she looked in my direction and the corners of her lips were drawing up into a half-smile. I spoke up:

"You should have taken an umbrella in this weather."

I approached her with my open umbrella and gave her shelter. She smiled. Then I said:

"Which way are you going?"

14

She was going the other way, but I wanted to act the cavalier. I said I would accompany her, and so I was late for work, but I told her that it was of no importance, that I was not obliged to come on time, that I had the privilege of coming whenever I wanted (at that time I'm sure she was asking herself *"Who is this gentleman!"*) I said:

"My name is Ottavio. My friends call me Otto."

Ah, friends. They also turned their backs on me. For no reason at all! Whenever I find a new friend, whenever I open up my soul, tell them about my poems, about my achievements, they leave. They cannot take it, my originality, the fact that I'm different, that I'm talented and I dare say, that I'm the chosen one … It's just too much for them.

She said:

"We see each other in the train every morning, so it seems like we are acquaintances…"

"Ha, ha, ha," I laughed heartily and, confounded, she asked me:

"Why are you laughing? What's so funny?"

I said:

"You wouldn't understand … and what is your name? You haven't told me your name."

"Carla," she chirped.

I said:

"Carla. Carla was my teacher's name. Ha, ha, ha." I laughed heartily once again, and she commented on my laughter by saying:

"You must be some kind of a joker."

I didn't know what she meant by *"some kind of a joker"*; was it supposed to be a compliment, or was she snubbing me? But I let it go at the time. I saw her to the door of her company and like greased lightning rushed back towards my office. The Big Tubby Chief was there to welcome me without uttering a word but just staring at me as if I owed him an explanation.

I said:

"It is raining, and there's been a stoppage of traffic," to which he replied with one of his quibbles:

"He who leaves on time always arrives on time."

I don't know whether he thought I should laugh or not, but I laughed and shut my umbrella, thanking God that I always remembered to carry it with me on days like this. Today it not only saved my hairstyle, but it also brought me closer to Carla. From now on I was able to greet her, to say, *"Good morning Carla, how are you today?"*

One morning, I ran into her. She was dressed in sports attire and I immediately realised that she wasn't going to work that day. I approached and said:

"You look very smart today."

She replied:

"Sportsmanlike. It's my day off today. I am going shopping and then I'll go for a walk, stop for a coffee somewhere, stop by at the library…"

So, elatedly, I said:

"What a coincidence! Imagine what a coincidence! I am free today, too! And I also plan on going to the library today. Actually, I'm going to have a talk with the librarian to see whether they would take my collection of poems."

"Your collection of poems? You are a poet?"

"Yes," I said, hoping she would not detect my own excitement.

We went on foot. That was how we had agreed. When we came close to a telephone booth, I said:

"Go ahead, Carla, I'll catch up with you. First I have a phone call to make."

I called the office and luckily at that moment the boss was not around, so I told Aurora that I was sick, that I had conjunctivitis and that my eyes were completely closed. After that I stretched my legs to catch up with Carla and told her:

"Nothing important, but I do apologise, anyway. I had to leave a message for my publisher."

It was so good to say *'my publisher'*, but he too never thinks of calling me, no, never to ask whether I'm working on anything new, or simply to ask me how I am. No sir, I'm of no importance to him, I didn't bring him any profit.

In Carla's company I thought less of *Her*. She almost ceased to exist. As I had already said, Carla was agreeable; she was very appealing. That's why, on the same day, I said:

"Carla, I will not address you in an honorific form, since I feel as if we are old acquaintances."

"It's better that way," she replied plainly.

She bought a dress; I carried her shopping bag, and when she proposed we go to the library, I said that I wanted to invite her to lunch. Did that lunch cost me! May it be understood it was not an expensive restaurant; an ordinary *pizzeria*, and we ate *pasta bolognese*. After that she ordered ice cream and coffee, and I drank a beer. But that was simply much too much, as a matter of fact, that made me nervous and I felt uncomfortable for the remainder of the day, but she did not notice it. I became taciturn and she said that poetic souls were fragile and I liked that, although it did not entirely get me into a better mood.

When we returned, I accompanied her to her house door. She said:

"Otto, next time the treat is on me."

I asked:

"And that is …"

"… tomorrow?"

Tomorrow.

Tomorrow was a Saturday; we went to see a movie and I held her hand when we came out of the theatre. She did not resist, and why should she? She found me attractive. If it comes to that, all women that lay eyes on me immediately find me attractive. I carried on as if I didn't notice it, but *I know*. They say I'm good-looking and the silent type. They say that I'm the silent type because I'm a poet; they say I'm introverted, *'unreachable'* or enigmatic; that's what they say, while I remain taciturn, no comment. I left a strong impression on Carla. She became my remedy, without a prescription. I decided to stop going to the physician, to listen to his boring questions:

"Otto, how are you feeling today?"

I now realise it was simply high time for her to get married. She was thirty, she was bored with such a way of life, living with her mother while she herself wanted to be a mother (it was my good fortune I did not get involved in that!). She'd been around! She wasn't as naïve as she seemed, no, no, no. She knew exactly what she was after. She saw that I was good-looking, that I had a good job, that I was talented; who knows how much she thought I earned from my collection of poems, and on top of that I told her that I was *'preparing something new'*. She surely thought that this was an opportunity she should not miss. Only three months had gone by when she said:

"Otto, will your ever propose to me?"

Humph! It wasn't easy for me. But, I was no longer thinking of *Her*. That's why I thought Carla would be the answer to my spiritual agony that was so violent I therefore readily responded:

"May 'ever' be 'now'!" (Which she particularly liked, stressing that only a Poet could say something like that), to which I added:

"… Carla, marry me!"

She embraced me and kissed me, and soon we began to make plans for our wedding. I explained to her straight away about my relatives being an unruly menagerie, and that there was no need to introduce her to that unusual assortment of wild animals, from geese to monkeys. She responded with a guttural laugh saying that I was *'silly'*. She could not believe I was telling the truth, that that was my most profound conviction, and so she asked, defiantly:

"Don't tell me you won't invite your own mother?"

"I won't."

And I did not. My mother said to me when she learned about my agony (when I lost *Her*):

"Otto, it's true you have no luck, but you're not in your right mind either."

Now then, that's what my own mother tells me! At the moment of my greatest suffering, she tells me that I'm an idiot and a loser. What kind of mother is she, I ask you? What kind? And now when I've found Carla, of all people I'm supposed to invite her to the wedding! The woman who said:

"Your only hope is to get the help of a psychiatrist."

She pushed me into the psychiatric clinic. I said nothing about that to Carla at the time, fortunately, for if she had known that detail, she surely would have defended her mother even more whenever I told her that her mother was an aggressive woman butting her nose into my life and offering advice: offering solutions, offering assistance that I was not prepared to accept. I was not willing. Please, don't shower me with advice; the easiest thing is to give someone free advice. Here is a prescription and you apply it. It's universal, works well; it's as if made to order for you. Yet only I knew what was good for my soul! And that's what I said to her mother, on the occasion of our first conflict; but she didn't take that seriously. She simply behaved as if she didn't hear me, as if I said nothing at all. She was the kind of chatterbox that hears only herself, the kind of parasite that sucks one's blood. Imagine what kind of life was in store for me! And should I then say that life is fair? Fair play? To play fair - are you kidding!

Right now, as I jot down these words on paper, I myself have begun to see what happened with greater clarity. How have the last dozen or so years of my life been?

Others have made it miserable without exception, starting from my obnoxious relatives to my insensitive mother and thereafter from *Her*, the woman who totally shattered my heart, to Carla who was average, without any specific intelligence, interests or talent and her mother, who was an everyday bitter pill that I had to swallow. Not to mention my worthy colleagues at the office or the boss who never even finished secondary school, yet comports himself as if he knows everything, full of wisdom and authority.

I'm a sincere person. I never make false promises, I don't encourage deceptive hopes, I don't nourish anyone's illusions. When the truth has to be said, I say it. Thus I said to Carla:

"Carla, this just won't do. I don't want to live with you any more. I can't bear your mother, the obligations towards your relatives, or towards you as a matter of fact. You're not what I thought you were. You are coarse and selfish, thinking more about others than about me. You ought to know that I loved another woman, and I thought I would forget her if I married you. It did not happen. For me, this marriage of ours is a lie. That's why I'm leaving. Ta-ta, I'm going ..."

You should have seen the hysteria! But I had to come out with the truth. The truth was burning me. The insides of my chest cavity seemed to be ablaze, as if I was being destroyed by fire. By the truth, or the lie in which I was living. That's why I had to tell it, I had to go - *"Ta-ta, I am going"*; that was the only way. I didn't even know to what extent she was tied to me. I thought her mother was more important than I was. She wept, had an outburst of hysteria; I couldn't even grasp what she was saying through her tears, through her screaming and mumbling. She really got on my nerves. I slammed the door and walked away. If something doesn't work, it doesn't work! Why the hysteria? I could not understand. We tried - and it didn't work out. Why all the drama now, the crying, begging, making up, the tears, tears, tears ... I don't need any of that any more. Nobody's tears, my own the least! Carla's are also pointless. How could she not understand; I need none of that any more. We weren't meant for each other. She didn't bring me peace, she didn't bring me relief, and she didn't make me forget. Forget, my foot! Actually, the more I became aware of how common Carla was, the more it was difficult for me to bear the loss of *Her.* What a woman! Therefore, Carla's mediocrity underscored *Her* unique quality. *She* was such an exclusive woman; that's why I loved *Her* immediately, from the very moment I met *Her,* the moment I laid my eyes on *Her.* I could see that *She* was special by the way *She* walked, the way *She* turned *Her* head. I could see it in *Her* eyes and in the movements of *Her* swanlike arms. Ah, how many poems I dedicated to *Her.* I dedicated all my poems to *Her,* including the ones that appear as if they were written for Miss Vivienne!

That day, after work, I went to our apartment to pick up my things. In the apartment I was caught in an ambush. Her mother! Actually, both of them, but it was her mother who blocked my entrance at the door she had opened when I rang. She said:

"What do you want from her?"

I replied:

"I want my things. I've come to get my things."

To what she said, *"Otto ..."* calling me by my real name for the first time *"... has anything gone wrong, has there been a misunderstanding?"* she said this time in a somewhat mellower voice (like a demoted general). I even imagined that she lowered her eyes. Again I felt that violent burning in my chest, and it suddenly dawned upon me that this was *a unique, actually, the only opportunity* that I would get to tell her *the truth,* to tell her everything I think of her, so I said with straightforwardness and satisfaction:

"Yes, something has indeed gone wrong. There has been a misunderstanding. That mistake and misunderstanding carry your name. Its name is Vanda! You are the mistake of our lives, hers and mine. A mistake that cannot be rectified; only (I wanted to say death, namely only death can remedy it, but I stopped at that, I really can't say why, perhaps because the violent heat in my chest had somewhat subsided ... extinguished.) So I said ... my departure can rectify it."

She slammed the door into my face.

W-H-A-M!!!

Again I could hear her, Carla, crying. I heard her shrieking. I strolled down the stairway empty-handed, but my heart was full. I told her! I told her, at last! Walking serenely down the stairs, I pondered over what else I could have (or should have) said, and I knew there would be no more chances for that. I was sniggering, particularly pleased with the shrewd way in which I expressed myself (indeed, like a real poet), namely … *"that mistake and misunderstanding carry your name."*

That will be a phrase that she will never forget. Who could she hear say anything like that ever? And who could have come up with such a selection of words? She only knew common people; she never mingled with poets to know how to put words together and give them deeper meaning, she knew nothing about personification, about poetic imagery. She once used to be a hairdresser. There, I married a woman whose mother was a hairdresser. Hairdressers are gossipers; everyone knows that. Women go to beauty salons only to evade their duties for five hours, using salons as an excuse to get away from their husbands in order to idly sit around and babble away while the hairdresser wattles some silly basket onto their heads. And the hairstyles! The worst thing for me was when my mother would come back home after five hours at the hairdresser's with some silly round ball of hair on her head. Everything was globular, each hair drawn up high into the air and then lowered in a wide arch down to the cheekbones, in places down to her chin, which actually no longer separated the lower jaw from her neck; an indication that my mother was no longer young. Still exalted from babbling and gossiping, exalted from all the compliments and looking adoringly at herself in the mirror, she would say:

"Didn't he, yet again, make an excellent hairdo?"

"No, he didn't," I would reply, half-angrily because of her absence for hours and irritated by her ridiculous appearance and divergent opinion.

"No, you look stupid, funny. You seem to have given in to someone more senseless than you are to do whatever he wants."

That's what I'd say to her whenever she came back from the salon. A reddish hue would then come out on her face and neck and made her look grotesque. That's the kind of mother I remember from my childhood and early youth. She loved compliments! Why do women like compliments? They would always like us to flatter them. To flatter even at the price of withholding the truth! They like to make liars out of us; that's what they like to do. I learned that lesson from my mother already as a child - that women are thirsty and desirous of compliments, even if they are fabrications. Well, not me! I never complimented anybody, I never flattered, never lied. I'd always say what I thought, like it or not …

But once, only once …

Ah, and that's what cost me my health, cost me my life.

Only once, only to one woman, only to *Her* … and *She*, what did *She* do?

What did She do?

She threw me into despair. Into the arms of madness.

But to get back to the story I wish to tell, the story of that so-called relative of mine. But, before I start, I must tell you how I met Miranda Mavis. Somebody recommended her to my mother, and mother advised me to go see her. At the time I had already severed all relations with my mother. However, when she heard that I broke up with Carla, when she found out what kind of mother Carla had and how they both had sucked my blood and exploited me, she phoned me. Her voice was tremulous, it immediately reminded me of some long past days; thus in spite of everything, her voice touched me even though I could not determine the real reason. Was it the pitch of her voice, the concern that trilled in its tone, the recollection of my childhood days? It's of no importance, it really isn't.

She said:

"Otto, come over so we can see each other. Do you know how many years have passed since we saw one another? Let's bury the hatchet …"

I said:

"I know what you want to say. Shut up! I'll come over."

I went. Everything was the same. How would I know the number of years that I had not crossed her threshold! Not because of her hairdo, but because of her attitude towards me. She carried on like I was somebody who lacked wisdom; yet she did foster affection for me. But I didn't want affection of that kind. I did not want her compassion and stomach-turning care. I wanted her to be proud of me, to believe in my abilities, in my talent. But no, she didn't. She'd say:

"Otto you'll never amount to anything."

And I wanted to become a poet.

And when I told her about my failed marriage, in a lachrymose voice, she said:

"My son, my poor sonny boy, I know everything."

I didn't want her to call me *'poor Sonny Boy'*, but since she was the only person that truly wanted to hear what I had to say and eventually to understand, I opened my soul to her and told her everything about my unfortunate marriage, about how Carla was ordinary, boring and selfish, and how her mother was inclined to be tyrannical. My mother exaggerated again by saying:

"My poor Sonny Boy, you have no luck."

No luck! No brains! No nerves! You lack power! You lack knowledge! You won't succeed! You can't overcome! You won't make it! You don't, don't, don't … you won't, won't, won't … my poor Sonny Boy!

When *She* abandoned me, my mother took me to a shrink. And now when an irrelevant and worthless marriage (because it failed to fulfil its purpose) fell apart, she was recommending me to some Miranda Mavis, psychologist! I wasn't willing to go. I was not willing, and I said:

"Mother, I'm not willing to go," to which she responded:

"Bah, you are not willing to do anything. But you shall go! Just look at the condition you are in!"

And precisely in such a condition I was unable to oppose her. Otherwise I would have. Otherwise I would have said, *"I won't go. I'm not in need of your psychiatrists and psychologists and I won't go."* But this time I simply shrugged my shoulders; she picked up the phone and made an appointment with Miranda Mavis.

In order not to travel from Milan to Bologna I decided to go on sick leave. The only thing was that I felt somewhat ... how can I put it ... somewhat awkward regarding what they would say at the office. Ah, always that stupid concern - what will they say at the office! What will that Fat Salami say! Nevertheless ... I had to concoct some tolerable reason as to why I'd be absent for a week at least. I knew they were already allergic to my sick leaves (as they would say, *"Yet again?"* even though I really was not absent so often), so I told him that my mother was sick, that I had no father, since he died a long time ago, and that I now had to care for my mother because there was no one else; she had to undergo surgery; she had only me, I had only her, and that I didn't want to lose her, God forbid, as a consequence of my negligence. A long pause of silence ensued, then he grumbled something I could not make out what, but it was not important since the moment he said, *"Okay, okay, Otto ..."* I said, *"Thanks, thanks a lot,"* and nervously hung up.

2

We went into a waiting room with a small reception desk situated in front of her doctor's office. My mother said:

"Sit down here, I'll speak to the receptionist."

She talked to her, then she said:

"I'm going now, Otto, and you come home when you're finished."

She made a gesture as if she wanted to smooth out my hair, but I stopped her by suddenly raising my right hand to defend myself from her attack: that was something I didn't like! I could never tolerate it - her combing back (or messing up!) my hair; I previously mentioned that my hair was naturally curly, that I smothered it every evening before bedtime with an ointment of gel and cold water that I prepared and thereafter I'd tie my hair with a bandana and put a cap on top of it. In the morning my hair would be perfectly straight. I never let anybody touch my hair. I couldn't stand my mother's motion towards my hair so as to … what? Smooth it out? I was the expert in that and didn't need any help, but on top of that, I simply *could not stand* anybody touching my hair!

When the receptionist called me, I went into the psychologist's room.

I told her my name and she offered me a seat.

I didn't like her!

She was a horrible sight. She was taller than I, in other words, too tall for a woman, of strong physical constitution, oversized breasts, big hands and fingers, and she had—curly red hair and a freckled face of the same colour. Indeed, I didn't even like curly hair on women, and especially, I could not stand redheads. I knew there was something evil and flaming in them. Her eyes were too small for my liking, although their colour was an unusual green similar to the little green pine tree in the corner of her room. I couldn't see the colour of her eyes very well because she wore thick glasses that did not suit her big face. She moreover had a big mouth and fat lips, and her teeth were also big and uneven and that made me turn my eyes away from her lips. The whole face, her whole appearance was not to my liking; the colour of her skin and freckles was repulsive and I didn't like those big hands and plump fingers. Why such big hands on a shrink, I asked myself.

She smiled. I didn't like her smile. Because of her mouth and teeth. With teeth like that she should not allow herself to smile. I immediately knew that I could not trust a woman like her.

In my opinion a psychologist must look entirely different. For example, if she were a more elderly woman, with a neatly buttoned up robe; if her face were an image of wisdom and patience, with a long and straight nose, thin lips whose warm smile revealed a set of white and straight teeth; if her hands were tender and wrists thin, fingers slender with well-shaped nails; if she were to speak in a low voice and her (oversized) breasts were not discernible, or let's say, that a slim neck adorned the small bun at the back of her head … then she would have been my psychologist. This way … how could I say anything to this redhead woman? To her with those excessively plump lips, with that flaming hair, with those bulky hands! She doesn't have the sensitivity that I require. How can she understand a poet, I asked myself. And when I told her, *"I have just been divorced,"* she asked me, *"Would you like to talk about it?"* just in spite, I replied:

"No, I would not like to talk about it! It was a totally misplaced marriage. For me it was a totally pointless and inconsequential experience."

She simply looked down nodding her head, and when she looked up again, I noticed an ugly and oversized red mole under her chin. I had not noticed it before, for it was located precisely in the shadow of her chin when she looked straight at you. But as soon as she lifted her chin a little higher, the red ugly mole came into view.

I would never open my soul to the likes of her, neve ever. I was just about to get up, I didn't want to talk to a curly redheaded woman that wasn't to my liking; I was almost on my feet, since I didn't give a hoot of what she would think of my walking away. I wanted to walk away and say, *"Ta-ta, I'm off,"* while thinking to myself, *"You find some patient who'll trust you … the way you are. That's not me!"*

Yet, something else happened!

A miracle!

It happened like a bolt from the blue!

His name!

But let's put first things first. She looked at me with those greenish eyes, similar to the colour of the pine tree in the corner of her room. She looked at me calmly, and her gaze made me feel uneasy. In order to hide my uneasiness, I placed my hands into my lap, clasping one into the other. I fondled them, calming the left hand with the right, relaxed them by squeezing the right one with the left; but my anxiety was visible in my eyes; only my eyes could show my restlessness and I therefore took in the items on her desk trying to find an object to fix my gaze on so it wouldn't wander, so it wouldn't betray my restlessness. And so I riveted my stare at a slip of paper. Something was written on it, but indeed I could not care less what was written there; the important thing was that my eyes did not wander, did not reveal my disquietude. That was the moment when she got up and said:

"Would it bother you if I opened the window?"

Still staring at the slip of paper, I quickly replied:

"No, it won't, just open it," and she moved towards the window in long awkward strides. I wasn't at all interested in watching her open the window with her big hands, but kept on staring at the strip of paper that was, as I said before, a mainstay for my wavering eyes. Suddenly the letters came to life. The letters formed a sentence. They spelled out a name. A name I hated. She sat down. I read what was written on the small piece of paper out loud. It was a message to her, turned towards her.

It said:

"Vilas Visconti called you."

She looked questioningly at me, so I repeated:

"Vilas Visconti called you."

"When?" asked Miranda. She asked me naively, as if she didn't know what was written on her slip of paper, so I said:

"That's what's written on that strip of paper, on your left and my right side," and I pointed a finger at the paper with his name.

She calmly nodded, as if that was completely in order. As if nothing dramatic had happened. So I repeated:

"Vilas Visconti called you."

Now she raised the reddish eyebrow over her left eye and said:

"Well, right now I'm dedicating my time to you. I'll call mister Visconti later on."

I asked:

"Do you know Visconti?"

She nodded, to which I said:

"Then we have nothing to talk about, because you are certainly on his side. Just like everybody else. I'm leaving."

I got to my feet and headed for the door. She also got up, got hold of my hand with her big hand, to my astonishment quite tenderly and asked me:

"Do you know Visconti?"

"I know him!"

"Are you gravely upset?"

I looked at her the way one looks at an opponent, sternly, with a dose of loathing. I thought I'd be able to maintain that stern look, that pre-scribed amount of loathing, but I couldn't. I burst into tears. They com-pletely liquefied my look and it drained away, flowing down my cheek. Miranda said:

"Do sit down!" and handed me a glass of water.

3

After finishing the glass of water, I went home. Anyhow, my mother had said that she would pay the bill upon termination. This *is* the end. I don't want anything more to do with that woman. She is without doubt in con-spiracy with Visconti, and my mother is surely a part of that conspiracy, of that deep-laid plot. I marched back to her house at a fast pace, fully pre-pared to say:

"I have not stepped across your threshold for years because of your always being up to something, scheming and hatching plots; but now I shall never step across this threshold again." Full stop.

However, I said nothing. I went inside the house, quickstepped into my room and began to pack my things into a trunk. She came in after me, with an *'as if'* worried expression on her face, as though she had no idea of what happened, and so she stupidly asked that very same question:

"What happened?"

"You know damn well what happened," said I, in spite of having firmly promised myself not to say anything. She put on an act, like she really knew nothing and repeated:

"Otto, is there anything wrong?"

I threw and pushed my things into the trunk, pressed its lid down with my knee, shut it, turned my back on her and left. She called after me to come back, to stop. I simply turned around and said:

"Ta-ta, off Otto goes." And I went.

I caught the train for Milan and tried to take an eraser. On the large screen of my memory once again I revived the encounter with mother and then I imagined how all of that was but a drawing and that in my hand I held an enormous eraser that could wipe away any recollection. I started by meticulously erasing every sentence, every one of her endeavours to be gentle or caring. Lies! All lies! Even after years of silence she still deals out the same lies. She takes me to some so-called psychologist; I myself didn't know the reason she used to justify the act, but I fell for it! And surprise, surprise: she's part of the conspiracy called Visconti-Mavis-Visconti! Why? Why does everybody hate me? Why does everybody want to hurt me, to wound me so deeply that I can never forget it? I can't forgive them, or myself, for being duped once again, for going to see mother again, for believing her that she had good intentions. I was meant to be alone. I'm the only person able to understand myself. Only my poetry - only My Poetry Is My Sanctuary!

I was a broken man when I reached Milan. A city I disliked; big, too big for a poet; dirty, too dirty for a pure soul; indifferent, not a home for a frightened person, yet I had no other. I sat down and cried. Not a single person to understand me, not a single friend, not a single soul mate! Carla came to mind; actually she wasn't all that bad. There were moments when she understood me; there were moments when trying to stroke my hair, she would say, *"Otto, you are such an eccentric,"* or she would say, *"Well yes, you are a true poetic soul; no place for reality!"*

What kind of reality, I ask myself? What is reality? Whose reality? Did Carla think I was supposed to live in her Reality? My Reality was seen with my eyes; I felt it with my heart and it beat to my heart's rhythm, moved to the rhythm of my breathing, resounded to the rhythm of my footsteps, restless with phases that are mine and smells of my sweat; and when it is blurred, it is blurred by the mist of my tears. How could Carla say anything about My Reality, how could she have comprehended what My Reality was at all! And how did she dare even try to tell *me* that I had—no place for reality?

And her Reality?

Employment. Bank employee. She puts on a black dress and blouse that's not too dark, although not too bright either, that's not buttoned up from top to bottom, yet certainly not unbuttoned *'where it shouldn't be unbuttoned'*; she wears shoes in which one feels secure because they don't differ in any way from those that others wear; her hair gathered at the back of her head in ponytail style does not allow it to be lively and free; she never uses too little or too much perfume, just the right measure that is needed and suits her (or the picture of her Reality). Her smile is made-to-measure for that reality, in other words gracious but not too friendly so that *'just anyone'* wouldn't dare approach her or talk out of turn with her. That smile is a barometer. Anybody who is knowledgeable about smiles knows the type of barometer that allows approach to a certain extent only. When I first met her I did not know about that barometer, but later on her Reality taught me what it was. Her mother was a part of her Reality, but not of mine. I simply avoided her and ignored her, as if she did not exist in my Reality. She was an occupant of the Reality of my wife, but I refused to acknowledge all the protagonists of her Reality. There was no room for her in mine; and when both women attempted to push her into my Reality, as I said before, I said, *"Ta-ta, I'm leaving since there isn't any room for you in my Reality."*

Perhaps Miss Vivienne ... So, after all, perhaps Miss Vivienne ... Maybe, only Miss Vivienne ...

I wanted to try; I wanted to leave a poem of mine on her typist desk. I imagined, in the morning, before she came in, I'd go into her room and leave yet one more of my poems dedicated to *Her* ... but something prevented me; I was afraid of something indistinct. Occasionally, I could hear her guttural laughter that was somewhat too loud. Maybe I was afraid of that kind of laughter ... it had a raucous resonance in my Reality. Nevertheless, with a twinge, each morning I thought, *"I can no longer look at this woman,"* as she would pass me by, saying, *"Good morning, Otto. I hope I haven't grown another nose overnight?"*

No, Miss Vivienne. You haven't grown another nose overnight. You look like *Her* and *She* was the Love of My Life. *She* was my only Reality, or at least, the only Reality that I wanted.

So, there you have it. That was the episode with Miranda Mavis, but as misfortune would have it, she seemed to possess certain supernatural powers, so redheaded and freckled, so indifferent and composed within, who knew that destiny would bring us together again.

I'll tell you about that, but I can't figure out where to begin since I also promised to tell the story of that relative of mine, yet who he is has now become so obvious. We even know his name. Namely, he is Vilas Visconti.

But I don't know whether to directly start with the Redhead, since she too, is involved in that story, in the Reality That I Did Not Want.

And I'd like best to say one thing only to that reality, as I have so many times before:

"Ta-ta, Otto's off ... to some other reality."

Simona

We were sitting at the table having breakfast. Father said:

"I have something to tell you ... Simona's pregnant ..." Upon delivering this sentence his face had become as red as if he had said something very shameful.

The very same redness spilt over mother's face; her neck, even her hands became red and sweaty and her fingers started to tremble heavily, which caused the tinkling of the spoon in the sugar bowl, and mother muttered a red-hot sentence from her flaming throat with a voice tinkling with excitement (everything, everything tinkled during that particular morning):

"You don't have to say a word, I know it all. You can go, but you have to know one thing—you are not going to take a single thing with you. Go!" Red and trembling she stood up and ran towards the bedroom where her tears had caught up with her after she had tried to keep them on the edge of her eyelashes while she was still at the table. When she slammed the bedroom door, silence was hanging over the table; the tinkling of the cups, the saucers and her own fingers had stopped, the tinkling of her voice had stopped, too, the only thing that could be heard was my father clearing his throat while looking at the cup of now absolutely cold coffee.

Simona.

We knew Simona well. Why did mother get so upset? Why did her fingers tinkle in chorus with fine china while the redness spilt all over her face? Why did father's face get so red that he resembled a little embarrassed boy who had just told a shameful lie to his parents?

We know Simona well; she is my father's secretary. And what a secretary she's been; father always used to say that *God, himself, had sent Simona to his office,* he used to say that *he would lose his head without Simona ...* I can't see why mother got so agitated … so what if she is pregnant, she is not irre-placeable.

I said to my father:

"Are you afraid that now she is going to leave because she is pregnant? Does it worry you to look for another secretary?"

He did not look into my eyes but rather somewhere around my chest, and with a still dull, quiet voice said:

"Otto, are you really that stupid or are you just pretending to be that way?"

I did not understand what he was asking.

He stood up and walked out without a coat into a cold Milan morning.

We knew Simona. She came into his office some five years ago, that's ex-actly how much older she was than I - five years. She was eighteen when she started to work for him. When I had laid my eyes on her, I thought, *"This is exactly how my future wife is going to look."*

Oh merciful Lord, she had the most beautiful smile, I had never seen a smile like hers. It adorned her face so beautifully that I was not able to notice anything else: the coulour or the shape of her eyes, the shape of her nose or chin … bah, what shape? No other shape was there to distinguish, nothing, there was only Simona's smile on that face. Simona's smile was always there like the sun in a cloudless sky.

Whenever I came to father's office Simona would treat me with choc-olates, which she kept in the first drawer on the left hand side of her desk. I would always take one, but Simona would not take any, for she would say she had already had one in the morning, which was exactly what she would allow herself to have (I marvelled at her discipline!)

My first cup of coffee ever! Simona had prepared it for me. I came to father's office carrying some papers which mother had sent on father's request. He was not there; Simona said:

"Sit down, Otto. Have a cup of coffee with me."

There I had enjoyed my first coffee, the sweetest, and I had never ever experienced that sweetness again but I had promised myself once again that the woman I was going to love would carry on her face the ever-present Simona's smile (was it good or bad luck, the devil knows; later I met *Her* with that smile which overshadowed even Simona's seemingly perfect smile.)

Whenever I would meet Simona my hands would tremble just as my mother's hands had trembled today. I never knew the real reason for the trembling of my hands … was it because of her smile or was it because of her pitch-black hair, combed and sleek looking as if it was made of tar … or was it because of the fireflies in her eyes which flew towards you as she talked to you or they flew towards the window to reach the wide sky? … Live fireflies in Simona's eyes.

When father had walked out without a coat (was it really too hot for him, or was he in such a hurry that he had forgotten his coat, who would really know now?) I had entered mother's room. I found her lying on the bed crying, I sat down on the edge of the bed without a word. After a short time she got up, wiped off her tears and said:

"Don't just sit there. I want to be left alone. Get out!"

"Mother, why did you get so upset about it? He is going to find another secretary."

She gave me one of her dumbfounded looks and asked:

"How old are you, Otto?"

"Seventeen."

"Are you really brainless or are you pretending to be?"

"I don't get you …"

"Your father is going to leave us."

"But why? It's not like he and … " I left the room without ending my sentence for my mother needed solitude. Only in solitude could she find peace and comfort.

In the dining room, everything was still the same as it was in the moment when we left it. Like some sort of theatre scene ... without protagonists ... it looked as if they had left in search of new roles.

Simona!

No, this is not possible!

This is what she thinks. That's why she said to him, *"You don't have to say a word, I know it all."*

This is not possible!

Simona! With her smile, with fireflies in her eyes, with her white teeth and dimples in her cheeks.

My father - the man whose face never showed a smile, whose teeth are brownish from smoking and age, and gum disease has left them rickety regardless of his daily hygienic routine and efforts.

Simona—one head taller than him, slim with a tiny waist and long, long legs and a little bottom like an Easter bun, with elegant hands and slim, long fingers adorned with numerous yellow rings.

My father ... stocky, short. He is already belting his pants underneath his sagging breasts. Short-legged, shortsighted, sullen, unapproachable and a know-it-all.

Simona ... with her pitch-black hair, dark but shiny, she looks like a perfectly crafted doll from some exotic place ... with her big almond-shaped eyes, the eyes of a child where fireflies are shining a light with their little brilliant torches wooing observers to drown in it.

My father ... half-bald but convinced that, yet, nobody can really notice it (nor can Simona), since he is combing his hair across his head, over the bald patch, from left to right avoiding the wind at any cost ...

No, it can't be true.

Can it be true?

***

My father, the most respected lawyer in town, the omniscient one, with no mystery left to be solved, the one who always knows and offers more, accustomed to be in the public eye, accustomed to obedience ...

Simona, my secret.

My first inspiration. A real woman of flesh and blood, the first one I had dedicated my poem to!

She would greet me upon coming or leaving with her magical smile, she would light up her fireflies in her eyes every time I walked into the office with an excuse that I was after my father.

She had that quality I had always admired in women - she was timid, for every time I asked questions about my father she would lower her gaze, she would blush or she would leave the room. If father was present, she would stutter timidly ... her unease would grow, knowing that father had caught us together alone in the room.

"Yes, yes ... Simona Verdi," that's how she would answer the phone. She would chirp:

"Visconti lawyers, Simona Verdi's here ..."

It must be a mistake. Some silly joke. Simona's not pregnant. Particularly not with ... no, no ... what is it that mother's insinuating, I have to talk to her, it cannot be that she thinks that Simona would ... and my father ... once again, I had entered her room and said:

"Mother, what is it that you want to say ... is it that Simona's ..."

"Leave this room at once, Otto. I want to be left alone."

I did not get the answer. Not on that day. But on the following one.

38

Mother said:

"I've known about that cheap slut since the day she came in."

"Simona's not a slut mother, she is a nice girl; I know that."

*"And what is **that** that **you** know, Otto? You are one very naïve idiot ... oh, Otto, how did we bring you up? Or, perhaps it was not of our doing ... could be that you are just like that—a naïve idiot!"*

"Why are you talking to me like that, mother? Why do you think that I am naïve?"

"So, tell me, you fool, why do you think Simona's a nice girl? Explain it, let me hear it, you imbecile."

I had never heard my mother talking like that. I kept silent; she was livid, screaming out loudly:

"Tell me, you smart arse, why do you call this little slut a nice girl?"

I stuttered:

"Well, she is nice ... always smiling ... always bright ..."

"Bright, huh? You are a real nincompoop."

"I am not a nincompoop, mother."

"Yes you are, a real fool, I can't understand what an idiot you have turned into."

I walked outside, then into the garden and sat underneath my poplar tree. I felt like crying, not knowing the exact reason why: was it because of my mother, was it because of Simona or because of my father who had walked out into a cold morning without a coat and without any explanation apart from one short sentence which did not explain much, *"Simona's pregnant"*?

Mother had sharpened herself for a bloody battle regarding the property, hoping that in this game she would use up all her mighty fury. But to my father Simona was more important than any property, so he signed over our family house into her name without a word. That was how he had left us and how he'd gone to live with pregnant Simona.

We were left with a house full of memories. Valeria Visconti, *Miss Pageant of An Anonymous Province*. That trophy she had taken into the marriage as a priceless dowry. How important it was to be beautiful and well dressed so that he could take her out showing her off to the most respectable people of the town! When they went out she would carefully select her clothes for hours, she would call her hairdresser to our house so that he could press her hair to perfection because she needed to look at herself in her own mirror and then she would ask it:

"*Mirror, mirror on the wall, who is the fairest one of all?*"

And she would hear its voice, "*Famed is thy beauty, Majesty …*"

(… but behold! A lovely secretary I see … rags cannot hide her gentle grace; Simona, with her beautiful, innocent face, is much fairer than thee…)

Simona. How withered away and old mother looked compared to Simona. Youth had left her, the collagen injections did not work miracles; the effects of long massages gave just temporary results, yes, they would freshen her up a little bit but she did not appear twenty-three years younger, exactly how much younger Simona was when put into numbers.

How to compete with Simona? With what weapons? The bosom had withered and the words were full of bitterness.

But, can she so easily let Simona sit on the throne?

Is it that everything could end just because of one little slut? Because of one pregnancy? What about all those years they had spent together? They even had their son together (right now, Otto Visconti is becoming important!); they acquired their property together, their families and mementos. But Enzo was not willing to live off mementos.

***

The next day I heard parts of her over-and-over repeated monologue, which leaked through the door cracks. The words were well laced with arsenic; the air was sour and her gestures quite uncontrollable. I had never seen mother acting like that. She did not notice me, for her gaze was quite absent. She got dressed while talking. Her speech was loud; she had spoken to Simona.

I followed her walking cautiously behind her, hiding myself even though I knew that her gaze was absent and hazy. It was not my mother; I had a presentiment about something of quite an uncertain outcome ... unpleasant ... She was heading towards father's office.

When she entered Simona told her that father wouldn't be back until well after lunchtime.

I saw discomfort on Simona's pretty face through the half-opened door; she took a few steps back towards the window but mother followed her with her flaming face throwing at Simona the countless-times-repeated monologue. In that heated speech she told Simona that she was a cheap slut with zero education and zero culture, and that all she had ever possessed were large breasts and a small, firm butt. She told her she was an amoral woman who was stealing from others because there was no one who could teach her any better. Then she told her that she, Valeria, would stop her in her dirty plan, for she was going to tell all their friends what kind of a woman she was, they'd know all before they even met her.

Caught by a merciless hand of contempt, hatred and jealousy my mother was blabbering heated sentences, walking to and fro with a crimson face pushing it into Simona's frightened face, gesticulating with her arms and in the end she grabbed Simona by the hair pulling it downwards as if she believed she could take off that perfect wig of hers. That was not all; she then grabbed her by the wrists squeezing them hard and after that she slapped her face swiftly with an open hand several times, then she scratched her hands like an enraged wild cat, kicked her repeatedly in the shins and finally started to spit into her face and eyes, while Simona was just standing there with hands covering her face crying, *"Please, don't do it, Mrs Visconti, please, don't…"*

I was standing there at the half-opened door with a full-opened mouth and, in this very moment, all illusions I ever had about my mother were dispersed, just as light clouds would disperse when caught in the web of my poplar tree crown. I came close slowly, as if I was walking through a dream, and tried to calm down that wild beast that was screaming from my mother's depths, truly believing that this was the first time I met her.

Even though the whole scene resembled a bad dream, even though I walked as a somnambulist, I felt that enormous shame entangled underneath my skin, which was adorned by goose bumps because of it. All I wanted was to close my eyes and fall asleep to be awoken in some other reality … but when I came close to my mother, who noticed me only then, she started to smack my face and head with both hands telling me what an idiot I was, asking herself why and how such kind of fool had happened to be her own son. She said that I was such a fool, even bigger than Enzo, and so enraged, she started to kick my shins and legs the way she was kicking Simona's before I tried to calm her down. The awakened beast in my mother could not slow down. Simona, scratched all over her face and covered in blood, rushed to my rescue, trying to calm my mother down by holding her hands and muttering with a beseeching voice, *"Please, don't, Mrs. Valeria …"* to which my mother went completely wild and screamed:

"Don't you dare utter my name, you prostitute! You little slut!"

All of that was way too much for Otto; I started to cry, begging her:

"Mother, don't! Please, don't call her by such names."

Those words had only brought a more intense attack of madness, so my mother had grabbed her by the shoulders and started to shake her as if she was a plum tree, her hair covering her sweaty face and her make-up smudged around her flaming eyes. She shook Simona, she shook her as she would shake a heavily laden plum tree, and after a while she pushed her with all her might towards the window, where Simona's head banged onto the windowsill and she fell down on her knees crying.

I ran to Simona's rescue; she was on her knees crying and holding her stomach, which did not look as a pregnant woman's stomach yet, with both hands. Simona didn't look like a real, beautiful and ever-smiling Simona, but rather like a while ago beautiful, but now broken doll, and as a sad child, I sat next to the doll and started to console her in a sincere attempt to mend the damage with words. I was hugging Simona, crying together with her, stroking her head and straightening her messed-up hair, wiping off her tears unaware that mine were rolling down my cheeks like a wild unstoppable river.

I heard my mother's screech, *"Traitor!"* addressed to me, her unfaithful son, and after that she left us wobbling out as if the whole scene had intoxicated her … intoxicated with what …?

Simona and I, we were sitting on the floor crying and hugging each other. My father had found us sitting on the office floor in tears.

Panic had painted a harsh mask on his previously placid face; he came closer to Simona while pushing me away. The same panic gave to his voice a different tone, so I could not recognise it as his voice:

"Simona, Simona my sweetheart, what has happened? What has this idiot done to you?"

Simona was drowning in her tears as if she had to cry them all out, right now; she was hugging my father unable to utter a word and he was repeating over and over without looking at me:

"What has this idiot done to you?"

I stood up slowly, wiped off my tears, and walked downstairs.

The morning in Milan was cold, foggy and full of filth.

And I, myself, felt like Milan: cold, hazy and full of filth with which I was dirtied by Valeria and Enzo.

The Death
of the
Poplar Tree

I wasn't sad to leave the house, to sell it and to disperse all the memories into the wind. Or to sell them together with the house; so let the one who was going to buy it inherit our past days. Therefore, whatever price they would fetch it would be way too costly! I had never expressed my view loudly, for who would care about it anyway? As a rule mother had always held my point as foolish and improbable.

It was the last year of my *Liceo* days and by the end of the year mother had decided to sell the house (together with the poplar tree, the only friend I ever had), but it never occurred to her to ask for my opinion.

Therefore, I had cut it down!

When she advised me that she had found a buyer for the house, I thought to myself, *"Go on, sell freely your past, anyway, it is so depressing, but I won't allow you to sell the poplar tree."*

On the very same day, I went to the hardware store and purchased a chainsaw and armed with it went into the backyard. When I came close to the poplar tree, I started to shed tears. It was swaying in the wind carefree-like as if it hadn't been aware at all that its tall, elegant body was going to soon fall down lifelessly. The mere thought that I was the one who was going to *murder it* made me feel the agonising pain which shook my hand in which I held the lethal weapon—the chainsaw.

You are going to tear my soul apart!
You're even taking the poplar tree away from me!

She wanted to move to Bologna. What would I do there? She never asked that question. She knew that I was about to enroll in a university course the coming year. She did not care. All she wanted was to go back to Bologna. Close to her sister. The very same sister who told her that she could find even a fifteen year younger man with such an inheritance and youthful looks. He was precisely the reason why she had left, not Pierina. He wasn't fifteen years younger, but eight; nevertheless, she went back after the house was sold, alas, without the poplar tree in the backyard.

Well, to continue my tale: I took my weapon—the chainsaw whose loud crying surpassed my own. My loud cries could not be heard from the merciless noise of the steal-cold killer that was turning around his sharp teeth ready to turn into pieces and sawdust the only one who had ever liked me, who had ever understood me …

I won't give away my poplar tree!
As I was cutting its very surprised trunk with watery eyes and from saliva uneven breathing, out of nowhere, red in the face, yelling and screaming, my mother had appeared. She waved her arms the same way she waved them on the day when she had thrown Simona down onto her knees, and I heard then, in the chainsaw clatter, in my crying and the poplar tree's crying, Simona's and her still-born child's crying, too. She walked toward me screaming, wanting to switch off the chainsaw, and the only word I could understand in that noise was the word *idiot*, naturally addressed to me, and I went straight to her with the chainsaw screaming as loud as she was, with the intention to cut her throat, perhaps.
"I'll cut your throat!"

She ran as fast as she could, she ran as if she was running for her life down the street, and I resumed calmly my ill-fated task of cutting and crying. I felt as if I was tearing apart my own soul; oh, if only you could have seen how the slimy blood was pouring out of its trunk while its soul was sitting on my shoulders pressing them down heavily; I heard the howls from its veins and twigs, the howls of its leaves which hadn't been swung by the rhythm of the wind but by the sound of the chainsaw.

I killed it; I killed my *road to heaven*!

Dead, it had collapsed down onto mother's car and smashed the roof, and the windows burst into a thousand little pieces. I couldn't have cared less, no, I could not—she'll sell the house anyway, she'll get her money, she'll get a new car. I couldn't buy a new poplar tree, couldn't buy a new soul or a new *road to heaven*.

The big hand of the clock in the sky, which was pointing me into the desired direction, was no more.

All I had ever wanted could not be purchased with money, and all she ever had and was able to give was measured only with money.

"I'll sue you, you idiot! You've smashed my car, you've cut my tree, you've damaged my property!"

I said:

"The car is yours, the property's yours, too, but the tree's mine. The tree is the idiot's!"

Now she looked at me without hiding contempt and disappointment: *Why did someone exactly like me happen to be her own son?* I knew her thoughts well, I saw what was written on her face, therefore I did not trust her tears when she started to cry. Regardless of the fact that I called those tears *the tears made for Valeria-Theatre,* for she would always use them effectively in her duels with Enzo, still, I was not fully aware that *it was only the cheap role of an actress of suspicious talent.*

She told and retold this *unfortunate scene* of my cutting down the poplar tree to all her relatives and friends countless times, saying:

"What did all this mean to him, who would ever know? Why did he need to do that and what did he want to say and achieve by cutting down the tree, that foolish son of mine? He isn't the one who can use words, the one who could explain what he needed, but simply, he has always been ready to shock us with his eccentric, totally mad actions … I can't turn my head around it any more, I simply can't explain who has made a mistake or when the mistake was made?"

I was—*the Mistake.*

Maybe the poplar tree had made a mistake by showing me the *road to heaven* … so, from that day on I have always aimed upwards, towards heaven … knowing that I do not belong low down … down low among weeds and the thicket.

Chapter Number One

I don't know what year it was. I don't keep numbers in my memory. Accordingly, I don't remember which date it was, for I don't feel the need for adding a number to a certain event. But if there is a need to implement a number to this particular event in my life (given that I put the events in order of their importance), then certainly I shall give a number to the chapter which followed that event, and its number should be the honourable *Number One*.

Mother had returned from Australia. I never knew she was there. Who, in their right mind, would want to go to Australia? The heat, the mosquitoes, the flies, the kangaroos, the little bears, the cockroaches, the rabbits, the English that nobody understands anyway, uninhabited, almost deserted … why did she hide that she was going there? Or to put it even better, *Why didn't she bother to tell me about her trip at all?* Yeah, that'd be even a better question! She couldn't be bothered; she couldn't care less!

That particular year when she had left, I rang her twice but she never picked up the phone. After the second time I gave up calling.

Sometime later that year my telephone rang, I answered, it was her. She said:

"Otto, how come you did not call me?"

"I called several times but no one answered my calls. How can anyone know about your walkabouts? Are you in Bologna at all?"

Through light laughter, she answered:

"We weren't here the whole year."

"Oh, I see …" said I.

"We were visiting Nick's family, we were in Australia."

"Oh, I see …" said I.

She asked:

"Aren't you going to ask anything? How was it there?"
I asked:
"How was it there?"
She said:
"Come over and I'll tell you all about it."

There we go! I went over that weekend.

I went to my mother's and Nick's who had moved into her house, the house she had bought with the money she had got from selling our family house.

So, there we are!

I found myself in Bologna once again. Knocking at mother's, by now Nick's too, house door, as a guest, as it is natural and obvious that I don't belong there.

The greeting is pretentious; mother's hugs are fast and nervous, the desire to tell and show about experiences doesn't allow her to pay attention to me. Once again, she is messing up my hair, I can't stand it so I am telling her, *"Mother, don't mess up my hair, it needed so much time and attention to get it the way it is,"* but she's only waving her hand half laughing.

There he comes, the virtuos Nick, he is approaching with an extended hand, with a grin so I can clearly see his big yellowish teeth and some strange contentment in his eyes (because of mother's house?); too fondly he is pronouncing my name ... no, no, no ... I don't trust him, I know that all this is just a theatre play and I have an insignificant role which is so obvious by their body language, by their looks which connect them in their conspiracy ... and it is so obvious by many small and big signs they are sending into my direction ... which throws me, straight away, out of balance ... I am getting prepared, I am nearly ready to get involved in their little games and plays ... we shall see where all that is going to lead us.

They were in Australia!

How exciting! Australia. As if Australia interests me. And who is really interested in Australia? To be clear and precise—where the hell is that Australia?

Yes, it is right down under, at the end of the world.

And who in their right mind, and why, would want to go to the end of the world?

Oh, no, no ... I am not even interested in a mere story about Australia. I am not the one who wants to travel. I don't want to go anywhere; even here in the heart of civilisation I would not travel, let alone to the end of the world, to the tundra, and sand dunes, to the Sahara or God knows what you call it. All of that is not welcome. Why would I care about their stories and adventures? I am not the one who would sit on a plane and travel to the end of the world, all with the aim to brag about it later, to show off that you flew from point A to point B. So, what did you learn there? What did you see? Nothing!

I see, I see, Nick and Australia, that's what's important!

Learning that, I said:

"So...what did you do in that desert?"

The spoon she brought to her mouth nearly fell out of her hand. On hearing those words, the spoon in her hand trembled and she spilt the soup onto her silken blouse.

I said:

"Look at the way you eat! You nearly dropped the spoon."

Nick poured himself a glass of wine and holding the bottle, he said:

"Shall we share some wine, Otto?"

"I never drink wine. It dulls the brain. I'll have a glass of water but you two feel free to enjoy your wine." Then I stood up and went into the kitchen to fetch a jug of water. I had cut several slices of lemon, put it in the jug and started to fill the jug with water when my mother entered the kitchen and uttered in a trembling voice:

"Otto, please, could you be kind? Nick is a nice man, for Christ's sake, be a bit kinder to him!"

I looked at her as if I was looking at a stranger. As if I was seeing her for the first time in my life—*what meaning did her words hold?*

Then after a brief observation of her utterly unhappy face, I said:

"Of course I am going to be kind. I always am!"

She squeezed my hand, trying to smile at me, picked up the jug and headed towards the dining room. Empty-handed I followed her. Fine, I got it, she wants me to be kind, so be it, I am going to be kind. But how come she never got it? —I was always kind.

So, I asked—kindly:

"Nick, do you like living in my mother's house? It is a beautiful house, isn't it? It is spacious. Mother had bought it with the money she had got from the sale of our old family house in Milan. I bet mother told you all about their separation, though they never legally got divorced but luck took our side so my father walked away empty-handed, never asked for a thing. Can you believe that he left us everything, for all he wanted was to save his own head ... ha, ha, ha ... I am joking when I'm saying he wanted to save his own head ... ha, ha, ha ..." I could not stop laughing.

Tears filled up my eyes, cramps crumpled my stomach, I nearly choked while stamping my feet and through tears and laughter I muttered to my mother:

"Tap me ... tap my back ..."

But she just sat there as if she was hit by a thunderbolt, looking at me dumbstruck. She looked like a bronze statue made by a distressed artist.

When I stopped laughing, there was a heavy silence hanging above the table, only, sporadically there were little disobedient *'ha's'* coming from inside of me, rising up my shoulders, and they sounded as if they were just hiccups.

Finally, when those disobedient *'ha's'* had stopped and when I had wiped off my tears, there was still that heavy silence hanging above us. I was looking at both of them for a while, then I said:

"What?"

They did not say a word, which confused me a bit, made me a little nervous, so I asked again:

"What? Are you mute? I made a little joke, didn't I? Isn't it good to have a hearty laugh? The finest art is to laugh at one's own expense. Only those who are not so vain, those without a big ego, can laugh at their own expense. Isn't it so?"

Silence.

"Isn't it so, mother?"

Silence.

"Isn't it so, Nick?" and with a somewhat quieter voice than usual but still with a strong accent, showing his yellowish teeth, Nick agreed:

"Well...it is, sort of ... good ... to have a good laugh ..."

"...even at one's own expense ...", I said looking at mother's still crimson face. She just slightly nodded her head and replied softly:

"May I be excused ...", stood up and headed towards the bathroom.

Silence prevailed. Nick gulped down his wine; quickly, I took the bottle and filled up his empty glass, saying:

"Cheers, Nick!" lifting my glass filled with water in the direction of Nick's unidentified gaze, which was balancing on the rim of his wine glass.

There we made a nice *chin-chin*, no harm was done, he had really understood my joke. Nick can get it with a little bit of effort! But I had decided to stop my jokes altogether. If they were really not up to jokes, I wouldn't force it any more. Why not spend lunch in the atmosphere they were keen to create? Let them choose their topics; let them talk about the desert and wilderness.

When mother came back she was dressed differently. Yes, I know, her blouse had been soaked with soup. She came wearing a colourful dress. I thought, *I'll pay her a compliment.* She liked compliments, plus she had a stony face. I said:

"*What a nice dress, it suits you well.*"

The little smile appeared on her face:

"*I bought it in Australia.*"

"*In Australia? Such a pretty dress? Oh, Lord, I thought they never wore nice clothes down there. Who would ever say that you could purchase such a lovely dress over there ... it looks like one of those dresses one can buy only in Galleria.*"

She changed the course, saying:

"*When we finish lunch you have to see the photos ... only if you want to ... Australia has such lovely nature ...*"

"*Greta Scacchi lives partly in Australia.*"

"*Who's Greta Scacchi?*" asked puzzled Nick.

"*My, my, you have never heard of Greta Scacchi?*"

"*No, I haven't,*" said Nick to what I replied:

"*Good Lord, he hasn't...*"

But mother hurried:

"*Greta is an actress. I think her mother is from Milan while her father's Australian ... or vice versa ... not too sure.*"

"*How come that you are not so sure, you've always read the cheap yellow press. You used to swallow up all those trashy magazines. Don't you remember, father used to tell you that you were not going to find anything clever in such magazines? Can't you recall his astonishment with your obsession with such filth? Nick, in such magazines one could have found all the trivial information and shallow lies about so- called public personalities, written in a very poor manner, bad writing style, naive and stupid, accommodated to the average reader, which really means, to the barely literate. Well, in such magazines one could find about Scacchi's cultural background, isn't it so mamma? Only what I wonder right now is that you are not so sure whether her mother was Italian or her father? I would say her father, for the surname says it so—Scacchi. Or, do you Italians, when you go over there claim that your surname is, actually, Australian? Nick, what would then be your Christian name?*"

"Nicollo."

"There you are, Nicollo, not Nick. Maybe that woman's father was an Italian born in Australia, but the thing is that, you people, you change your background easily ... you sell your soul ... trade it off."

"I can see your point, but let me say that everybody has the right to feel the way they want to feel about who they are."

"Bullshit! That would be the feeling of those who sell themselves straightaway. Why would you call yourself Nick when your real name is Nicollo ... Nicollo what?"

"Vidal."

"Vidal? What do you mean—Vidal? Can't be, this is not an Italian surname. What we are missing here is a letter at the very end of the surname, right?"

"Well, you are quite right, our family name was Vidalle ... but father had made a very slight change ..."

"He had made a slight change? You've lost your identity, for you are not Nicollo Vidalle any longer, but Nick Vidal. This is an example of alienation; this is exactly the way they take our names, our people ... the weaklings without backbone."

"Why don't we change the subject?" in a quiet but obedience-seeking voice mother had suggested.

But Nick Vidal was not ready to be obedient yet:

"We don't have to change the subject; I'd like to have the opportunity to explain to Otto what would be my opinion on such matter, for we have heard his. Don't you agree, Otto?"

"Go on, I am keen to hear your opinion and those like you who easily change their background, their family name and so forth."

"Firstly, please, do not judge how easily we change anything. Secondly, a man was born in a particular place, within a particular nation, which gives him a certain identity, a feeling of belonging to such a place or nation. But the world in which we live is on the constant move. When people migrate to some other land and their children are born in that land, then I am asking Otto, what he thinks, how do those children feel about themselves? Does Otto know?"

"I don't know. And how would I know how they feel about themselves? All I know is how I fell about myself. Full stop."

"I am the one who knows how they feel. And if you allow me, I shall explain it to you. The children who were born in a different land to their forefathers adopt this land as their own and the process is called assimilation, Otto. And what does assimilation mean, exactly? It means not to be too different from the others. Ask the children who are 'different' how they feel about it? Ask those kids with a surname too difficult to pronounce or with a name nobody ever heard of, or when their family has customs which really don't serve any purpose any more. Do you really think then, my dear Otto, that one left-out letter at the end of someone's surname makes for such a catastrophe? Do you think that it was a sacrilege of the Holy Sacrament when my father had left the last letter out of our family name all with a good aim that people would remember it easier, pronounce it more easily? Do you really think that Nick is so different a name from Nicollo? This is just a shorter name, the same as yours Otto is short for Ottavio, isn't it?"

"No! It isn't the same. Otto is short for Ottavio, but both names are Italian, while Nick is the anglicised version of Nicollo. Can't you see the difference?"

"Well, I do live among Anglo-Saxons."

"I do not and never would want to. I think that people who leave the country of their origin are deserters, they change their names, customs, they come back with a thick accent ... and why, why now, when you are here in the country of your origin, you still insist on being called Nick Vidal instead of Nicollo Vidalle, trying to cheat the world?"

"For me, this is the very same name, just slightly shorter."

"Yeah, yeah, try to find as many excuses as you can ... you and your kind are traitors. I have never had my name changed and never would want to ..."

I have to admit now that at this point I was so agitated by this so-called Italian, so-called Australian, my blood reached boiling point ... and my mother ... she was not ashamed! She was quiet while he was blabbering, trying to find excuses for his own stupidity while admitting that he had no identity or even worse—he was proud of it, claiming that he had a right to choose. So be it, let him choose!

And mother? She had the right to choose, too. So, she had chosen to be on Nick's side when she said:

"Enough is enough! Are you going to argue now endlessly? Nick is right. Every man has the right to make his own choices, especially a man who lives in two different places, two different countries, in two different cultures. It is only natural that everybody has to assimilate to their environment."

Oh, mother's comment was just what I needed; I was looking straight into her eyes when I asked her:

"So, what about you? To what did you assimilate? To Australia? You were the one who could assimilate effortlessly to anything—any situation, any person. Any person, except the one ... called Ottavio Otto Visconti! Yes, it was I, the last fiddle in your orchestra of easy and popular music ... everything came before, the last was Ottavio Otto Visconti. Try to roll this film backwards, back into your son's childhood, now put the events and people in the numerical order according to their importance: Enzo Visconti, your sister Pierina, Mauro, the hairdresser, Tulio and Marco your cousins, then Gavina, Stella and Anna, then it would be bridge or scala quaranta by whatever name you have called it, the beautician Dina, father's friends with no apparent numerical order, parties, parties, parties ... never-ending parties, cheap magazines with lacquered biographies of so-called stars and models ... where did you place Ottavio Otto Visconti? In this turmoil where had you misplaced him? I am asking you now—where has your son been all those years? Which place did he occupy on your priority list at that time and which place is he occupying today? Yes, right now, in this very moment? Just as always, as countless times before, so as today—you are taking sides with some stranger who you're yearning to charm, as you've always longed to fascinate people ... I don't quite know with what ... all, except one—your own son. Ottavio Otto Visconti, where is he? He is in Milan. What is he doing? He is studying. What is he studying? Oh, dear people, I don't know what ... I am paying for it, I do pay for all my obligations and responsibilities, I do and I always have. Obligation. Ottavio Otto Visconti. How are you, Otto? What did you

do all those years? Were you deeply hurt by father's leaving? Were you hurt by my silence, by my indifference? Yes, mother, I was hurt by your silence! I was hurt by your indifference! I haven't heard a word from you for the entire year. I've been in Australia, I'll show you the photos, you'll see the beauty of nature, I've bought a dress.'

Mrs. Visconti, I've had enough of this theatre, I do not wish to be a partaker in it any longer, not even a passive observer, I am leaving. This very moment, right now. Here, look at me once again, the last time, and off I'll go to Milan, to my tiny rented room, and you can be free to enjoy your comfort together with your worthy friend, Nick Vidal, I am leaving and perhaps I would, by mere chance, somewhere on the streets of Milan meet my father who will look at me full of contempt and I would never know why? Or, do we know why? Weren't you the one who had convinced him that Otto was the 'incapable one, nincompoop, poor sonny boy, a misfit?'

So, my dear Mrs. Visconti, my dear indifferent mother - that would be my monologue. The monologue I was carrying and rehearsing over and over silently all those years, the monologue I was repeating in my dreams, dreaming that I was reciting it to you as I would recite some poem learnt off by heart. From the heaviness of this poem I had started to whine, had developed asthma, a constant inflammation of my lungs which came as a result of those congested sentences ... no, no, I can't afford any longer that my own sentences suffocate me; these are the very last words I am about to say in this house you had bought with the money you had got from the sale of our family house ... so, enjoy it, together with your friend, Nick Vidal, enjoy sharing this expensive wine he is sipping effortlessly ... off he goes, Ottavio Otto Visconti, off Otto goes, ta-ta." While saying that, I had stood up, cleaned up with a serviette the crumbs which had fallen on my pants, finished up the water in my glass while staring directly into my mute mother's astonished eyes, talking so quickly that she would not get a chance to say anything.

All this time Nick Vidal's lifeless hands were resting on the table. He did not move them one inch. They were lifeless from the excess of alcohol, not from the shock. I don't think that he was prone to shocks; he was more prone to alcohol, precisely—to wine.

I turned my back and walked away; I heard her crying, and it looked to me that I could have cried easily myself too, but why tears when this time my words had said it all: every feeling suppressed for years, hence, there was no room for tears...with a light step I let myself down the street and it was the first time that I felt as if I was breathing with full lungs, as if they were not squeaking at every breath-in and breath-out, and it seemed to me that the wind could blow easily through my light lungs, freed from the trampled sentences which started to rot after years of being trampled, sending out the odour of withered and dead thoughts.

La storia è finita!

And now, there we have those several years of icy silence. It had spread between us as some sort of thick, sticky fog enveloping those years when I did not belong to anyone.

I never wanted to belong to anyone!

That sentiment of not belonging had tagged along since my early child-hood. I had never felt as belonging to anything, even though, on that very day I had argued with Nick calling him traitor while emphasising my national pride, all of that was just a theatre. I had never been defined by any rules. I did not really care that I was born in that particular city, of that particular background. The mere notion that I belonged there had never brought along the feeling of belonging. Maybe that was the real reason why I had tried to accuse Nick of being a sold soul; I could have sold myself easily only if I had had a chance, if only somebody had wanted me!

Who wants me!?

I wanted to scream:

"*Who wants Ottavio Otto Visconti!*" Again I could see those words written on my huge screen where I would always see my sentences to which answers were never found.

Let her have Nick Vidal, let him have this woman, my mother, let them be happy ... let them belong.

I'll go alone ... alone I came to this world ... I'll go all alone!

Mother had Nicollo Nick Vidal, father had Simona Sargente, I didn't have my poplar tree any longer, I had cut it down.

Mother's Death

When she had died I had forgotten everything: all I had ever reproached her, all what had ever made me mad with anger, only a heavy sense of remorse kicked in—why hadn't I allowed her to see me regularly all those years, and in the end, why did I get mad to such an extent that I just walked out of her house, that last time when I saw her, resolved to never see her again? There were those periods of time when I had not called or seen her for several years, not even when she had called or sent one of her pathetic letters.

Death!

What to say about death? We are never prepared for death. Neither was I prepared for it that morning when the telephone rang. It was a call from Pierina, with whom, I have to say, I had not talked precisely ten years.

She said:

"Otto, Pierina here."

"What do you want? Why are you calling, and who on earth gave you my number…(and the permission to call—I wanted to add, but I didn't, it hung onto my tongue.)

Pierina said:

"Valeria has died."

'Valeria has died' —I saw those very words written on the same screen from which I had wiped off, with a big eraser, all memories about my mother the last time I travelled by train from Bologna to Milan.

It became reality. Valeria had died. I hung up without saying a word and commenced a sad cry for my mother to whom I had turned my back and all offended walked out for good.

I went to the office and said to the Big Wig that my mother had died. He looked at me without a word of consolation. He asked:

"For how many days are you going to be absent this time?"

I said:

"*Only because I am racked with pain I can't hear the ring of cynicism in your question. I am going to be absent for one week. And may I ask out of curiosity—how many days would you be absent if your mother had died? Perhaps—none!?*"

I said exactly that, that was the exact wording I had used, and in all that despair I was quite proud of my quick wit and courage. I have to admit, it took me off guard, even me, I would not have expected such a brave response.

The feeling of remorse, actually, had accompanied me throughout all of my life, but when my mother died this feeling took up the central place on the stage of my, rather delicate, feelings, and then as a sovereign king it was crowned on the invisible throne of my brittle self-esteem.

The voice of remorse accompanied me unceasingly whispering, —*You are guilty, Otto.* There were so many reasons for feeling guilty, so many wrong deeds and decisions and every new minute I was more aware of my tremendous guilt and responsibility of betraying mother, betraying her expectations, never visiting her, getting angry whenever she would tell the truth (it was actually the truth) that I was *incapable*, that I would *never succeed*, that *I would never amount to anything worthy* ... and so on and so forth. And as it is, it looks she was right, she knew it, and I dare say maybe she had died because of all my wrongs ... I faced the truth finally but there was no way back. There was no way to negotiate or to bargain with death: if only you give me back my mother, I will admit that I am a *nincompoop,* that *I will never amount to anything worthy,* I will admit that I am a nut, an eccentric—give me back my mother, I repent!

No! There was no such game in anyone's reality. Death has its own reality, ungraspable to us.

Only remorse is what's left to mortals.

Even though I had turned my back to church, priests and all other beasts long ago, I had promised myself that I would see a priest when this pain subsided … maybe he would find a way to tell it all to my late mother.

There were so many reasons for remorse. All the way from my childhood. A different Otto they wanted. I was a defiant child. All I wanted was to be unique or exceptional, even as a little child all I wanted was to be a poet … but, in their reality, in the book of their desires it was written—Otto is going to be a lawyer. Same as his (holy) father. He will inherit father's business.

Oh, no, no, no statutes! No uniforms, court-clerks, policemen, decrees, no big books full of boring, identical sentences, grey suits, ties, authoritative tone of the omnipotent. No, Otto doesn't want that!

But, there was no mercy! Who was going to ask a child, anyway? Who ever asked Otto what he wanted to be? Nobody! My father used to say just to anybody who would or would not ask him about my future, *"My son is going to be a lawyer."* That inner voice (back then I did not know that it was going to be called *the inner voice of remorse*) was screaming, *"No, no, no, this is a mistake, Otto is going to be a poet,"*… but I was the only one who could hear this voice. While the expression on my face was telling that it had nothing to do with that tiny voice (there was a smile on my face), my eyes were looking down hiding that secret. And always the same: whenever my father would state, *"My son is going to be a lawyer,"* I would stretch my lips into a twisted smile and would look down at the tips of my shoes. But both mother and I obeyed father's wishes without a remark, for there was no place for expression of our own wishes, dreams and hopes … I left all of that for *some future time.*

In my early years I wouldn't mention my own desires (waiting for *some future time*), I would only nod my head and lower my eyes, but when I found myself all alone, I would sit in the garden and gaze at the crown of an old poplar tree that was showing me to which side the clouds were sailing, and the crown itself looked like the big hand of the clock in the sky which was going to show me—*the road to heaven.*

And to me, Otto Visconti, the only *road to heaven* was to be travelled on *the wings of poetry.*

Only on *the wings of poetry* I could survive in such a reality. I was the laughing stock at school: I was the smallest, thin as a twig and timid. When I had to say something, I would stutter, and there was a hot dumpling in my throat, which wouldn't let my words out. The dumpling's heat would colour my face and the temples of my head red. There was nothing yet invented which could have eased that heat ...

The only ease I could find was to sit in the garden and gaze into the crown of my poplar tree, pointing to *the road to heaven.* My poplar tree was my only friend, my only counsellor and comforter, and only I knew that that the poplar tree had *a soul.* How to explain that to a lawyer-father? Or to a mother who was preparing me to be his carbon copy? I could express myself *only to my poplar tree.*

Therefore, I had named my first, never published, collection of poems—*Only To My Poplar Tree.*

She

She said she had to hurry to catch *Her* train. I knew *She* would have to say that sentence, I knew I was going to shiver as a leaf played by the wind. There was no way I could have taken this sentence into my mind and assembled it into my system easily, naturally. This sentence was repulsive to me, it was obnoxious, it caused me a headache and a sensation of sharp pins in my heart. I knew, from the very moment I met *Her* that day, that our time was limited and that *She* was going to say fairly soon that sentence: *"Now I have to go, Otto, to catch my train."* While saying that, it was almost as if *She* was spilling out venom which was finding its way into my system, poisoning it.

I wanted *Her* to say:

"Otto, I'll miss this train. I want to stay with you a little bit longer. You are the actual reason for my visiting Milan, not my cousin, she was an excuse, but you were the real cause."

But *She* never said that. Such a thought had never occurred to *Her* …still, I could not penetrate into *Her* mind, into *Her* hidden thoughts, but that was even better, for I might have stumbled on my way there onto the adjective *"muddle-head"*, which I would have easily sewn onto my name— Otto. The sentence *She* uttered had not even slightly changed *Her* placid face. Well then, is it true that the face is the mirror of emotions? The mirror of internal storms? What was telling *Her* placid, motionless face? Absolutely nothing to me. Only, it seemed to me that *She* said it so simply, unpreoccupied with thoughts or feelings.

She had to go. *She* couldn't miss her train.

So what if *She* did miss *Her* train?

There are other trains!

What if *She* missed one?

I would have said, *"Fine, I'll keep you company, you can stay with me as long as you wish."* Big deal—*She* missed the train! (Countless trains have been missed by Otto!) So, it means I am not worthy of one missed train. I am just someone *She* paid a visit passing by, with whom *She* spent a few hours before catching *Her* train.

She didn't even want to think twice; *Her* face was calm, not a single line on *Her* forehead, not a single worry or a slight dilemma.

And what did Otto's face look like? What was written on Otto's face? Was it reflecting a storm of emotions and nightmarish questions which were arguing in his head?

Otto nearly started to cry.

Whatever he wanted to say, he could not deliver a word!

Not a single word! I, me, Otto Visconti, was mute, as mute as my phone, which was mute for days until *She* finally rang. Such was my silence: no words, no tones, neither ringing nor buzzing came from me. I was silent and scared of my own voice: *She* might understand, might read from my buzzing that I was on the verge of tears, on the edge of despair. I stood up and wobbled to the waiter giving him a ten-euro bill with my shaking hand and telling him to keep the change. Why would I need the change! Petty cash! Always some petty cash in my life! Why always petty cash for me? So I said to the waiter:

"Why would I need the change? I don't need petty cash!"

He only replied:

"Grazie signore!"

(… ma, che grazie … ma, che signore!!)

Fine, in silence we sat in the taxi. As always, *She* was first to speak:

"It is a long way to Trieste. I thought I might read your book on the way back. Is it out yet?"

In disbelief, with a quiet voice, I asked:

"Do you really like my poetry?"

"*I really do, Otto. I am not a professional reader but I do know what good poetry is.*"

I shrugged my shoulders.

She asked:

"*Are you tired?*"

I am not tired, I am sad, that was what I wanted to say, but I didn't. All I said was:

"*It could be said that I am tired …*"

"*Are you working too hard?*"

"*It could be said that I am working too hard …*"

We were standing on the platform, oh, how much I hated this moment of parting! I never used to have a problem with departures; I would leave with a light step, especially when it came to my family … I would simply go away, away from all of them. But this was the first time in my life that I understood what was the real meaning of going away from the one you care about.

I gathered all my might and asked:

"*Are you going to call me?*"

"*Sure I am going to.*"

"*Are you going to call or write a letter?*"

"*Whatever you prefer … I shall call you.*"

"*I am looking forward to it. When are you next coming to Milan?*"

"*Not so soon … I am spending more than I am earning …*"

"*So … when am I going to see you again?* I asked seemingly in a casual manner but my voice was trembling, and I honestly feared that I might get teary, to what once again, with a casual and cheerful manner, *She* said:

"*Who knows, maybe next year again … we'll see, maybe some coincidence again …*"

"*Yeah … some coincidence …*"

"*I'd better be going now, the train is about to leave soon. Thanks for the company, thanks for carrying my bag to the station.*"

"That's the least I could do for you."

She hugged me as one hugs a brother. I hugged her as I would have hugged a sister. There! We hugged each other! I deeply sighed, but *She* didn't. *She* only checked her wristwatch and said:

"Ciao Otto, see you again."

"See you again ... ciao ..."

Yep, see you again! Rest assured—I'll see you again!

The train slowly started to move; *She* waved to me through the closed window without getting up. *She* smiled at me. I smiled back. But I did not feel like smiling. The train station became real: ugly, huge and dreadful, full of busybodies ... Milan became the very same city as it was before her arrival.

With her leaving, all the colours had left, too.

Only greyness remained.

Do you think *She* rang?

No, *She* didn't.

I could have died from sweet sadness. I could have written yet another collection of poems on that particular evening woven with threads of sweet sadness ... but, I'd decided to do something else. I'd decided to take the poems I had written that summer for her and weave those threads of sweet sadness and painful longing into their body.

There you have it! That was my panacea: to tell *Her* with my heart, with my poetry about my pain, which was caused by *Her* unconcern.

I cried my eyes out in the morning when I read my poems altered in such a way. I knew then that I had weaved into their body all of my finest feelings and the most sophisticated expressions; I knew then that any publisher, surely, would want such poems.

I knew then that *She* was going to read them in hardcover.

That thought was my driving force to knock on the publishers' doors. I had spent so many sleepless nights waiting for their answer, waiting to hear how impressed they were with my words, how surprised and pleased to finally find a real genius … I was waiting, burning, I was walking through dark alleys, praying to an uncertain god to find a publisher who would make her immortal in my poems … and then a miracle happened! I found him!

I found him or he found me … but it did happen.

A wave of newly found self-esteem came over me. I am worthy! Much more than my mother ever believed, or especially my father, much, much more than some so-called Nick Vidal believed … I don't know whether that was his real name, I had forgotten it and all about his Australia … I am worthy! My poetry was acknowledged!

I have a good reason now to call *Her* again! I shall write *Her* a letter and tell *Her* that my publisher (I even have his name now!) was planning to publish my poetry by the end of the year. I shall invite *Her* to the book launch. I can invite *Her* cousin from Milan, too.

Could anybody imagine what my days were like while they were preparing my book for publication and organising its promotion?

Truly and literally: sleepless nights, nightmares and foolish self-talks … Oh, what I could have dreamt of in those short spare moments when sleep did close my eyes for a while … What brave visions I had! I saw myself on the covers of the most prestigious literary magazines, oh, well—I am not a person cut for the cheap, yellow press! I had seen myself surrounded by masses of admirers showing their admiration openly, but yet, they did not dare to touch me as if I were a demi-god or to be more frank—as if I were a real god; indeed, poets are gods, very special souls, with very special talents. I saw my name *Otto Visconti* written among the most famous names, shoulder to shoulder with *Pablo Neruda, Federico Garcia Lorca or Lord Byron* … my name next to names like *Allan Edgar Poe, Maria Rainer Rilke* … yes, shoulder to shoulder with the most acclaimed, the most talented, the most tragic ones … so, my illuminated but at the same time tragic name—*Otto Visconti* among them.

Yes, that was the way I felt right then.

Everything became so trivial. Especially trivial appeared to be material things which my father had carefully collected and treasured all those years, so that my mother could scatter them, give them to her relatives and to that silly Australian puppet … Everything became so trivial. I learnt *why* I was here—to pursue my poetry. I was here to create, and I knew how to do it, I was the creator. Ah, with what ease I found my publisher! You should have seen the way he rubbed his hands. I was silent as a seer … what was I supposed to say? I had said it all with my poems. But I only said it to those who could understand it, for it needed a subtle soul to grasp it. *She* understood it at once; *She* had that subtle soul which recognised the genius as soon as *She* met me. *Oh, my beloved, I shall reward you, as you deserve - how easily you have recognised the genius!*

And the genius knows how to reward you!

Now that I *am* a poet, I have to change the way I dress. I look too formal, this clerk mentality and spirit I was exposed to for so long has damaged my image. I don't care any longer, I won't be coming to work dressed the way they expect me to be dressed! No, I won't! I'll come dressed completely different to them! I'll dress as a free person! I don't want to wear a suit any more; I don't want to wear stripy shirts with two little buttons on the collar. I don't feel like tying those ties of complimentary colours any more … this is not Otto any more … not the real me. I have never had the courage to dress the way I like to dress. I mean, the real me … Otto's coulour is—black. I always felt the best when I was wearing a black turtleneck skivvy and black jeans (well, that's exactly the way Giorgio Armani dresses himself, so, why shouldn't I dress the same way?)

On one occasion, I had bought black pants with vertical purple stripes. My, my ... did I look smart, so powerful!? With such pants I put a black skivvy and, listen, - a black beret. It was the time when I just grew a little moustache ... boy, was it stunning!? But, you know, when they had seen me, they gossiped about the way I dressed, they reproached me. Yes, I heard them, I did, they talked, whispered. Yeah, I would hear those whispers as I was passing by or when I would join them in the common room; they would all stop talking ... and then upon my leaving, I could hear murmur again. Whispering, whispering ... I would look at myself in the mirror and I saw a very pleasant reflection; I thought how original I was ... one hundred percent different to them.

Well, all of that happened in the first years of my employment. In the first year of my service, I still had the courage for individualism, for I wanted to be different ... but those whispers, those constant murmurs. The constant little laughter which came from those dressed properly in their suits, with ties, and the ladies with not-so-good copies of Chanel suits, with their skirts just above their knees ... yes, my respected comrades who looked so alike that you couldn't distinguish one from the other. They laughed at the best pants I ever owned! There you have it—it was their favourite entertainment! Some time after, I thought—no, you are not going to laugh at me. No, you are not going to laugh! So, I became the same as they were. My look was not any different to theirs - so no one could ever consider that Otto was a poet. Who would ever think that there, inside of me, I was capable of wearing my striped pants and a black beret forever? I even thought, back then, that I could grow a little moustache *à la Dali* ... but I really did not have the courage at that time ... why not now? Why wouldn't I give myself, right now, permission to change everything?

What would they say? My office mates?

Look at Otto, for heaven's sake, he has published a collection of poems and he is a completely changed man now. He is totally unrecognisable now. But I would think—

yep, but this changed man was I the whole time, I have never changed really, just expressed myself in the right light, this is who I am, indeed.

But what if they laugh at me? Loudly and sweetly. What if they say *Just look at Otto …*

I want to change the way I dress, the way I comb my hair and I want to grow a little *à la Dali* moustache … to be more—myself. I want that from the very first glance at me it is apparent that Otto is somehow different, somehow disobedient … that he's a poet.

Otherwise—there is that split. There is that outer image—the image of a clerk who is all combed and neat, seemingly all ready for collaboration, while inside, there is the other one - uncombed and untidy, with wild hair and wild imagination, apparent in the way he dresses, in the way he speaks and the way he carries himself … there, that Otto I want to let out of the cage in which he was caged by his own mother, his father, then by the society which never fed his self-esteem, which never said that it was good to be a poet, never said that poets were needed by society, that they, indeed, were a panacea for it. But quite the contrary, actually. According to their view, a poet is a weakling unable to face the real world around him; a poet is a confused and lost soul on the edge of a psychotic breakdown, too gentle for reality, a misfit, maladapted … I am asking you once again:

Which and whose Reality are we talking about?

Who has the right to hold an exclusive view of Reality, to interpret it with their limited means? Who's the one who has chained us to civic reality, the prison from where even poets can hardly tear themselves apart? I don't want such a reality! I long for a different one. My own reality, so be it: laugh at me - I accept I am a Puppet! Laugh at me, my reality is where you can never find it … you clean, obedient citizens, I am renouncing your reality, for it is boring, it is imagination-killing, creativity-and-zest-for-life killing! To me, your reality stinks! You won't, ever again, push Otto into your box ... no, no, I have seen through it all. This reality is a plain lie. I desire not to live the lie!

This is why I had cut down the poplar tree! Only the poplar tree had a soul. Only the poplar tree resided in my reality, therefore I had never let mother sell it, cut into pieces, kill its soul. What did she ever know about matters of the soul? Just as she generously gave away father's ties, she gave away the soul of my poplar tree and my own. What did she ever know about matters of the soul? What did she ever feel? She went away and marvelled at Australia: *You should have only seen the palm trees; they were touching the sky* ... Oh, really, the palm trees! What about a poplar tree? You never had an eye for a poplar tree; you never had a soul to connect with a poplar tree which had been touching the sky for the past twenty years in the frame of your window! You never marvelled at it; all you wanted was to sell it, give it away, walk away without a word ... so, I had cut it down! There is no more poplar tree, so be it! There is no more family house; there is no more poplar tree. She marvelled at palm trees! She marvelled at everything that was never connected to her soul, because she was never connected to her own soul as if her own soul had lived somewhere else. How is it possible that a soul could marvel at the palm trees which the eye had seen for the first time, but never notice the poplar tree which should have swayed her soul each time she looked through the window, I am asking now?

My poor mother, she has died ... but what I was talking about was about her when she was alive and her soul was in constant alteration between the two realities, between the palm and the poplar trees and it could never meet at a common point ... but my mother has died and I hope that her soul has flown to the place where it belongs; maybe she carried there, within her soul, the poplar tree; maybe she carried me there, maybe she has forgiven me, maybe she has forgiven us all ... she should have forgiven just as Otto has forgiven … yes, he has forgiven her for leaving for Bologna, leaving for Australia, forgiven her for Nick Vidal, for the poplar tree and has forgiven that unbearable scene when she had attacked and beaten up pregnant Simona, so consequently the poor soul had lost her baby, as we had heard some time later.

Yes, Otto did forgive all of it. He had forgiven himself and her … for he had to … my mother had died … the regret had eaten me all up; I had to forgive.

But what about Enzo Visconti?

No, I have never forgiven him. He didn't even show up at her funeral. He knew that mother died. I delivered the news. I called up and told him so. After twenty years I heard his voice, I almost hadn't recognised it; he did not recognise mine. He even didn't remember my name. When I finally got him that day, I simply said, *"Otto's here,"* to what he questioned, *"Otto who?"*

After a well stretched out silence, I replied:

"Otto Visconti, your son."

What do you think he said?

Nothing.

He was silent for a long time. A very, very long time.

It was as follows:

With a shaky voice Pierina announced that my mother had died. At the first moment I was completely blunt (I had never expected that she could die; neither then nor at any other time would I have been ready for her death) but after the initial dullness ceased, I started to cry bitterly. I had cried for days after it, but on that very day after a good, long cry I decided to call my father. Now eighteen years precisely had passed since I talked to him or saw him. I had never even bumped into him, for Milan is too big a city for such encounters, plus we belonged to different classes—where would we ever meet?

His secretary answered the call (by now, it was so clear that it wasn't Simona any longer). I asked if I could talk to Visconti but she said that he was not in his office. She told me to leave my number, but I didn't want to. So, three times the same scenario had played out. Finally, I got him at twilight. I heard the voice I didn't recognise just as he did not recognise my name. I said:

"Otto's here."

He asked:

"Otto? Otto who?"

Me again:

"Otto Visconti, your son."

He was silent, silent, silent. I allowed him to be silent. I had allowed him to be silent long enough while I was silent too, consciously and deliberately creating uneasiness in interstice, giving generous opportunity to the time in which my father could press his own thoughts onto his conscience.

He cleared his throat, still silent; I was counting the seconds; I knew he must have been pressed by his thoughts, for they took him off his guard, they boiled his blood; I knew, for his blood would boil easily, quickly (which was only known to us—his own family) … I let the silence irritate him; I let him clear his throat once again and when he opened his mouth, his voice still sounded harsh as if it hadn't been cleared:

"Otto, anything new?"

"New? Well, if I only start to recount, everything would be—new, to you. But there is only one thing I'd like to tell you, the reason for my call. My mother has died. Your former wife. That's all I wanted to tell you. The funeral's on Friday … in Bologna."

"This coming Friday?"

"Is there any other Friday … please, tell me!?"

"Oh, yes, yes, I see, coming Friday. But I am in Palermo the coming Friday … I should be at court …"

"All I wanted is to let you know, I really couldn't care less what you are doing on any Friday ... that'd be all, just called to tell you that she had died ... your son's mother has died ... so, that'd be all—father! Good-bye."

I hung up without giving him a chance to say a word, to say *'good-bye'*. He said his *'good-bye'* eighteen years ago without giving me a chance to say anything. Yes, that's what he did, he left without a *'good-bye,'* leaving us without wishing us well ... leaving us to cope the way we could cope, leaving us the house as a possible and acceptable *'good-bye'*. The house which mother had sold, the poplar tree which I had cut down! Yeah, that was his farewell!

On that particular Friday he didn't come to Bologna. He didn't attend the funeral; possibly, he was in Palermo. He didn't come to say the last *'good-bye'*, he didn't have the courage to face me. Or to face her family? My father Enzo Visconti, the respected lawyer about whom daily papers wrote regularly - thus I knew I had a father, I knew he was alive - never came to my mother's funeral.

Instead of my father, Nick Vidal attended the funeral.

Nick Vidal and Pierina were standing on the house porch when I came.

He extended his hand; his eyes were filled with tears and compassion. I started to cry; I hugged him while he patted my back. He smelled of cologne and wine. He smelled of cigars. In any other circumstance it would have irritated me, I would have told him that he smelled of acid and of inferno. I said nothing. I simply allowed him to embrace and comfort me regardless of the smell, which came from him and enveloped us like some kind of sad but safe shield. He said:

"I share your pain, it is equally painful for me ... right now, just when I met such an extraordinary woman ... right now, when I fell in love with her ... why now?"

I said:

"My mother has died."

"I loved you mother."

"Not as much as I did ..."

"... no, not as much as you did, Otto ..." hesitantly, Nick agreed.

I knew that I had to forgive her *all*, because I couldn't forgive him for *anything* that he had done (their trains were frantically speeding in opposite directions, but without me in any of their carriages). Therefore, if I do not forgive, un-forgiveness will eat up my heart. I would die young from *'old heart disease'*, with the heart full of bites and holes like fine Swiss cheese. And yes, my heart was pierced already; it already looked as a piece of cheese gnawed at by a little, invisible mouse that chewed persistently, wholly dedicated to his task. His fine work of gnawing went on and on for days, months and years ... and it could have gone on and on until he had eaten it all up and eventually, one day, it could have been read in the obituary that Otto Visconti had died young from the disease of an old and worn out heart.

And my mother had died too young. She had died, too, from the disease which had eaten up all of her internal organs, perhaps the named disease had caught her in that train which carried her in the opposite direction to the one she wanted to travel to, in that empty train she travelled without her descendants, without me—Otto Visconti, so, why then was I crying?

Why?

My mother had died.

Regardless on which train she travelled, how many stations she had missed, she had died ... my mother had died.

Oh, I did not know what to think, I did not know what to say ... I did not know anything. I cried alone, hidden from her family's eyes, hidden from everyone; I sat on the park bench and there above me, standing tall was a poplar tree and I let myself cry as I would before a dearest friend, before someone who would know how to soothe my pain, as if I was crying the very first and the very last time. For her!

The Book Launch

They called me to take a photo for the back cover. I decided to buy new clothes for the occasion. I had tried to find the very same pants (or at least similar ones) I had worn to work when those fools had laughed their heads off. Those little pants in which I really felt so good about myself, I felt like the real Otto, as a poet. The black pants with tiny vertical purple stripes … then, if I could only find a black skivvy, let's say, edged with a tiny purple trim around the sleeves, then, a beret, of course, a black one (*black is Ottos' colour*) as it goes well with my complexion, it emphasises the colour of my eyes, it makes me appear strong and sharp. I wandered through the inner-city shops but I couldn't find what I really wanted, yeah, I didn't have much luck. But anyway, I had found something similar enough, though the beret wasn't exactly as the one I pictured in my head. Neither were the pants the right ones, nor the skivvy … it was just a plain black skivvy without any colour around the edges, let alone purple.

Well, whatever it was, it was way better than if I had showed up in the grey suit, the one I wear to the office, daily.

All those new clothes I had bought in one of those ultra expensive shops … it cost me an arm and a leg … a real fortune, but nevertheless, it wasn't the time to be stingy, anyway, I was going to wear those clothes to the book launch. I had to look stunning because of the public, myself and above all—because of *Her*.

Several photos were taken, but when I saw them I wasn't pleased. It wasn't me. There was something missing there; I told them that I wasn't pleased with the photos, so we took new ones but alas, neither the new ones were the way I wanted them to be: my hair was not in the right order, my eyes looked sleepy, there was a shy expression on my face … that wasn't me. I wanted my hair to be sleeker so that none of my hair was out of place, I wanted to look straight into the camera so that that strength in my eyes could be seen (the strength which was bursting out from my creative soul); I wanted my smile to be relaxed but not too wide, to appear just in one corner of my lips as if I wanted to say something but had changed my mind and was keen to keep that wisdom to myself.

That would be—the real Otto!

I had explained it all to the boy who was taking the pictures; he looked up at the ceiling and said:

"C'mon, get your act together: fix your hair, the smile, the expression … c'mon for the love of God!"

Even though I didn't like the way he treated Otto the poet, I sighed deeply, and tried again to please this young lad, so he had taken a few more shots … yes, one of them wasn't too bad, it was the closest to the idea I had in my heart. But again, it wasn't me; once again my smile was somewhat lukewarm, my eyes were too meek, but I have to admit that this time my hair looked OK for I had tamed it, and if I couldn't have tamed it, I wouldn't have had the picture taken without the beret. Firstly, I wanted to have my picture taken with the beret but I gave up this idea, fearing what would happen if some of my acquaintances saw this picture and would not recognise me just because of the beret. *It would be better for the first time to show fully that it is me, and for the second book I could have a photo with a beret on my head.*

By then everybody would know who is **that** *Otto Visconti.*

The impatient youth had told me that it was a good photo, that I looked good in it … but I wasn't reassured; but nevertheless, they did put that photo on the back cover and underneath it a short biography. I said that I didn't desire anything too long. I mentioned I was born and bred in Milan; I mentioned our family house and the poplar tree; I never said a word about my schooling, for I wanted to learn something else, I wanted to be someone else, surely not some sort of office scribe … so we'd left that out.

So, it came …

… my big day …

Yep, it came … and thank heavens, *She* came, too.

Now first things first.

The day and the place of the big event was established, and I took advantage of knowing the details and rang *Her*.

"Otto Visconti's here."

"So early … Otto?"

So early? Did *She* really *have to* prick the balloon of my enthusiasm?

I called *Her* too early! I checked my wristwatch, OK, it was early but not too early, it was already seven o'clock in the morning, Saturday, and I was awake from five waiting at least two hours to pass so I could ring at a decent hour, speculating that at seven *She* could be up already. I said:

"I am sorry, I haven't woken you up, have I?"

"Actually … you have."

Only silence was there. I said:

"Well then, go back to sleep … I'll call you later."

She said:

"Yeah, call later, I am so sleepy, went to bed quite late. Ciao Otto." *She* hung up.

She was sleepy. I would never tell *Her* something like that even if *She* rang at five in the morning. I would say, *"Don't worry, you can call any time you want."* Well, anyhow, *She* said something else. *She* said that she was sleepy, that it was too early—so be it! *She* said that *She* went to bed very late! Damn, where was *She*? Why did *She* go to bed very late? Where did *She* go? It was Friday last evening, where did *She* go on a Friday night? What was the time when *She* went to bed? Midnight, two hours after midnight, three, four? Ah, women! I was so enthusiastic to let *Her* know about my book launch: when and where it would take place. I wanted to organise the transport, offer a taxi, buy *Her* a bunch of flowers …

Never mind, in the end it isn't a catastrophe of such great proportions. I'll let *Her* sleep a little bit longer, then I'll call again. Or … should I call at all? Should I put *Her* on ice for a change? Put *Her* on my waiting list? I said that I would call later, what if I simply don't call back? I'll do that—simply nothing! I'll let *Her* sleep, and then when *She* calls me, simply, I won't answer *Her* call … but is it a good idea? What if Maurizio calls with some new details? No, I'll get the call, but certainly I am not going to call *Her* again. I want *Her* to experience how that feels. I will let *Her* wait for my call. I will wait for *Hers*, too. Noon would pass, then one o'clock, two, three … I won't call. I'll let *Her* worry, I'll let *Her* wait and ask herself, *"What on earth has happened to Otto, he said he would ring again?"* I'll make *Her* wait and tire of waiting so *She* will say, *"I am going to call him now, I can't wait for his call any more."*

The hours had dragged slowly. I was waiting while *She* was sleeping. Eight had passed. I decided to go out to buy the papers and a *brioche*. I changed my mind: what if Maurizio called or God forbid herself? But, no! It was too early for anyone to call; maybe I should go down and get those papers and a *brioche*. I didn't even have any cigarettes. Yeah, I had to go and get some cigarettes. I put some clothes on and found myself on the street. Saturday morning, the street was still asleep, just as all its residents were still asleep (just as *She* was, too) because the night before they went out and came back so late. I walked the street listening to the sound of my own steps. I was counting the steps and it sounded to me as if I was listening to the melody made by my own bare feet on the pavement. I started to sing. Quietly, then a little louder and in the end from the top of my lungs. The song itself had altered my mood. I asked myself, *"Why should I hurry home when I can sit in a coffee-shop, enjoy my coffee while reading the papers?"* Sure Maurizio was not going to call me that early; if he really needed me, he could call a bit later, in the end, he was the one who needed me now … and when it comes to *Her* … *She* was fast asleep, *She* came home late last night. Why did *She* come home so late and where was *She*? Yeah, where and with whom? Would I ever be able to summon the courage to ask *Her* who was the one *She* was going out with? Would I ever be able to summon the courage to ask if there was any man in *Her* life? No, I couldn't believe that, *She* wouldn't be so kind to me, *She* wouldn't be so happy to hear me, to accept my invitation to the book launch … No, no way, I knew *She* was waiting for me, *She* was counting on me. I had illustrated my life to *Her* with such ease. I laid it all before *Her* feet: it was clear that I was living alone, that there was no one there, that I was a hardworking man who wrote a lot … *She* knew all about me.

But, what did I know about *Her*? Nothing!

All I knew was that *She* visited Milan occasionally, for *Her* cousin was living here. I knew that *She* worked for some broadcasting company … and that was all. Full of mystery - never willing to talk about herself. When I asked anything of a private matter, *She* would simply change the subject, anything but private stuff. How could I know, then, where I stood? How could I know that?

So confused I was sitting there sipping my first morning coffee, smoking and reading the papers while pretending to understand what was written there. I couldn't understand a single sentence; I was reading it over and over again. Reading in vain. In my thoughts only—*She*, in my head and in my heart; *Her* image was floating in front of my letters while I was reading. I gave up reading: *'Well, I AM going to think about Her while I am sipping my morning coffee and smoking the cigarette of an endless chain, at least I am not sitting next to the phone, I could be tempted to call Her right now, at nine o'clock in the morning while She is still fast asleep, telling me that She came home very late.' She came late! Damn, where was She? Maybe She didn't go anywhere, maybe She simply stayed home and watched television till the late hours … maybe She watched herself … isn't She a TV presenter after all? Could it be that She watched some movie, or that She wrote a letter to someone (to whom?) … probably She ironed her clothes or did something plain and common!? I have to go out and stretch my legs.'*

It is a pleasant morning, chill in the air, but it seems as if the sun is going to come out from the thick smog … I'll have a brisk walk, maybe I'll manage to run away from my thoughts! The best would be if I ran the fastest I could; maybe by running I would shake off all my thoughts never to catch me again. But I am the one who doesn't like to run. Not only that I dislike running but I never liked any kind of physical strain: I have never visited gyms, never lifted heavy weights, nor have I ever run or ridden a bike. There is that mass obsession with the idea of *'being fit'*, hence everyone is doing some sort of exercise: running, hopping, skipping … I don't feel like hopping! I would only run if I were certain that I was going to run away from my thoughts, particularly this morning's thoughts because they are accompanied with rotten feelings; the rotten feelings are accompanied with rotten ideas, and now, that makes me afraid of myself; I am afraid that I might give in and bring my rotten ideas to fruition. I'd better stretch my legs; it would be better to walk because when I walk I leave less opportunity to hear the chatter. There is an unceasing dialogue in my head; it is loud, particularly when I am sitting doing nothing. Then the record goes endlessly on and on: blah, blah, blah … blabbering, blabbering, blabbering …

Here I am, I've got to live in Otto's body and mind … is there any way out?

A prisoner!

A prisoner of my own mind! Where did I get such a mind? Is it the conductor of my pessimistic thoughts, does it dictate my moods and my wrong decisions? Who was directing my mind, myself? Was I programmed to be *Otto il poeta*, then where and when did it happen? How can I get rid of it, how to enlighten this mind enveloped by dark fog, by dark thoughts? Is there a way to be someone else? Would I have become *someone else* if I had only changed my thoughts, my dispositions? But I wasn't even sure if I really *wanted* to be *someone else*. On the other hand, nor was I sure that I wanted to continue on with this Otto. Who is Otto: a toy or victim? Is there any possibility that Otto becomes a creator? What if he *was the creator* who had decided to create the very circumstances where he had found himself? Consciously? Unconsciously? With his mind? With his heart? *I don't wanna be a victim!*

"Hey you, up there, are you playing me like a game?"

Hey God, do you hear me, or do you have more important business to mind? Is there a piece of me in your book, in your plans? Were you the one who had tuned my mind to this frequency? Why this Otto? Why do you need me the way I am and what do you want from me at all? I know … there is no God. Then whose creation am I? The creation of Valeria and Enzo Visconti, the provincial Gods whose brains are bashed by the uncontrollable winds of lust.

Oh, piss off … just piss off!

I want to cut that long story about my waiting short because it only takes me back to my bad mood and it weaves my nervousness into a thick rug.

I just wanna say that; I went home and *She* didn't call, neither did I on that same day. On the following day *She* didn't ring, *She* wouldn't ring ever, so I called *Her*:

"Otto's here," I said shortly, to which *She* replied:

"Otto, I thought you'd call yesterday."

Yeah, you *thought*, but why didn't you call me … I wanted to ask, but refrained, all I said was:

"Had no time yesterday, there were too many things to do."

"I thought so."

Hmmm, *She* thought so! Does it mean that *She* was waiting for my call … does it mean that *She* was really thinking of me … that sentence had changed my mood for better. All I said was:

"So, how are you doing?"

"How are you doing, Poet, on the eve of your first book launch?"

I really wasn't glad that this was my first book; I would be more self-assured if it was my second ... or third book ... I said:

"*Actually, this is the reason I am calling. The launch is on the 10ᵗʰ of March.*"

"*March? Didn't you say it was going to be in February?*"

"*Ah, publishers ... they would tear up your soul, they are often irresponsible liars ... but to hell with them, tell me, are you coming?*"

"*Oh yes, I really want to be a part of it ... who knows what will yet become of you, Otto?*"

O-ho! There we go! *She* said, *Who knows what will yet become of you, Otto. She* believes in me. *She* is well aware of my talent and my prestige. *She* respects me! Yes, yes, who knows what yet Otto is going to achieve, above all when *She's* on my side; together we could burn this world: *She* and I. Humbly I said:

"*Whatever will be—will be; the most important thing is that you are coming.*"

There was a cold silence from her side, so I added:

"*... among the others ...*"

So, there we are.

Do I have to emphasise how slowly my days were dragging, or is it only natural to understand in what kind of fire I had lived? Oh, sweet anticipation! Double anticipation: I was going to be a recognised poet and the woman of my dreams was going to witness it.

Those days prior to the launch had become the brightest days in my pessimistic book.

Even though I had pleasant dreams and visions while I was daydreaming in those days prior to the launch, I felt some sort of dull pain, somewhere in my stomach, or in my guts, or around my appendix, I couldn't locate it precisely, because the pain was walking unhurriedly as if it was walking through the promenade of my inner labyrinth. Because of those promenades I couldn't eat. Whatever I would put into my mouth it was travelling up and down through my digestive system only to come back into my mouth again causing heaviness in my stomach, then hotness in my head and in the end causing tachycardia. Yes, my heart raced as a wild animal, particularly so when I had dinner and went to bed on a full stomach. My hands were sweating; I was repeating the speech I wanted to deliver on the day countless times, changing it from minute to minute in the belief that it was shallow, that it wasn't spontaneous and that it was full of meaningless sentences …

I didn't want to write down my speech, because my thoughts were always clearer and made more impact when they were in my head, but when I would write them down, they'd only be a vague interpretation of what Otto wanted to express. How to let my heart speak its un-encoded language, which I didn't have to interpret into harsh words? Only in that language I wanted to tell the *woman of my dreams* what my heart was dreaming of, yeah, only in that language.

The Saturday had arrived, the 10th of March. I got up earlier than usual. I got up at 5 am precisely, anyway, I couldn't close my eyes the whole night, so I got up to end that nightmare. I could hardly wait for the arrival of that holy afternoon; the hours were dragging, I checked my wall clock and wristwatch twice to be sure that they were still ticking … that they were still counting seconds in their usual way but not in some other rhythm today as if they both had decided to get broken and to stop right now. But alas, they did not break; only the time was dragging in its usual pace.

Yesterday, I called *Her* to make sure that *She* was coming, that there was nothing which could interfere with her arrival. *She* told me *She* bought the train ticket. *She* is coming! Because of me! Because of my book launch, because of Otto *She's* coming! An endless happiness. I was prone to believe that God himself existed, that he was full of mercy and endless kindness, that he kept me in his books, that he hadn't forgotten or forsaken me. And in the grip of such ecstasy, I hastily thanked someone I had never seen and I would never see.

Do I need a rehearsal now? I am going to get dressed. I've got to try out my clothes to see how I am going to look. Regardless of the fact that I have been in those same clothes in front of my mirror repeating those sentences which are meant to be my speech, I need one more—the last rehearsal. I have even put on my beret, counting that misfortune might find me and bring on lousy weather; that the air might be full of moisture or God forbid that it might rain. Oh, how well my clothes suit me! I look so cool in my black pants with purple stripes, in my black skivvy (the one without the purple edge around the neck and sleeves, because I couldn't find such a skivvy). The black beret suits me so well giving to my face a different expression: sharper and more serious.

Black always suits me best, good that I have chosen it.

A few hours earlier I strolled downtown. I couldn't stay in the apartment any longer … and what for? To stare through the window? To stare at the clock hands which weren't moving?

I couldn't stand that, hence I went downtown earlier. I was walking through the streets of the city which looked to me now dear and unique: full of colours and distinctive, it was my city, I belonged to it and it belonged to me, I loved it and I convinced myself that it loved me back. I convinced myself that this city of mine was going to adore me even more when all the papers brought the news of my book launch, when I became *the best poet Milan ever had* … Oh, heavens, what a future was laid out there for me! Who knows, maybe I was going to be so rich that I wouldn't need to work any longer in such a boring company with such boring and uninspiring people. Maybe I was going to be a millionaire, maybe my poems were going to be translated into all world languages (or at least the majority of them); maybe I would be asked to travel all over the world to be a distinguished guest at world launches, maybe to open some important, distinguished gatherings; I was going to be a celebrity, hence I started to act as one while I was slowly walking the streets of Milan with a happy smirk on my face, and when a passer-by would look into my eyes, I would mildly smile, nod my head in agreement, so that he could retell later the unusual encounter with the kind, humble and talented poet who never hesitates to mingle with commoners. Rumour has it that Pablo Neruda was like that. As much as I know about him: he was a communist, but I wouldn't go as far, that idea stinks to me, look at all those communist countries; they stink, they are all poor, they failed … the mere idea is a failure … but I won't talk about politics, I am *the Poet*.

I came one hour earlier than my publisher told me. They offered me a drink, which I accepted at once; I needed it badly. Oh, how good that sweet bubbly was! I liked it, it stretched my lips wide and every time I thought about *Her*, I would take another sip, which added to my much-needed self-confidence on that evening. Yes, yes, self-confidence. I didn't want to think about my mother's unfortunate sentences with which she would diminish my self-worth while they were echoing within my mind every time my self-worth was tested. I said to myself, *Otto, all this is happening because of you!* So it was! I knew it, all this commotion, all those people who were going to rock up: the journalists, professors, gentlemen who were going to talk about my poetry, the applauding audience, and all and sundry were coming because of me—Ottavio Otto Visconti!

Yeah, I liked that thought! Just that sentence—*Otto, all of this commotion is happening because of you!* And … because of *Her* … I thought. Because of us. Our future. In *Her* wildest dream *She* couldn't dream what I was planning. What a brilliant future I was planning for *Her* … for us!

Well, I will pause right here to impose one question: *What happens if we know the unknown?*

I feared it. Fear always accompanied me like a dark shadow, which I could notice only on the façades of houses when the twilight sneaked in, finding me turning my head around to check if anyone was following me. Fear stuck onto me like slime on a newborn. I felt as if this slime was never washed away but it grew into and under my skin and became my own shadow, which followed me around all the time. A slimy shadow of fear written on the building façades, on the shop-windows, in the pupils of my interlocutors where I could see my reflection, in the raindrops where I could see my own face and its shadow of fear, in the after-rain puddles where I would stomp deliberately not to see my own reflection and the shadow of fear in it … fear of everything.

Here, it is present in this very moment. The fear of the book launch, fear of public speaking, fear of the possibility that *She* won't come, the fear of laughter, tears… fear of the fear.

I drank a little more of that sweet bubbly wine and said to myself in a semi-loud voice, *Otto all of this commotion is happening because of you*, and I added loudly:

"She'll be here, She will!"

I tried to think of some other thoughts but those two.

I said earlier: I didn't know what kind of future there was for us; I thought an exceptional one, what else could have been in store for the two of us?

What happens if we know the unknown?

If I had known the unknown, I am asking myself now—would I have committed suicide right there and then in an attempt to stop once and for all those immeasurable troubles of my poor torn soul, troubles of a little pitiful heart? Right then! If I had only known!

But, I didn't know.

I didn't know, so I walked naively, madly, with open arms and a trembling heart into the embrace of my misfortune.

Do I have to say that from the beginning till the very end of the whole event I was unceasingly thinking only and only about *Her*, that I had heard *Her* words (which *She* never uttered but I swear - I heard them)?

Do I have to say that I was looking only into *Her* face and while talking addressing only *Her*, at this rather small gathering (because the crowd was not as big as I had anticipated)? Do I have to say that I read my dearest poem *The Poplar Tree's Heart Woman* only to *Her*? Do I have to admit that I had cried, no, not because of the reason others assumed caused my tears, but because of the fact that *She* was there. That *She* came because of the poet Ottavio Otto Visconti; what kind of poetry could have matched that fact? *She* with *Her* girlfriends, with the invitation in *Her* hand; I saw *Her* chatting with someone and then, when *She* saw me, *She* started to walk slowly, elegantly towards me; my heart started to tremble like the trembling leaves of my poplar tree on that day when I walked towards it with a chain-saw and cut its trunk, separating it from its veins which were tying it to mother earth.

Yes indeed, when *She* headed towards me I heard music. Yes, I saw *Her* walking in a long white dress, I saw a white veil covering *Her* face, the veil just slightly lighter than the lightest strand of *Her* hair; I saw *Her* bare-foot, meek and ready to give *Her* youth and *Her* life to me, and in giving me *Her* youth and life, *She* was injecting into me everlasting youth and eternal life.

I saw *Her* floating and I, myself, started to float towards *Her* across the hall; drops of sweat were running down my forehead, my eyes were moist and the palms of my hands were nervous and moist too; tightness gripped my throat so that I couldn't utter *Her* name at all, I just managed to stutter whilst kissing *Her* hand:

"*You ... came, you did ... come ...*"

I can't state for sure whether *She* was as elated as I was, *She* didn't hug me (I expected at least a hug); there wasn't any particular kind of excitement in *Her* voice when *She* said:

"*Of course I came, I told you so.*"

And everything just faded away. Professor Ruggieri lengthened his speech but I was not aware what was happening, what it was that he was telling us; he was talking about some metaphors, about the poplar tree that grew strong within my soul ... hang on ... it grew in our backyard ... but all I was thinking about was how attentively *She* was listening, how gently and approvingly *She* was smiling ... *She* and *Her* girlfriends ... all of them were here because of Ottavio Otto Visconti who was standing next to the professor, bah, next to the professor—he was standing next to himself alone, without a word, intoxicated with the words of others, intoxicated with *Her* eyes and sweet wine.

Gently, I was smiling wanting this moment to stretch out indefinitely …

Well, it was my turn to say a few words about myself and about my poetry, so I said:

"I haven't prepared any speech for the occasion. I am not a speaker; I am a poet. Perhaps you are expecting from me to hear something extraordinary, different or something what was important to my creativity. But all I wanted to say (there I started to stutter thinking that *She* would think of me as of an idiot and laugh at me; I thought what if *She* really got ashamed of me and questioned *Herself why she came to such an idiot's launch;* I asked myself why the crowd was so insignificant in their number, why all the eyes were pointed into my direction; I asked myself was I really ready for something of this proportion even if *She* was there to see me … was it all worthwhile … and I was stuttering more and more) … *all I wanted to say … I wanted to say that … I am not a great orator … only a modest poet … I am …"* and rescued there I was by professor Ruggieri's words:

"And because of it, it would be the best just to read Otto's poetry. He is a modest chap but the beauty and the tenderness of his soul can be found on the pages of his collection which, I believe, as stated earlier, isn't the last one but quite the contrary, it is just an introduction into the rich creativity which is going to sway in the crown of Otto's poplar tree sown in his restless swaying soul …"

Applause had woken me up from that semi-paralysed state. Everyone was clapping their hands but I was gazing only at *Her*; I saw her big teeth *She* showed in their regular beauty while *She* smiled warmly as if *She* was proud of me - *She* was proud of *Her* friend Ottavio Otto Visconti.

Absolutely, completely, I was intoxicated. Intoxicated with love, with fame and with that sweet bubbly wine. It was perfect complete ecstasy.

Time meant nothing to me that evening. I was simply dull from the happiness and rapture. As dull as dishwater. Might sound strange to say that someone was dull from happiness and rapture, but me, Otto Visconti, I was dull and blind from ecstasy willing only to smile, to nod my head and to wish only for one thing: that this evening should never come to an end. I wished that *She* stayed there forever clapping *Her* hands and showing *Her* pearly white teeth to me while I felt as one who had earned precious pearls by his own wisdom and merit.

Oh, what a pleasure it was to sign my own book; I smiled to photographers; there were people in the audience who wanted to take a picture with me … I smiled proudly.

I didn't even think of my mother at that moment. What would she have thought if she could have seen me … what would my mother have said who used to say—*You will never amount to anything, Otto,* my mother who used to say—*You are simply useless matter, Otto* … No, I wasn't thinking of her; *She* was there, in *Her* white dress as if *She* had come to a wedding, my dear faithful friend.

Let me say one more thing:

While I was signing the books, I noticed that *She* and *Her* friends had gathered some crowd around them. If my launch wasn't in question, I am quite positive that I would have experienced a wave of rage: redness in my head, sweaty palms … but in these circumstances, I thought I'd let *Her* talk, most probably they were talking about me, anyway, most likely, *She* was telling them that *She* was my friend, perhaps *a very good friend* … I saw *Her* being very proud, I saw *Her* being flattered.

She approached me finally followed by *Her* girlfriends. *She* introduced them one by one, and I nodded my head only.

She said:

"What a lovely event, Otto. Congratulations and thank you for the invitation."

I said:

"I got confused a bit … then, while speaking … didn't I?"

In a very casual manner, *She* shrugged her shoulders and said:

"That's—you Otto. Everything was in your real manner."

If I hadn't had drank such a quantity of sweet bubbly wine, I would have questioned at once what *She* meant by saying *'That's—you.'* I would have surely questioned what *She* meant by saying *Everything was in your real manner*?

But as I stated earlier, I was already drowning in my sweet ecstasy caused by intense feelings of love, fame and sweet wine, smiling gently with absolute awareness that *'She does love me and accepts me just the way I am. Yeah, exactly that manner of mine is what She adores, hence leisurely, She's shrugging Her beautiful shoulders, yes, yes, just that poetic confused manner of mine is what She loves … or should I say my charming way is what She loves … and from that mere thought I get so much esteem—my stuttering is my charm indeed, something very unusual, quite unique … let it be so … let it be'*, I thought.

That short sentence *'Everything was in your real manner'*, let it be a story itself, the story *She* wanted to narrate.

Poets have style. Poets have charisma. I didn't feel awkward, why would I? I was a poet, not an orator!

I had signed quite a large number of books, I put my name down, a scribble, and while signing, I imagined that there was no end to the queue, to this crowd waiting to get my scribble … the number of people doubled up, tripled … they were all there because of me, because of my signature, my words of dedication … thus a man said to me:

"For my girlfriend, but would you mind writing something nice and personal … almost as if you knew her personally?"

I knew it! I always knew it, but was never believed. No one ever believed me; no one ever took me seriously … I was a laughing stock in my family

... they were not aware of my *insight,* that *I knew it all,* so I said to the young man I was signing the book for:

"*I knew it ...*" made a little pause, looking straight into the youth's eyes, and he said:

"*Igor ... like Igor Stravinsky ... I was actually named after him ...*"

"*I knew it all, Igor Stravinsky ... I always knew it.*"

We shook hands, he tapped me a few times on the back, we took a photo together, his friend took the photo, maybe his name was Bedrich ... after Bedrich Smetana ... While he was taking the photo, I was smiling knowing that it was a sign from the Heavens, a subtle whisper from my destiny which was whispering that I was going to stand shoulder to shoulder with the great immortals—with Igor Stravinsky and Bedrich Smetana.

It seemed that everyone, everyone wanted to shake hands with me, it seemed as if that was only the beginning of handshaking and that the only thing I'd do in the future would be handshaking and smiling to the camera. There was no end to handshaking; at that moment I wished that I were some hundred-handed Hindu deity, the goddess Kali or the Lord Shiva ... yes, years ago I read about those multi-handed Indian gods or demi-gods, and I felt as one myself and at that moment it wasn't important any longer that I didn't possess four hands, I extended those two I had to everyone, to every side, letting them touch me, feel me, whoever wanted, yes, there I was with enough hands for everyone, with enough knowledge, with enough divinity within me ... *Touch me freely, feel my presence!*

Only *She* was standing apart from the crowd, in the corner of the room, turning the pages of my book with *Her* slender elegant fingers. With those long elegant fingers of *Hers, She* would regularly comb *Her* hair backwards or tidily put it behind *Her* ear, therefore I was able to see *Her* gentle everpresent smile. *She* was smiling; I knew that my verses were falling down onto *Her* soul the same way the morning mist falls onto just awakened rose petals; I had poured myself another glass of bubbly wine and while it was streaming down my throat and giving me the ultimate self-esteem, a thought occurred: *In that white dress She looks as if She is going to a wedding—I'll propose! This very evening, I will!*

By sheer luck of the mad one I didn't propose to *Her*, the opportunity didn't present itself. But that had only lengthened my uncertainty; it only postponed the noxious moment of truth … A bitter truth. Therefore, it was all just a lie. All of it! *Her* white dress, *Her* gentle smile … I even thought that *Her* teeth must have been fake, because they didn't resemble pearls any longer; it was all fake, a lie, all that was there was darkness, abyss, nothingness which was swallowing Otto, rendering him to the darkest voids of desolation, and the only honourable way out of it was—suicide.

I want to say that the truth didn't come out all of a sudden. No, he didn't come at the same moment, my malevolent relative, not that same evening, willing to tell me the whole story. The story, which upon its hearing, firstly shocked me, it took my breath away, I could not believe it … knowing him well … I could not believe him …

Knowing *Her* … no, it couldn't have been true …

Lunch with Gabriella

Well, it is said that from every ordeal something good comes out of it.

Mother had sold the house and I ended up in a tiny room at university campus. I met Gabriella there. Only a thin wall stood between us so I could hear her breathing, I could imagine how she looked while she combed her hair, I could imagine the tip of her nipples barely noticeable underneath her semi-transparent nightgown in which, actually, I had never seen her, if I don't count my dreams. She was the dream of all young men of my generation. Seldom would she talk, she would only lightly nod her head while smiling, and I would imagine the sentences which stayed locked in the privacy of her beautiful head. I would play with those imagined sentences; I would turn them around and fit them together as a child does when playing with Lego blocks.

I was putting those sentences together into little poems, I was writing for Gabriella that particular year.

Gabriella had never cared for any of us. She simply could not have cared less.

She was as pretty as an image on the cover of some expensive magazine, and I think that was exactly what she was dreaming of those long past years ... oh, Gaby, Gaby ... you were even prettier than Simona, who was the measure with which I measured women's beauty until I met you ...

Only once had I summoned up all my courage to knock on her door, which she kept half-closed while she talked to me. I only managed to see one of her eyes; I had asked her about some notes which I could not manage to take, for instead of taking notes I was writing a poem for Gaby, which she never knew was written, not even on this very day of telling my story.

She said:

"Tomorrow, Otto. I'll bring them tomorrow."

Mad I was from the sheer happiness, drunk like—*she knew my name!!!* *Otto!* Oh, how sweet it sounded coming from her child-like lips, pouted out while pronouncing my name …

I met her in the corridor on that particular afternoon embraced with an unknown man. It was a real shock for me! Gaby with some man! No, it was not one of us, a student. What could a student offer to Gaby? She deserved a film-producer or an editor of some glossy magazine!

The face of the handsome man who embraced Gaby looked so familiar to me that that was the exact reason why I thought he was a public figure, someone I often saw on television, perhaps. I could have bet I knew him, seen him many times. I was standing there with my mouth open, looking at both of them so beautiful and harmonised: my beloved Gaby to whom I was writing my poems and that handsome actor whose name I could not recall. In slow motion they were approaching as if they were filming some romantic movie right there and then. I was in awe looking at them approaching in slow motion, envy rising up towards this handsome man who was cuddling my *Muse* and *Inspiration,* and when they were just a few steps away from me, Gaby said:

"*Otto, here you are, the notes I promised yesterday.*"

I was still standing there as if struck by lightning; I couldn't understand the sentence she just said so she repeated it once again while I was staring at that handsome man cuddled up with my Gaby, who said in a voice I had recognised from the TV screen:

"*Otto! Is it really you? Our, silly, muddleheaded Otto?*" making a gesture as if he was going to hug me.

I still could not recognise him, I still could not understand who the handsome actor was. I was trying to figure out *where he had noticed me, where he had met me.* I even thought it could have been one of his well-mastered roles, smiling and ready to give me a heart-warming hug as one gives to an old pal.

He said:

"Gabriella, Otto's my cousin."

Vilas Visconti!

While I was still flabbergasted, he clenched his arm around my neck and started to squeeze it as if he was going to suffocate me. He started to squeeze his arm tighter and tighter around my neck, choking from laughter, and I gasped for air waving my arms around trying to remove his off my neck. Gaby said:

"Hey Vilas, you'll strangle him."

Vilas had loosened his grip and started to pinch my face and give me slaps all over it, saying:

"Otto, Otto, I have hardly recognised you. The little muddle-head … look how fine you have grown … ha, ha, ha, Otto, who would expect to stumble upon you … ha, ha, ha, the same muddle-head, just a bit bigger … ha, ha, ha, I haven't seen you for years."

I didn't have a word to say. He slapped me twice or thrice on the left, then the right cheek, and I did not know that was a token of closeness, but my cheeks were torrid, my hands were hanging down lifelessly as if they were pinned to my body with pins, and my lips were the lips of a wooden doll unable to utter a word.

He asked:

"Are you living here?"

I only nodded my head, and he continued:

"I heard that you were living with your father."

"Father? Which father?"

"Which father? You muddle-head, your father, not mine … ha, ha, ha, you are always the same silly little Otto … ha, ha, ha, which father he's asking."

Cool as steel, a voice came out of me:

"Father has died."

He looked at me in disbelief. He could not know whether I was lying but he looked at me astonished, and as I said, full of disbelief:

"I did not know that."

"Well, you know now."

"I am sorry …" he said, and I answered:

"It is just a phrase, not your genuine feeling."

They exchanged their glances and Gaby said:

"I'll wait for you downstairs, Vilas." She came on top of her toes and kissed him.

I did not have any word to offer him, so he said:

"Join us, let's have something to eat."

Should I say how desperate I was to have lunch together with Gabriella even at the cost of Vilas's company? But what I wanted to clarify as well was: what kind of relationship the two of them had. It couldn't be that she had fallen in love with this selfish, self-centered creature. I thought I was going to warn her what a selfish and self-adoring person he was, utterly indifferent to other people's feelings and emotions. Yes, I had the intention to tell her that for sure! She better be warned! I saw this lunch as an opportunity to get to know her better and when the time was right I'd tell her.

The lunch itself was a real Visconti-comedy.

According to her choice and wish we walked two streets down to the local *pizzeria.* In peculiar silence we walked there; Gaby walked in between us, keeping her lips sealed as she felt that strange tension in the air which had spread from my direction toward Vilas's and vice-versa … perhaps.

We all ordered *pizza* but when Vilas said that we were all going to have a beer, I protested:

"A beer, not for me ... I never drink alcohol."

Upon hearing those words, Vilas had turned himself into that small, mean little boy who used to always repeat my sentences with a little girl's voice:

"I don't drink beer ... I don't drink alcohol, so, what do you want—aqua minerale?"

So, that's exactly what we ordered: two beers and *aqua minerale per lui*.

He impersonated me, my sentences, my intonation ... only this time he did not pinch my thighs and my rear end but was pinching and squeezing Gabriella. He squeezed her cheeks, pinched her hands, her thighs under the table while she was just laughing and stretching out her limbs as some contented Persian cat. I could hear her purring out of sheer pleasure as she observed him with eyes full of adoration ... that game between the two of them was so easy and sweet, never trying to hide their excitement and lust, so, accordingly, they started to act as if I was not there at all, as if I was just a silly painting on the wall across from the two of them. A painting of a clown. Even I, myself, was able to see that painting: the dry mouth open wide, the big eyes—red, the red nose, the drops of sweat rolling down my crimson face even though it was not hot, I may say—it was rather cold but some inner warmth forced those sweat drops down my brow; I was sipping my *aqua minerale* without a word, only trying to clear my throat just as my mother used to do when I would deliver a sentence which sounded silly to her. That's why I kept my mouth shut, fearing that I might say something stupid again because of that incredible heat which could not be cooled down despite those sweat drops which dampened not only my brow but dampened my hands, too.

Before the waiter had brought the tree *pizzas*, Vilas ordered two more beers and *una acqua minerale per lui*.

At the table they were kissing, hugging, squeezing and groaning, as I said already—completely ignoring me as if I was not there at all. She was telling him:

"You naughty, dirty boy ... you bigamist ..." but she laughed while giving him those compliments and he laughed too as if she was telling him the sweetest verses ... and her words sounded as the sweetest verses delivered straight from her sweet, soft lips ...

When the warm *pizzas* had arrived, we started to eat with the fewest of words, but their conversation continued with their eyes and their touches under the table. I dedicatedly ate my *pizza;* I almost gobbled it up in three gulps while Gaby was still blowing onto her second bite.

Vilas said:

"You're already done with yours'. Do you always eat as fast? Look at you: skin and bones, would you like another pizza, you dissolute one?"

"No, I'd better be going."

"No, I'd better be going," once again Vilas was talking with a little girl's voice and he continued explaining to Gabriella:

"This was the way my dear cousin Otto would talk when we were children: No, no thanks I wouldn't want to ... please, don't do it, Vilas, it hurts ... no Vilas, thanks, I'd like to go home ... I wouldn't like to eat right now, thanks but I am not hungry ... I don't want to play, I'd rather read something ... My, my, how much this one could have read! He could sit still for hours and read. As a child he used to read books which I don't want to hear about even today. Classics! Then some sort of poetry written who knows back when ... ha-ha-ha ... maybe in the fifteenth century ... ha-ha-ha ... fifteenth century ... but he was so well read, he would recite poems, you know, I would spy on him, sneaking behind his back while he would recite one of Byron's poems, then I would kick the hardcover book underneath and when the book (and nearly his heart) fell down, out of astonishment or fear, his tears would flood his eyes, he would stutter Vi ... Vi ... Vi ... Vilas ... ple-ase ... do-don't do it. I would laugh so hard. Could you imagine a child of seven or eight sitting the whole afternoon reading and memorising poetry? Gaby, can you picture it?"

"No, I can't." she said.

"What passion, what interest ... being seven and reading poetry!"

"And what were your interests at that time? Little girls?" with just a hint of reproach Gabriella asked him.

Vilas said:

"Certainly, little girls and little girls only. Even now I am with the most beautiful little girl ..."

Her next sentence was addressed to me:

"My dear Vilas likes little girls, so he has always several of them."

"Oh, c'mon Gaby, c'mon ... it is not the way you say it."

"Really? What's with that 'bella stragniera'?"

"Ma che bella stragniera? Cosa parli? Dai, che bella stragniera?"

I heard those rumors too, that Vilas had a girlfriend ... a serious relationship with the girl who came to his parent's house ... but now, there was Gaby, she came as a new contestant to this worthy game, and I was curious to see how this fine game was going to end.

I said:

"Don't worry, Gaby. You are a new member of the worthy team and we shall soon see who is going to win the title."

Vilas protested:

"What's wrong with you? What are you talking about? What team, what game and what title? While saying this, a winner's smile was adorning the lips of our little *Casanova.*

Vilas did not let me pay my share; he said it was his shout. Before I left, he said:

"Call in sometimes."

"Where?"

"Well, when you're in Bologna."

"I don't go there ... have you met Nick?"

"Haven't met ... but heard of him."

"What did you hear?"

"That he was a family friend."

"A family? No, he is my mother's friend, not a family friend."

"Otto ... take this life easier ... like ..."
"... like you ... for example ..."
"... like me ... for example ..."
"Thanks, Vilas ... ciao, Gabriella."

Take this life easier!

What, as some sort of game? Like some sort of mucking around? As one who only takes from life? As one in constant search for fun? As Vilas Visconti?

I am not a superficial man!

I am not the one who plays with others' feelings. I am not taking unscrupulously. I am polite, I am patient, I do ask, indeed I do beg. I am cautious, considerate, kind and ready to please ...

Take this life easier!

I looked at them as they were leaving, never turning their heads back ... as so many times before, my piece of cake had fallen into Vilas's lap regardless of how he had earned it, with what kind of wit or cunningness he snatched it from the kitchen bench ... my piece of cake had fallen into Vilas's lap once again ...

But those were not all of Vilas's sins. No, those were not all!

Vilas Visconti
(The Beautiful One)

Bologna, school holidays at uncle Lorenzo's.

Vilas Visconti and me. Two worlds so apart, there was not a bridge which could bridge our differences.

Vilas was willful and a self-loving child.

Astonishingly beautiful, his face was delicately crafted and looked as if it had emerged from one of Michelangelo's paintings.

The expression of his face was angelic: small pretty lips and big chocolate-coloured eyes edged with thick dark lashes. His cheeks were pale-pink and his hair was silk-like. The silk-like hair he had inherited from his English mother. The two of them spoke only English at home, and it looked to me that the English language was a very strange and difficult one, understood only by unusual and difficult people (no way kids could ever understand it!) Back then, I thought *'it wasn't a language for poets, for people with soul.'* Simply, there was no melody in it which would nourish one's soul. Yes, that was what I was thinking while the two of them were exchanging some polite sentences full of obedience.

Visitors, visitations, family or friends' gatherings were a heavy burden to his mother. I knew that intuitively, reading this story, by the signs contained in her movements, gestures and mannerisms, and even though she uninterruptedly spoke her English, I knew exactly how she felt. The heaviness of her sentences was measured by the bitter expression of her face, by her tightened lips and by her monotonous voice stripped off any trace of excitement.

When we were alone, Vilas used to pinch my thighs and bottom, leaving dark marks on my skin to witness, for days afterwards, that I was maltreated again.

I would tell him, *"Don't do it, Vilas, it hurts,"* but he laughed mimicking my voice (speaking in a little girl's voice), *"Don't do it, Vilas, it hurts,"* walking behind my back and watching for the moment to pinch me again.

For me, the only worthy of mentioning entertainment in the house of the Viscontis was reading books. I would take one of my uncle's books, sit in the garden under the shade of a tree, and read. There is no need to emphasise now that, every time, when Vilas found me reading my book, he would sneak behind my back and kick the book out of my hands, laughing hysterically. I would say, *"Don't do it, Vilas, it's not nice of you ..."* then he would repeat in a little girl's voice, *"Don't do it, Vilas, it's not nice of you ..."*

He was ready anytime for any kind of malice: to take a hose and soak me wet, take his toy car and sink it in my soup, in the morning hide my trousers and socks to make it impossible for me to get dressed and come down for my breakfast ... as I said earlier, he would pinch my buttocks and bottom until it really hurt, take my piece of cake and run with it into the backyard and while doing that, he would mumble something, with a teary voice to his mother, in English:

"Mummy, mummy, blah, blah, blah ..." pointing his index finger at me. The English Lady would say something in a very calm voice and collected manner without even looking at me, while he laughed maliciously staring into my face.

Those days at the Viscontis were a real nightmare for me. My poor father naively thought that I was enjoying my holidays at his brother's house. The way he saw it was completely bizarre: he was convinced that Vilas and I got along so well as two brothers would. There almost wasn't any age difference, Vilas was older only by seven months, but that small advantage gave him permission to feel and act as if he was seven years older, not just seven months.

Once, only once, I had complained to my father and mother that Vilas was treating me really badly when we were alone. I told them about his pinching, about how he pulled my beanie down to my chin, holding it there until I suffocated, until I cried and then he ran away … to what my mother had replied that kids' games were sometimes quite cruel and that I'd better get used to it. She said that Vilas was my cousin and that he was only joking (he wasn't joking!); she said that I was a softie, like a girl … there, that's what my mother had said.

Not only was he a very, very pretty boy but also she believed that he was very intelligent, entertaining and unusually funny as well. She would point out how charming he was when he wanted to be, knowing exactly what he wanted, even when he was only a young boy.

Well, the whole truth was in this: that even young Vilas Visconti knew exactly what he wanted from others and he knew ways to obtain it. He manipulated everyone around him, kids in particular, and kids were, as paradox has it, the ones who liked him best. He was the best loved in any group, he constantly manipulated his father, my parents, myself … but in some strange way he had a lot of respect towards his English mother. In her polite manner and her monotonous voice she would say something barely hearable and Vilas would go all serious and stiff as a wooden little soldier, saying:

"*Yes, Mother. Certainly, Mother!*"

It seemed to me that that name—Mother, suited her best. In those rare moments when he addressed her as *mummy* it looked to me unthinkable in relation to this woman who never spoke much and when she spoke, she talked in short sentences without warmth or melody. *Mother.* When Vilas would stress it as '*Yes, Mother*' I knew that he was called to obedience without a hint of doubt. That demand could be read in her upright posture and in her monotonous voice with a slight but firm allusion of authority. When I said *a slight allusion* it could be only to the one who didn't know this voice and intonation, as indeed, it was a voice of absolute authority and I knew it better than Vilas, her own son, that this voice sounded like one which asked only for absolute obedience and one and only acceptable answer to it could have been—'*Yes, Mother; certainly, Mother!*'

In that house of torture, I would spend the whole week each and every year. It seemed that time had stopped in that house; summer days were dragging on endlessly, at a snail's velocity, promising that they would never really come to an end. I, in particular, hated the afternoons lengthened to eternity; the sky looked as if it was ever blue without any prospect of getting pinkish on the horizon, of getting darker … *Is it ever going to get dark?* I used to ask myself while counting the hours the way soldiers count their hours in the barracks, where they never wanted to be, the last days of their service.

It was precisely the way I had felt around that woman, as a soldier in barracks I never wanted to be in, a prisoner in the tower of obedience.

Vilas's father, my father's brother, was mostly absent. He worked all day long and when he came home at dinnertime, he would exchange a few words with his wife. Just a few cordial sentences, and I believed back then that the reason for it was his lack of English. It was almost normal and totally acceptable that she spoke only English as if she lived at Trafalgar Square, not in the Via Vittorio Veneto … she had never learned the language of the country where she came to live and believed that intelligent, learned people spoke English anyway … anyway, the others never counted.

Lorenzo Visconti knew almost everyone in the town. The window of his living room was always open to allow him to see who was passing by and to invite people to have a glass of *bevanda* with him or to join him for dinner. Often, I would sit in the corner of the room and observe with what joy he was celebrating life. He was celebrating the little things which add meaning and joy to life, because of the '*big things*' he had already missed out on. He enjoyed good wine, fine food, great conversation and above all great jokes he shared with anyone.

In such an environment *Lady Mother* looked like an ambiguous but very fine lady from an old English movie put in a plot where she never belonged, but found herself in the midst of it by some terrible mistake. She looked like a sophisticated waitress or the most elegant servant who found herself there only temporarily because there should be a better role for her, the one for which she was trained and prepared for years before.

Well, it was known that Vilas enjoyed mother's company more; his father's society and his friends were too loud for him. It was well known that I had preferred Lorenzo's company, there was an obvious zest for life in him, and it was obvious he was a soulful man. But he was never present in the house, he had found so many different interests and was always ready to pull one out of his sleeve as an excuse why he wouldn't be home so as not to disturb the perfect harmony which Vilas and *Mother* had weaved by simultaneous politeness.

I had never called her by her name. Well, I didn't know what to call her! I never had a need to call her, to ask her for anything. I would think *'I'd rather be seven days hungry than ask her for anything.'* For the very same reason I would wear the same clothes for the entire stay at the Viscontis, because I didn't know where to put my unclean singlet and underwear. I would take my unclean clothes back home with me, and my astonished mother asked:

"Are you sane Otto? You haven't changed your underwear for seven days?"

I would shrug my shoulders. How to tell her that I didn't know where *Mother* kept dirty clothes? How to explain that if I asked her she would only look calmly into my chin (not into my eyes!) and, most probably, she wouldn't say a word? She would turn her back as straight as a candlestick and with a light step walk out on me. Only her long dresses were rustling like in some old English movies about imprisoned princesses.

I had never witnessed her exchanging any kind of tenderness with anyone. She never ever hugged or kissed her son, or mess up his hair the way my mother messed up mine. Maybe that was the reason why my hair was so curly—often my mother would mess it up while saying:

"Otto, Otto, where, for God's sake, are you living?"

Epilogue
(The Malevolent Relative's Story)

The doorbell took me by surprise—who could call in on a Saturday? Blood rushed to my head—what if that was *She?* Maybe *She* was visiting her cousin here in Milan and wanted to surprise me. Anyway, *She* had a habit of coming unannounced; last time *She* did the same. It could be *She!* Do I have to say at what rate my heart was beating? At the same moment I questioned my looks: the way my hair was arranged, so I ran to the bathroom to glance at myself in the mirror, got some water into my hands, a little bit of hair gel and mashed it, then evenly spread this mixture onto my hair combing it first with my fingers, then with a thick comb, then again poured a little bit of water onto my hair and one more touch of the hair gel—*voilà!* The doorbell rang once again, I shouted *coming* as I was heading towards the entrance door, but then an idea changed my direction; off again I went into the bathroom, took a bottle of *doppo barba cologne* and hurriedly but generously poured some of it behind my ears and down my neck, and after that once again I went toward the entrance door, repeating *coming, coming* with a sweet voice full of anticipation.

I opened the door!

I saw his face: it was handsome, attractive as sin!

I was taken aback, not knowing what to do at that moment; should I have closed the door for he never came with a good intention? No, never! Not Vilas Visconti!

But, the door remained open. I just stood there staring at his placid and good-looking face (I said already—as sin itself it was attractive!). Yes, I was staring and there in the corner of his lips stood a little mysterious smile. A kind of smile I had *never* seen on Vilas Visconti's face. And all his little smiles; peculiar and provoking, his big, perfect-teeth-showing grins I had seen so far countless times; all those years since I had known him I could read all of his smiles, but today his little smile was mysterious, yet strange, as if I had never seen any of his smiles before.

It looked to me as if Satan himself was incorporated in that strong, young, handsome body, in his hypnotic gaze and his mysterious little smile which sent an electrical current running down my spine as I was staring into his eyes, aiming plainly to penetrate into his mind before he could even open his mouth to let out of it his lies as if he was letting out white birds as a sign of his warm welcome.

He had almond shaped eyes but they did not have the colour of almonds. If I were to describe their colour I should recall the patch of the sky in the darkest night, there were even several stars imprisoned in that patch which filled the almond's shell. It looked as if the night stillness too was caught in his eyes, the night deafness, its horror and its shriek. All of that was reflected in the dark mirror of his eyes, even those imprisoned stars were mirroring in their own reflection on that dark surface of his eyes which looked as if they were made of the darkest agate stone with particles of mother-of-pearl.

I feared his eyes. This fear overtook me a long time ago.

Back to the story; as I said, there was a little peculiar smile vibrating on his face. I could not read it, for I had never had the pleasure of meeting this little smile before, this odd expression on his face regardless of how many of his smiles I had met and had known so far. I had known almost all of his ill-intended cynical smiles in all given situations, even when it was the cruellest of the cruel; it was different to the one he was showing now.

What did he want to say to me with that smile?

The little semi-smile reminded me of the smile which vibrated on his lips when he said that he had *forgotten who Gaby was*. On my own shoulder, Gaby had cried as I was tenderly consoling her, full of compassion and remorse on behalf of Vilas … on whose lips the little smile was playing when asking, *"Gaby who? I've forgotten ... no, no don't remind me ... it really doesn't matter now ..."*

While he was standing there, on my threshold, I saw in his eyes the whole scene again: the crying face of Gabriella which I wanted more than the *Madonna* herself when I was still so shallow to swallow un-discrimina-tory mother's tales. Mother would say that the *Madonna* was going to come when I fell asleep, that she was going to put her hand on my forehead and stay by my side till dawn came. My mother would come to my room and I would plead with her to stay a little longer. Her visits were only short and I would squeeze her hand while burning with fever, begging her:

"Mamma, stay with me ... mamma, stay a little bit longer," to what she would reply exactly as I said earlier:

"Calm down and try to sleep. When you fall asleep Madonna is going to come. She is going to put her hand onto your forehead and stay next to you till dawn. Calm down and try to sleep."

Upon saying that, she would leave the room, closing the door behind her, and I would look at the big window, believing that the *Madonna* was going to come in through the window to avoid causing any disturbance of the household and was going to sit on my bed and tell me all those sweet words of getting well again ... the words I wanted to hear from my mother's lips ... but somehow my mother kept the belief that such words were the *Madonna's* duty, not her own.

But however it was, let's get back to Gabriella, let's get back to Vilas who said that he had never known her indeed. Gaby had left my life as if I had wronged her, and I have never seen her since. With her, she had taken all of my dreams and all of my yearnings, too ...

Ah, it was only a platonic kind of love (even though I loved her a lot), it was completely different to the kind of love which *She* ignited in my heart.

She was the one that no one could have ever torn apart from me! No, in particular not some Vilas Visconti, even if he resembled Apollo himself, *She* wasn't attracted to that kind of man; *She* was after finer qualities, after a kind soul, substance, *She* was after art and poetry, *She* was searching for human goodness and genuineness … after all, these qualities Vilas has never possessed. Oh, *She* would easily see through an upstart like him …

Yes, this time my love was something absolutely different.

A mature one and reciprocated.

If love is not everything, then it is—nothing!

I loved this woman deeply and utterly, for *Her*, I was ready to do anything, just as *She* came only because of me to Milan, to my book launch, *She* brought *Her* cousin with *Her* … all of that had added to my self-esteem; looking at Vilas standing at my door, I called to mind my poetry collection (why would I be bothered by Vilas's vacant stories!) and I started again with much attention to analyse that expression in his mocking eyes (which had changed yet again), and his little curled up smile, in the corner of his even more mysterious lips.

Let me clarify this: His gaze was clear and bright as if he had just got enlightened … as if he had discovered an extraordinary secret and was ready to share it with the world. In his eyes pleasure and victory shone.

Stars fall, heroes fall but Vilas Visconti was ready to fulfill his destiny.

I could see that clearly manifested as a light in his eyes, I could see that written in his little smile, which indeed wasn't that mocking smile of his, that smile on his lips twisted by cynicism, wickedness or twisted by something I had not recognised and experienced earlier on Vilas Visconti's lips.

That smile was something completely new, something that I had to experience without impediment. So, I walked towards my own destiny governed by the desire to get to know this unique smile of Vilas Visconti.

Now I demand your trust, because I am going to retell the story exactly

114

the way it had happened, which means, the story isn't polished by the passage of time and it isn't altered by a number of narrations; I am telling it right now, for the very first time, without any intent to fascinate or charm you, or ask you to take my side or anything like that … but, first things first.

All of my might went into one sentence:

"Vilas Visconti."

I said, *all of my might*, because every time I found myself in Vilas's company my might would leave me at once. It looked precisely as if his mere appearance, his persona, was sucking my blood and energy, leaving me absolutely exhausted and empty. Intellectually dull! Was that phenomenon occurring each and every time because of his persona or because of his unbelievably strong energetic charge which would make me weak and limp as if he, with his mighty energy was sucking my own into himself? Let me be more precise: every encounter with him meant not only total physical and emotional exhaustion but it brought a terrible dread while anticipating—what kind of storm he was bringing now! Because he never came alone, but accompanied by dark clouds, heavy rains and thunderstorm. He never came without a sly little smile or an evil plan.

In order to calm my heart down, which was beating like a drum with overstretched skin across it, in order to calm my fingers down, which started to tremble like leaves of my dead poplar tree, in order to give a deeper, soother tone to my voice, I called up the image of *Her* face, I brought to mind the cover of my book, I had refreshed my own worth and importance, then much more composed, I looked into his dark windows rimmed with almond shaped frames.

(*Mercy!* Inside I screamed, *Mercy!*)

But that one had never known the word *mercy* because it could never be used together with a desire for cruel entertainment at someone's expense, hence I pushed the word down to the depths from which it had arisen on the surface of my consciousness.

In my stomach, nausea had taken place. With one hand, I grabbed my stomach; nothing was there yet except the content of two cups of coffee and the smoke of several cigarettes, if that is what could have been counted at all. To say it again, my stomach was practically empty and because of that emptiness and lightness it started to travel upwards, then back downwards as if it was some sort of elevator, causing by such travels light vertigo and nausea. Light, said I, because it was a light vertigo in that moment (but with a visible tendency to worsen: to escalate into severe shakiness, an extreme nausea, the absolute sickness ...)

First things first.

Accordingly, I squeezed his name through my teeth sighing it out, *Vilas Visconti*", and while keeping his little eerie smile in the corner of his lips, he almost repeated the sentence changing the first name, and instead of his, he pronounced my name:

"Otto Visconti!"

Upon saying that his smile became even more peculiar; he sized me up as if he was seeing me for the first time, he smiled at me as if he had heard me for the first time ever. I didn't know where I was at that moment. Fine, I knew I was on the threshold of my home, but I didn't know on what unstable land I was standing. Shaky for sure, but how shaky?

He extended his hand and I, carried by the impulse, extended mine in an attempt to shake hands with him, but he quickly pulled his hand back and combed his hair backwards with it, twisted his little smile into a grotesque expression and said:

"A Poet, hey?"

Oh, that was the reason for your coming over, Vilas Visconti!

116

You came over with the kind of smile on your face that I was witnessing for the first time because you were surprised by me being a poet. Were you mocking me or was it envy? Of course, I didn't ask him these questions, I asked myself these questions as I tried to resolve his mysterious little smile and the 'combing hair' gesture with which he clearly wanted to show that he was playing with me when he pulled his hand to comb his hair carelessly, the hand I wanted to squeeze and shake. My hand was left hanging in the air and my mouth hung half-open. The expression on my face should have been the one of an idiot, the very same expression on the mask Vilas always wanted to paint onto my face when he would meet me.

I called upon *Her* vision which gave me more confidence and said to myself, *He is not going to paint masks onto my face, he is not going to suck my energy with his cynical questions and remarks, he is not going to do this to—me!*

I didn't want to capitulate so easily, no, not this time: *I have my own collection of poems, I have Her on my side, I have something I've created. I have created all of it alone! Vilas Visconti is not going to laugh at me! What has he ever created? He has always destroyed, never created. He has destroyed others' dreams, others' lives; I know that for sure. This time he is not going to destroy with his brazenness my readiness to defend my ... my dignity, let's say.*

I've decided—I won't talk! That'll be the wisest stand! Whenever he asks or comments on anything I will award him, firstly, with a long stretch of silence, followed by a very short sentence without any particular meaning. Let him try to find the meaning in it. Thus, for example; if he asks me about my new book (as I see he has already learned about it):

*"How did that happen, that **you** published a book?"*

To that I could say (after a long, philosophical silence):

"There ... there, the book was launched ..."

*"...well, where did **you** get those ideas..." (he thinks that I am an idiot), and I could answer after a long philosophical silence:*

"...ideas, ideas ... they are floating ... through space ..."

If he asks me:

"Why didn't you invite **me** *to your book launch?" (It could easily have been the reason of his visit today! Perhaps he wanted to be proud of me now ... perhaps he wanted to brag around Otto Visconti's my cousin ...)*

Once again, I will implement a long philosophical silence and answer:

"... many were invited ... many ..."

While I was thinking and turning around, in my head, all the possible questions Vilas might ask me, searching at the same time for the best suited answers to them, Vilas asked me:

"You are going to let me in, aren't you?"

That little, ever-present smile glued onto his lips looked to me peculiar for yet another reason: it looked like a smile which belonged elsewhere, as if he had cut it out of newspapers and glued it onto his face. Even though the little smile showed signs of cynicism and self-contentment, it didn't compliment his face. I anticipated only in a split second that this smile was going to turn into a bitter one, or some sort of twisted expression accompanied by a cascade of abusive words, for I knew that this strange smile, this facial expression of contentment was short-sighted and deceitful. I was waiting for the transformation of his face, and he said in a louder voice:

"Are you going to let me in or are we going to stand here ... as two ...?"

I said, moving to the side of the door:

"Please, do come in ..." With his ever-present smile he repeated *please, do come in ...* and his eyes started to walk up and down the walls of my one and only room scrutinising every inch of them. He looked at the walls and sized them up as if he was measuring their height; he was observing the paintings on the walls; he came closer to the bookshelf and started to look at the books and the titles while I had the impression that he was after a particular book. He propped himself on the tip of his toes, leaning his head to the left, then to the right; he would bend his knees, or even squat down as he was thoroughly examining my little library (which was adorned by the most recognised poetry names of the last two centuries: Lord Byron,

Shakespeare, Milton, Spenser, Goethe, Schiller, Chaucer, Wordsworth, de Quincey), and at the end of his observation he said:

"Did you ever read any of it, or does it serve only as décor?"

All of my philosophical answers, all of the long and short pauses in between words which I had aimed at Vilas disappeared in the conflict with my insecurity, hence I said:

"Well ... I've read it, nearly all of it ..."

"You've read nearly all of it ..." Vilas repeated my words.

"What about poetry?"

"Who do you care about in particular?"

"Who do you care about in particular? From whom are you stealing your words, from Lord Byron? As I can see there are mostly his words ..."

"Stealing? Stealing what?"

He laughed at me with squinted eyes. He was observing me methodically, I hated his penetrating gaze which crawled up underneath my hairline and brought restlessness to my thoughts. A lengthy period of time, he gazed into my eyes which became so nervous that they started to stride along his suit, slipped down to his shoes, climbed up to the ceiling and once again marched to the bookshelf where Lord Byron books were laid. Right there, my gaze found its refuge; Vilas asked:

"What about a Muse? Do you have a Muse?"

Prior to such a question he had already swung my nerves which swayed like leaves in a pleasant breeze. Yes, I felt my own nerves dancing on my face and causing ticks around my eyes and lips; I felt my fingers swaying, my nostrils widening and my chin trembling.

What does he want? He came with a motive. What Muse? He was not going to hear a word about Her from me. That is for sure! Whatever he touches he soils; She is a demi-goddess for such an unscrupulous monster. Oh, no, no, he can hear from me anything he wants; when and why I started to write poetry; I'll tell him the poplar tree story, even the bit when I had cut it down; I'll admit that I fell in love with Gabriella

that summer when he was kissing her in the adjacent room; I'll admit how much resent-
ment for him I harboured in my heart while I secretly envied him; I'll try to convince him
that I wanted to invite him to my book launch, but it wasn't my duty to invite the
audience as the publisher did it on my behalf … I'll say whatever he wants to hear and
much more than I am willing and prepared to recount and admit. Only to spare Her
… never to mention Her name!

Not to Vilas Visconti!

Still, his gaze was fixed on my out-of-rhythm trembling face, while I
thought that each and every muscle followed its own dance routine without mutual coordination, understanding, agreement or harmony. There
was utter muscle-dance disharmony on the stage of my face while my
hands were dancing, yet each one in a perfectly different rhythm as if they
were about to crash onto the keys of a piano. So danced my facial muscles
to an invisible music a dance without my agreement, for I never wanted
this particular choreographer to chose the music and its dance. *I* wanted
to be **the one** who was going to decide … but alas, they danced the way
they danced, and probably they would end up dancing that way regardless
of the effort I might put in. While I was trembling in disharmony of my
muscles, my thoughts started to tremble the same way, and when he asked
once again, *'Do you have a Muse?'* I started to laugh uncontrollably, deafen-
ingly, cramping all of my muscles trying to put them that way in some sort
of order, into the same rhythm so that they could contract and relax at the
same time sequences, that they could dance to the same music of laughter,
which I had started by my own will this time.

That laughter was the best possible choice. It was indeed, for my muscles started to crumple and relax simultaneously and in the same rhythm,
and I felt that I was, once again, in control of my own face, but then, from
such hysterical laughter my tears started to run down, and we both couldn't
figure out whether I was laughing or crying. By both possibilities I was
awarded, hence I took advantage of them; while laughing I was shedding
tears, which in some way brought me relief.

Yeah, I said, *in some way ...*

... because there was no mercy!

I said it before—not with Vilas Visconti!

He wanted to know it all. He was of the kind who had to be always in control. Or at least, in control of—me. I couldn't stand being under anyone's control, but here I couldn't do anything. Absolutely nothing. Not with my own willpower, nor with any other kind of knowledge (which was anyway unknown to me).

Vilas asked:

"Do you have any beer?"

"Not sure, I'll have a look," answered I, while wiping off my tears which, as I said, I didn't know if they were tears of laughter or tears of anger and weakness.

"You're not sure ... not sure if you have beer ... then, what are you sure about, Otto?"

"I don't know ..."

"I don't know ..." he repeated after me in a mocking voice (the one from childhood).

I didn't have any beer and told him so, to what he rolled his eyes (keeping on his lips, still present, that odd smile, keeping in his eyes, still the same splendour—more intensified and stronger as if he had reached a rare secret), then he said:

"You don't have any beer, what do you have then?"

"Coffee?"

"Fine, coffee, Ottavio." (Making it long—Ott-aaaavio).

While I was preparing coffee, he continued examining the titles of my books.

We sat down. We drank our coffee without a word. Only his gaze was articulate as he was sipping his coffee and looking at me without blinking. He started:

"As a matter of fact, you are, Otto, one sweet fellow. Such an affectionate creature, one would press you tight onto one's chest, just like that, just to be your friend ... you are a refined soul, a shoulder to cry on, a poet ... so, that's who you are."

From his mind, Vilas Vicsonti wasn't talking.

Those were someone else's words, the words of someone at whom he was laughing, right here, in front of me.

I was looking at the empty cup silently. I lifted my eyes and looked in the direction of the bookshelf; I looked at Lord Byron's book of poems; my thoughts were with *Her*, no, no, *She* had nothing to do with all this theatre of his, how would that be possible? What did he have on his mind? To whom belonged those words, which he was cynically turning around and shooting them like he would shoot arrows right into my chest?

Whose words are those—it tormented me!?

Whose words are those? They are not his own. What does he want to achieve with them?

Whose words are those? Why does he slowly torture me?

"Whose words are those?" I managed to summon the courage to ask as my face started again this utterly disharmonic dance: every muscle danced on its own accord, even my ears danced, each to a different rhythm as if they were not a pair of ears but each ear had its own will to dance the way it wanted ... once again I felt as if I could become the victim of my hysterical laughter ... or ... the prey of hideous crying.

"Whose words are those, you asked, didn't you? Whose? You think they are not mine? Is it then you think I don't keep you in such high esteem? You think those words belong to someone else? So, why do you think I am repeating someone else's words?"

Once again, silence prevailed. Once again my face was shaking and trembling, yes, that merry stage on which my muscles were shaking as in a trance, but each of them had their own trance, there was no unity.

"Why?"

I didn't have an answer.

"Why Otto?"

He was staring at me and that stare had intensified the trembling of my voice:

"Well … well … those are not … your words …"

"Bingo! So, whose are they?"

"I don't know, but they are not yours."

"You've guessed it right, Ottavio. They are surely not mine! I don't think that you are a sweet affectionate creature, a poet, a sophisticated soul who needs to be hugged and pressed onto one's chest. Of course, I wouldn't think anything like that. You know, too well, what I think of you, for me you were always and always will remain Ott-aaavio … then, what do you think whose words are those?

I shrugged my shoulders. I sincerely didn't know. It could have been that he had met Gaby again, maybe she told him how I had consoled her on that day when she showed up teary at the door of my dormitory. On the very same day when he should have consoled her, or at least given her a kind, empathetic word—that task he left to me. It may be that he came to tell me that Gaby told him about my kindness and empathy when I stroked her hair and kissed the top of her head telling her that *every little thing's gonna be all right*, wiping off her tears, even though I knew back then that when Vilas Visconti went, nothing was good any more for the one who stayed behind in the ruins, because he leaves for good, destroying all the bridges mercilessly.

Maybe he had met Gaby!?

Actually, he did meet Gaby, so I said:

"Maybe you met Gaby, only she could have told you that."

"For Christ's sake! Gaby who? Is that the chick who lived on the campus? Gaby? Gaby who?"

His words made me mad with anger, so I felt red hot spots spreading across my face like little button mushrooms after a generous rainfall of Vilas's light insults. I must have resembled a self-portrait of a frustrated painter who ruined his masterpiece by his own disliking of it.

Getting up, Vilas said:

"Let's get out and stretch our legs, I've had enough of being stuck in this little hole of yours. Let's get some fresh air, if there is any fresh air in this city of yours. You see, Ott-aaavio, you got sick here … let's get out to fetch some fresh air.

I put my shoes on and started to tie the shoelaces like a robot. I was always obedient to his voice, *why*? Should I rebel against him this time? What would be the worst thing to happen if I now rebelled against him? What would happen if I simply said *bugger off*?

But I said neither *I don't agree* nor *bugger off*, I was just tying my laces while he was standing above me with hands in his pockets, whistling some melody, which wasn't in the rhythm with that dance of my facial muscles either.

How to stop that dance—that was now my first and foremost concern. Yes, how to stop that crazy dance! How to calm my nerves!? To get some fresh air! But alas, there was no fresh air anywhere, I couldn't inhale anything fresh, especially when he was right on my back monitoring every breath-in and each breath-out, and such breathing was the breathing of an ill little child who was gasping for air, battling an unnamed vicious lung disease.

Without a word we were walking, when all of a sudden, he pulled me by my sleeve in the middle of the street, and my first thought was that he wanted to get me killed; he wanted to push me under a car, but he pulled me all the way till we crossed the street and led me to a near-by café.

When he had seated me (to repeat it: as one would sit a little ill child who was battling an unnamed but severe lung disease, unable to get enough air) he went to the bar. He returned carrying two pints of beer. The froth was alluring, and I licked it off straight away. As I was licking this thick foam, I felt his sharp eyes resting on the back of my head and he shouted a warning:

"You are repulsive, stop licking it, drink it as any normal man would, you are licking it like a dog!"

I leaned back onto the chair and looked up into the sky (not into that tiny patch of sky which was imprisoned in his dark eyes), but into that grey sky above the little café, the grey sky which looked like it was about to cry over that miserable destiny of Otto Visconti.

May I impose one question here?

I've never been given an answer to such a question.

Is there a destiny, written up there in the, by mist and smog hidden, stars or are we indeed the creators of our own fate?

For … if I knew that I was the creator of my own fate, then I would act differently.

I would say to Vilas:

"Go away!"

I'd order him as one orders a dog:

"Get lost! Get lost from my life you bloodsucker!"

In his total astonishment maybe he would wander away for good. All ghosts are like that; all bloodsuckers are like that, when you shout at them, they disappear never to return. Was Vilas Visconti just a phantom that would vanish if only I howled at him?

If only I had known that I was the master of my own destiny, I would never have allowed him to play with me.

I would have said to Vilas:

"Hey, Vilas Visconti! S-T-O-P! Stop it! This wasn't written on the page of my destiny, because nothing, anyway, is written anywhere, hence I will not allow you to write

onto my blank page the scenario you have chosen! No, I do not allow you! Back off from my scene, back off from my film, I don't need you in it, not even as an extra."

Well, in such a case I would have the courage and knowledge, in the case of knowing that I was the creator. But in that other case ... all was already, I thought, well planned, I got the role of—*Otto.*

In such conviction I was cemented once again by Vilas Visconti's firm voice:

"Do you remember, then, what we were talking about?"

I only shrugged my shoulders; if my answer, too, was written in the stars I could have told him, *"I know, I know, we were talking about my Muse. You've asked me if I knew whose words you've repeated ... so, whose words were those words if not Gaby's if you really haven't forgotten all about her?"*

But, what if the answer was not written in the stars? Then I am presented with thousands of possibilities by my own intelligence. What if it was a matter of my own personality or my character, my individuality or my own alter ego, the real Otto who I knew existed deep down within me ... what if such Otto once and for all wanted to say to Vilas Visconti ... *No, I don't remember what we were talking about, and what's more, I can't give two hoots about it. Look, now I'll get this pint of beer and will pour it down your head, out of sheer pleasure to show you how it feels when someone pees down your neck. I don't remember your question, I don't remember what we were talking about, what you were trying to recall, I don't remember any woman called Gaby, nor do I remember anything in connection with you. Go away, I've had enough of your following, you've been following me like a dark shadow all these years ... all these years you've been pissing down my neck ... go away, you are only an apparition, a phantom, in my world you do not exist at all.*

I was turning my thoughts around and around, being silent for too long before Vilas's voice brought me back:

"Then, who was the one who said that Otto was a soft soul, a poet, a dear heart, a sweet nincompoop ...? Would you ever guess it?"

"Don't torture me any longer, Vilas, do tell me, why did you come in the first place?"

"Am I? Torturing you? Oh, yes, you are a refined one, a poetic soul, sophisticated, charmingly confused, the sweetest, well brought up … idiot."

"Vilas why? Why are you talking to me like that?"

"Vilas why? Why are you talking to me like that?" once again he started imitating me with a mocking voice. That was the first time since I had known him that I saw him absolutely aggravated. I'd noticed that his good-looking face started, just as mine did, to shake and tremble so that his handsome features started to mold into some strange crimson mask; it wasn't Vilas Visconti any longer.

I reached for my pint and gulped it down all in the one gulp.

He did the same; twice he sighed out through the nose, twice through the mouth.

We looked at each other as if we had just taken a short break form the terrible battle chest to chest. We were now sizing up one another in antic-ipation who was going to start the battle again.

The silence lasted; I noticed his attempts to calm himself down, to collect himself again; it was the first time ever that I saw Vilas's face painted crimson, first time his hair uncombed, his eyes flaming as stars from the stolen night sky; it was the first time ever that I saw Vilas Visconti angry, a nervous wreck, fuming.

No, I never saw him like that.

The nonchalant kind he was.

Never would he get upset, not Vilas Visconti; he waltzed through life as if life was a never-ending party. As if the table was laid out only for him with all those beautiful culinary delicacies, with desserts of creamy cakes and colourful delicious lollies … all of that right there just for him, that splendid light, heartwarming music to which he danced liberated from any concern, he danced and he snatched, he celebrated and he moved with his light dancing feet from table to table, from function to function, from wedding to wedding, from party to party, never looking down at those who collected the crumbs which he wasted under the table ... Such kind of person was Vilas Visconti, therefore there was my utter astonishment to Vilas Visconti's new, never seen before aspect of his persona—he was irritated! I saw him for the first time in such light.

All of a sudden, he got up and disappeared in the café. He was absent for quite a long time; I entertained my mind with thoughts of leaving; I thought how would it be if I just left, ran away?

But, he would come and ring my bell: redder, madder than he was now. He came out of the Gent's room, went to the bar and came with two more pints and the words:

"*You didn't escape?*"

"*To what use? You would come and haunt me, wouldn't you, cousin?*"

"*You are right—Visconti!*"

We almost smiled at one another. We carried the same surname. Our fathers had the same father.

Except contempt, I didn't feel anything for Vilas Visconti. Since I could remember I always had the contempt in my heart for him.

Without a word, all in one go, we finished our beers, to what Vilas remarked:

"*It's your go now, bring two more!*" and when I readily got up, he added:

"*We never drank to toast your book launch.*"

I gave in without a word, brought two more pints which we gulped down in no time, again I got up and took those empty pints and brought them back topped up.

After four pints of beer Vilas's eyes sparkled differently, his hair flattened onto his head and face because he combed it with his fingers several times (ah, if only I had such kind of hair, dark and smooth, it appeared as if some shiny cream was applied through his hair ... and mine? ... curly, as curly as an old lady's hairdo) and his smile was a little bit more familiar to the smile I used to know on that vagrant's face as appealing as sin itself.

Vilas got up and took out of his pocket a small book.

In the middle of the book it was written:

Only to My Poplar Tree

and underneath that title my name was written: *Ottavio Otto Visconti.*

He placed the book on the table and I was staring into it as if I had seen it for the very first time. *Why?* I asked myself. *Was he jealous?* Couldn't believe in that, *jealous of me,* no, not Vilas Visconti. No, not because of my small book! *"Patience Otto!"* I commanded myself , *"Let's see what he has to say."*

He opened the book, turned the first page slowly, with caution, as if he was going to find there the biggest revelation written by my own hand:

"To Alenka … just as to the poplar tree … to Alenka" (underneath, there stood my shaky signature, all uneven and wobbly as if I had just signed it, that very moment, with my unstable rickety hand … and my soul was rickety and shaken by this small book, shaken by the dedication *("To Alenka … just as to the poplar tree … to Alenka")*.

There it was, my little book opened on page One where the dedication was written to the woman I loved with the same might I loved my poplar tree, as if they had the same soul, as if they both belonged only to me.

(If love is not everything, then it is—nothing!)

After that the longest silence prevailed. As long as the longest afternoon I had ever spent together with Vilas Visconti. My childhood afternoons spent with Vilas were measured by minutes elongated as hours, by hours elongated as days … elongated to the extent of physical pain, just as now when it seemed to me that all of my long childhood afternoons at the

Viscontis were gathered together in one long endless afternoon which was never going to untangle, just as my letters tangled into a signature written underneath the dedication to my one and only true love, to—*Alenka Dorinec.*

The beer I drank had dulled and slowed my reactions. My brain was operating at a slower rate; my hands, even though they were trembling, didn't tremble at the usual velocity, I'd rather say they were slightly jolting, my heart was jolting and my thoughts were jolting; hence I put together some of those jolting thoughts into one sentence which squeaked out through my tight and dry throat, leaving a sharp burning mark (because of the former's stiffness, perhaps!):

"Where did you get that from?"

"What do you think, where did I get it from?"

"Who is the one who gave you my book of poems?"

"Isn't it written on it, as clearly as only a poet can compose it - "To Alenka ... just as to the poplar tree ... to Alenka"? What do you think, who has given it to me: Alenka or the poplar tree?"

"Where do you know her from? Where from, Vilas?"

"Where from do I know her? Oh, Otto, you naïve simpleton: I know her from Lerici, I know her from Bologna, Milan and Trieste ... I know her from my youth, right from my heart, I know her from my bed, from the story called Vilas Visconti and Alenka Slavina."

Silent I was. That particular wording had fallen the hardest onto my heart and onto my soul, *"... I knew her from my bed ..."*

Silent I was. *Alenka Slavina.* He said that he knew her from his youth. No, no, it can't be the *same* woman! I remember, Vilas had a long-term girlfriend, some *Slavina* she was, it was so long ago, so long that I have forgotten that his mother called her *Slavina* ... no, no, that wasn't Alenka ... no, no, that wasn't Alenka, not *my* love!

I stuttered:

"How come ... how come the exactly ..."

His way to shut me up was by grabbing my wrists and squeezing them harshly. His grip was hard just as his stare was penetrative and hard; there, in his eyes were no stars left, in his eyes only darkness prevailed, darkness without a glimpse of light. He said:

"I'll retell you the tale ..." then neatly he started to narrate the story about him and Alenka *Slavina*, his first and only love. Without omitting anything, he started the story from his high school days, when he met her so young, how they spent blissful four years together and he told me he never stopped loving her. The very same Alenka: who I, Otto Visconti, loved more than my own life.

He continued the story by mentioning his mother, asking me, *"You remember mum, don't you?"* Oh, good Lord, did I remember her! How many countless summers I had spent in their house of politeness astonished by her everlasting silence; she behaved as a captured princess ... then he told me, reminded me how much his mother despised *Her*, trying to break him with her constant despondency, suspicions and accusations ... he told me that his mother got what she wanted in the end ... she wanted to rescue her prince, hence Vilas Visconti became her real prince, but consequently Alenka had lost *Hers* ...

As if one can love ten times!

It was well known that Vilas Visconti had loved ten more times, and then ten more after that; women loved and adored him, but in all that race and entanglement with quantity and numbers, he was never again able to find the same harmony and love which was lost in that hidden space and time to which he never again knew the returning path.

Ten years he had spent with Annamaria Monte. Exactly ten years of Annamaria Monte, exactly ten years of Alenka in the shadow.

No, not My Alenka! (She wasn't, She couldn't have been Vilas Visconti's lover!!!)

Not My Alenka!!!

I said:

"We are not talking about the same woman, right?"

"Oh, yes we are, my dear Otto, the very same woman, the one to whom you have written your little dedication ... the same Alenka ... as same as your poplar tree ... the very same Alenka ..."

There we have it! I heard it all: I heard that he met *Her* once again on a train to Milan; *She* was reading *Her* book; years had passed since they saw each other; he went to one of his lectures, he sat next to *Her*, some strange scent took him back to the Adriatic coast ... *She* travelled to Milan to visit *Her* cousin ... he told me that his long-time-dead heart skipped its beat, it started to beat as if some invisible mechanic, right there, had fixed an old and rusty outdated mechanism. He said they cried together ... on that very same night in the apartment of *Her* cousin ... he said that right then he decided never to leave *Her* again, never to let *Her* leave him again ...

He told me about their passionate rendezvous in Milan; he told me that *She* followed him on his business trips and lectures wherever, whenever he went ... he was recounting the story telling me all the details as we were drinking countless pints of beer ... we drank those pints of beer, we slurped the froth from the top, but I slurped my own tears while his face was of a strange colour, it was sort of greenish - he looked as if he wasn't a creature from this planet, thus I looked at him in bewilderment ... there within me there were all sorts of emotions mixed up; actually, all emotions I ever knew brewed inside of me, and they ranged from contempt and hatred, then progressed to repulsiveness and the greenest jealousy, and they extended into understanding and absolute empathy. I almost thought I was him, and it ended with admiration and awe-stricken envy.

At the end of his story it seemed to me that the corner of his eyes were glassy, moist.

Mutely, we looked at each other.

On his face there was no expression.

It was a face on which it was written that all of his emotions were just used up and that there was left only a blank board on which stood his tired eyes and his even more tired lips which resembled a withered piece of fruit.

I didn't know what to say.

My breathing was heavy as the breathing of a child who was battling a fatal lung disease or taking air through a straw. I heard my own lungs squeaking as if there were rusty doors attached to them and they closed up with every inhalation and opened up with every exhalation ... but not fully. So I was squeaking and piping, looking at my fingers which were laid next to the dedication written on the small book titled *Only to My Poplar Tree,* to the woman called—*Alenka.*

After a long, long silence which could have lasted, perhaps, for hours, I said:

"And ... where do you stand now?"

"Where do I stand?"

"With those women? Where is Alenka in your life, where is Annamaria?"

"Annamaria is my fiancé, Alenka is my love."

"Is she ... a lover?"

"She is my love, not my lover."

"What is going to happen to Annamaria?"

"What do you think should happen?"

"What is going to happen to Alenka?"

"What do you think should happen?"

"What did you want to tell me ... what's the point, what's the moral of this story?"

"What do you want from Alenka?

"She is ... a friend of mine."

"A friend? You are in love with her ... you nincompoop."

I got up, left the table and headed home with a wobbly, crooked walk.

Vilas Visconti.

Is our destiny already written down and has it been given to Vilas Visconti to follow me as a dark shadow in my attempts to find love?

I was the one who consoled Gaby when he had left her pregnant, because he already had his big true love—*Alenka Slavina.*

Who will ever console Otto?

There was no more Gaby, no more *Slavina!* They both took with them, in their hearts, Visconti ... but not Otto, the other Visconti they took - Vilas Visconti.

Part Two

Selected Stories

Pia's Poem

My memory's fading. You tell me what's real.

My story began long before my remembrance. My remembrance was as long and winding as a dirty country road.

I told you my story, but was it really an objective one?

I remember the day when someone brought quinces and put them on the table. Against the dark mahogany table they looked like they were made of brass. They looked rather unreal, as if painted in 3D technique.

I told you that I was happy on that occasion, their smell made me feel loved for some reason.

Yes, I told you—I was happy, but I wasn't. The quinces' smell brought lots of sadness to my day. It was the day when they tried to conceal Lila's death from me. They tried to mask it with a smell. Yes, we mask things with smells.

While the brass quinces were still perfuming the house, it proved to be a rotten day, concealed by all that sweetness and by my mother's forced laughter.

My father said *'no real man cries'*, and the relief he obtained by saying it was expected to be my relief.

They brought in the quinces and I said I was happy; again, there was an expectation of gladness from my side, for they thought that I loved quinces. I said the same to you, on that day when I started to recount my story.

My story was made up.

Stories are made of feelings, not of events.

I told you the events, but through the prism of false feelings.

I can recount it to you now, but shadowed by different shades of feelings and you'll see what a difference it makes.

On the day when my father was taken to hospital I was happy. They told me that I was going to get a bike, instead. Instead of the truth, that's what I meant when saying *'instead'*. Yes, I was happy; I was going to ride a bike.

It was grey. I didn't like the colour, but I said I did.

I came to the hospital a month later riding my bike. The hospital wasn't far from our home. Mother was walking and I had already learned how to ride. On our way to the hospital she cried, but she blamed the wind, blamed the little fly, blamed the onion-sticky fingers. She plainly cried. I was riding my grey bike.

Dad never came back.

They told us that we couldn't see him—yet. Maybe tomorrow.

I rode back whistling. Mum cried. She blamed the wind and the little fly. And I wasn't really aware of the proportions of reality and feelings.

They said Dean had left for Amsterdam. What the hell!!! Amsterdam! Why, out of all the destinations this world offered had he chosen Amsterdam? Bobby was killed in Amsterdam: some car ran over him. As if he was a rabbit.

I blamed the car, the lousy driver, the wrong weather and the laws in Amsterdam. But, I never blamed Bobby. He smoked. I never knew it. Mother said not to blame anyone as he had freely chosen such a script. Bobby never liked *'happy endings.'* I did, and believed if we said so, we'd believe so ... if we believed so, it was real then.

When they said that Dean went to Amsterdam, I wasn't ready yet to show my real feelings. I kept on pretending to read the label on some jar. The jar was red; even though it was made of clear glass, it was red. The content was red. I was reading the label keen to figure out what was in it. Strawberries. Sweet strawberries. They sweetened his departure. I buried my head into the dish and ate two jars of strawberries with extra sugar on top.

Mother cried. She blamed the menopause.

I couldn't blame anyone. I just ate and ate as if this was going to be my last meal. After that, after his departure, I hadn't eaten for more than two weeks. My mother cried. Begged me, telling me that I was *'everything what was left to her'* as if I was some, quite dear, piece of furniture. She loved her antiques. It was a firm confirmation that we belonged to the *'right family'*. It looked as if I was the last piece of antiquity in that household.

I said—I wasn't keen to see the Rembrandts, that I was *'more than happy'* to stay with her among the antique furniture.

But I wasn't.

I concealed my feelings with the red strawberries.

Bobby used to conceal his feelings with grass.

Dean—with his travels.

I said I was predominantly happy throughout my youth. Mother took good care of me. Besides, she had money and antique furniture. She had everything. She even had me. We were both conscious that *'having everything'* makes one feel absolutely happy.

I started recounting my story telling you how happy I was. Blissfully happy: we always had *'everything'*.

Dean never came back. He went in search for Bobby. Bobby was already *'elsewhere'*, but by that time Dean believed that he would find him. I was happy for him, even jealous (only a bit), for I thought *'How on earth could he sustain such faith?'* But Jesus resurrected!

Bobby didn't. No one did. Father didn't. Even though they said they were *'expecting a miracle'* because father was a strong, healthy man and had a brilliant, focused mind. They said he had a *'perfect family'* worth fighting for. He wasn't as lucky as Jesus was. Or the family wasn't as perfect as it needed to be to summon a mighty wish to fight.

We were blessed. In a way.

He lived a month longer than doctors really expected. I learnt to ride my bike just to tell him that I did, perhaps to make him proud of me, or … maybe, somewhere in my childish mind I believed that this fact would somehow enhance his recovery.

It didn't.

That year I was utterly sad. Beneath it was all dark, perplexingly deep, but I concealed my utter sadness with reading books. I assume that I had learnt a lot, who wouldn't learn a lot from Dostoyevsky? He wrote about death and sadness. He worked it out all for me, so I was just a passive reader. Death and sadness thus happened to someone else, in some other stories, Dostoyevsky's .

I lied to my mother about my choice of literature. I told her that I was reading something else. I found a writer whose name I had forgotten long ago and told her that I was reading his simple, uncomplicated and entertaining stories. The ones that all other kids read at that time. Back then everyone watched *Pippi Langstrumpf*, later some kids went on reading it. I didn't. I kept Dostoyevsky's book under my bed, wrapped in a scarf, as if he was a dead seer, hidden, not discovered yet. It was Lila's scarf I wrapped him in. I suppose that, too, was a way how I mourned her death. I never knew where she was buried. Mother said that it wouldn't be appropriate to bury Lila in our garden. The garden was always perfect, and death wasn't. It was scary; I denied death as if it wasn't real. How brave, arrogant and naive that attempt was: to deny the only certainty!?

I told you that I had six girlfriends but I never loved any of them (that's why I left each of them … except the last one).

But this wasn't true, either.

Mother liked none of them.

I met a girl named Appolonia.

Those were the times of *'The Godfather'*. I met her on the street. Unusual place to meet Appolonia—the daughter of an Italian immigrant. They didn't walk the streets just like that. There was not any scene from a romantic movie on that day, on that street when I met Appolonia.

A figure of infinite beauty.

I saw her eyes and my heart raced. My feet raced and I foolishly followed her. She turned her head twice and hurried. I hurried and she started to run. I ran, caught up with her and breathless said:

"Don't be afraid, I am breathless not because of running but because of your beauty."

I squatted down, picked up a daffodil from someone's garden and extended it to her. Her eyes were pretty, big with wonder. They shone. She didn't say anything; she just took the daffodil. It was yellow, like the quinces on our antique table. I walked next to her speechless. When I summoned enough courage to talk, I said:

"I am not speechless because I am dumb … but, because of your beauty."

She smiled.

I smiled.

I took her bag and carried it to the park. When we reached the park, she said:

"May I have my bag now, please?"

"When am I going to see you again, beautiful, nameless girl?"

"I walk this road every day … Appolonia."

"Appolonia Road?"

She laughed.

I laughed.

But I really believed in that moment that it was the name of the road. I walked that road many times before, but when I met her, I had forgotten all the names. Including mine. She asked what my name was and I said:

"Call me Michele, *Appolonia."*

She just smiled gently with tight lips, shaking her head barely visibly as if she knew that I fell madly in love and that she triumphed again.

Bobby told me not to *'mess with Italian girls'*.

Bobby was jealous. He always was. He was a readhead and short. He had a bad temper. He was quick as quicksilver. Once he got in trouble with Stefano. Yes, he was Appolonia's brother.

Mum said not to *'mess around with Italians'*. When I told my mother that *'I loved Appolonia'*, she just waved her hand unwilling even to consider the possibility of loving an Italian-immigrant-daughter. Waving her hand meant *'we don't mess or mingle with Italians'*.

I said that to Appolonia and she said that her brother didn't like us, either. Appolonia's father owned *The Gelateria*. I used to buy an ice cream there occasionally. One day, upon my entering the place, he came quickly and said:

"Leave her alone."

He didn't have a gun, or anything that a seventeen-year-old scared boy might have imagined after watching *'The Godfather'* over and over. *'That particular look'* in his eyes was just enough to convince me that there might be some unpleasant consequences if I didn't obey.

I loved Appolonia and that gave me courage. So, *'that particular look'* was not enough to convince and ward me off, even though I was scared. I didn't say a word to Appolonia but daily I kept on carrying her bag to the park where the bag exchanged hands and we exchanged our kisses.

Shaken by the certainty that God was never present when he was needed, I lost my occasional and weak trust in him: on my way home I was beaten—badly. I couldn't walk for days. Mother said that she told me not to *'mess with Italians'*.

Appolonia changed schools. A year later she went to Rome to study. I had never been to Rome, never wanted to go—why would I care about the Sistine Chapel or Caravaggio's work?

From that day on, the day I was badly beaten, I never met Stefano again. Bobby said if he ever met him, he was going to *'kill that Italian bastard'*. I was happy that Bobby never met him again. What a terrible, terrible temper Bobby had. Paradoxically, he had a mellow heart, and as sweet as dark-yellow quinces.

I never talked about Appolonia again.

Then the four girls followed that I really didn't love, but I did care for them in my own way. I remember their names because I had written their names in some sort of diary. I had a thick book where I would write some sketches of my daily life. Not on a regular basis, not in structured sentences. More like—jotting down:

"Failed exam … Bobby's a bastard—he stole from Dean … Al Pacino said, *'Cavalleria Rusticana!? I think I got tickets to the wrong opera. I've been in New York too long …'* got to memorise this line … Beatrix gets on my nerves, can't stand her high-pitched voice … Four library books due on Monday … Cathy called … shall I or shall I not??? Shall not? Not pretty enough? … Tuesday cinema with Dean …"

That's how I could still remember their names.

I ended up going out with Cathy only because she wanted me so badly. I liked pretty girls. One can't date an angel like Appolonia and not care about a girl's appearance after that. But Cathy! Was she an artist in the art of opulent persuasion? Oh, yes. All I learnt from her was plainly sexual. Fine!

Then I met Emma and after her Simona.

I hoped Simona would awaken in me the same sweetness Appolonia did, but Simona was *'just another pretty girl'*, there was plenty of intellectual vacuum around her.

I don't want to talk about it any longer because I never want to leave the impression that my speech might be absolutely derogatory when it comes to ex-lovers.

Emma and I, we lasted the most. This time mother didn't mind the girl's background but she had found other faults as time went by. Mothers are skillful in finding faults with girls, their potential rivals and threats.

Bobby liked Emma. For hours, for days they could laugh together. They had the same sense of humour. They behaved like they were brother and sister. But then he left without any warning or need for any explanation. He just said he wanted to live *'elsewhere'*. Yet another battle he had won without glory. I said that I didn't miss him at all because he was always a troublemaker. But I missed him terribly. I feared for his future knowing him too well, knowing his temper, I wanted to say.

In 1990, I met a woman I fell in love with deeply. From my side it wasn't an ordinary love - it was pure madness. I never told anyone how much I loved her, anyone—including herself. I wasn't even prepared to admit it to myself.

I read her poem.

It blew me away.

I read her poem before I met her and thought that it was written by an older, experienced woman and even though the poem was fresh and mellow, it had that depth which can come only through a number of different life experiences.

I learned it off by heart.

I walked in its rhythm, whistled it often as if it could have been sung. While whistling and reciting it in my head, I would imagine the woman who wrote the poem. I gave her the face of Meryl Streep: she was beautiful, mellow and mature enough to come up with such a perfect order of words and emotions. I even called it *'Meryl's Poem'* although it had a different title.

Dean used to write little poems. When I think better of his poems, I might correct myself and rephrase it: Dean used to write soulful, meaningful verses which could easily bring memories of my father, which could at the same time easily sadden and mellow my heart. I used to love some of his poems but I never admitted it, for I believed that it might show some of my hidden weaknesses.

It was quite a cold evening. Dean was coughing the whole day. He asked me to accompany him to a poetry evening. It was held in a small dark café downtown. I was hesitant because he was almost ill and this place was full of smoke that one could cut with scissors. Dean has those big brown eyes and he knew how to look in one's eyes if he wanted to make one do what he wished. He looked in my eyes with the right dose of sadness, precisely enough to make me change my clothes without a word and get the car key.

I was driving; he was coughing.

I said:

"Do you really ..."

"I really do!" he cut my sentence and I started to hum *'Meryl's Poem'.*

As soon as we walked in, Dean lit his cigarette and ordered a beer. I just swung my head helplessly; my eyes were already hurting.

Dean read his poem and I was close to tears. He had his way with words, awakening feelings of sadness, awakening pictures of Father's departure, of Mum's absent-mindedness written on her face like on a blackboard with blunt dirty-white chalk. It looked to me that evening as if he had known a long time that he was predestined to write this poem, to awaken those exact feelings in my heart.

I pleaded, he was coughing, smoking and drinking cold beer, but I pleaded to no avail. When Dean starts to drink his beer, you'd better not plead.

Sulky I sat in the dark corner while he talked to one of his friends. He introduced me to a young woman. Yes, she was pretty and I was sulky and unfriendly, I couldn't care less, all I cared for was Dean's cough and his reluctance to go home. Father used to cough a lot the year before his departure. Dean had Father's nature: independent, stubborn but subtle in a way. The pretty woman was a quiet one. She didn't talk a lot. Without saying a word, she stood up after a while. She took the mic and started to read. I didn't care; all I wanted was to take Dean home.

But I recognised the poem.

It was *'Meryl's Poem'*.

She just renamed it. She had stolen it! I stood up quickly and came closer, to hear it better, or to see her better.

Shamelessly, she read *'Meryl's Poem'*.

I almost protested, but as I came closer and looked into her eyes I stopped as if I was trapped by her melodic voice and her purple eyes. In the dark her eyes looked purple.

I came when she ended her reading and said:

"You read it so expressively."

"Thanks!"

Her name was Pia.

Pia.

She said in the poem that she *'was dethroned from love'*.

Half-drunk on our way back home, Dean told me that Pia didn't just read the poem, but that she wrote the poem. She was a Poetess.

Pia was a Poetess.

It wasn't Meryl Streep's.

It was a young woman's poem.

A beautiful young woman of few words. Probably she spared her speech, she spared her words for her poems.

I changed the title. I wasn't calling it *'Meryl's Poem'* because it was now, rightfully— *'Pia's Poem'*.

145

Since that day when I met Appolonia on Forest Hill Road, I changed the road's name. From that day on for me it was - Appolonia Road.

I met Pia on Appolonia Road on 22 September 1990. She never noticed me and I simply said:

"Pia."

She lifted her glasses up looking puzzled.

She looked absent-minded; she didn't remember Dean. She didn't know who he was. I said *'sorry'* and walked away. Pia yelled:

"Wait up!" She said she just remembered, but she never called him Dean. I never knew that his nickname in those circles was Jacques. So, my Dean was Jacques. Like Jacques Prevert, perhaps.

There, on Appolonia Road I fell in love with Pia, but still wasn't aware of it. It took me a few years to admit that. I considered it to be a stroke of good luck that among a number of fruitless encounters the only woman who would embody the beauty and brains would be Pia the Poetess.

I said that I was happy the day when I fell in love with Pia. That day was shadowed by yet another death.

We got the news—Bobby was run over. I cried in the shed as one would cry for a real brother.

The first time when I kissed Pia, she said:

"Don't expect me to love you. I don't fall in love, and I don't see myself sharing my future with anyone. I am free and independent; I have never stayed long with anyone because of the fear that someone might get to know me. The art of loving is not my art, I can write poetry and that's the only field where I feel knowledgeable, confident and surrendered. Otherwise, I don't surrender."

"I never wanted you to surrender. All I want is to be friends ... may I say, I want a lasting friendship ... even when you go ..."

She looked at me long before she repeated my last words:

"A lasting friendship ... even when I go?"

She shrugged her shoulders and headed towards the park down Appolonia Road. Although I used to carry Appolonia's bag to the edge of the park, I had forgotten carrying it; her brother had beaten out of my brain most of the memories containing slides or pictures of Appoloina ... except for the Road I named after her.

I said I was happy with such a relationship.

But I wasn't.

Everyone believed that we both wanted the kind of relationship we had. I never wanted it to be that way. I wanted to tell her how much I loved her ... I wanted to tell her all those sweet verses lovers say to each other. But I never did. Pia reserved all those words for her poems, I always felt like a stranger on her pages. They were not my home. The verses were written for someone she was yet going to meet, that someone she yearned for. It wasn't me.

But I loved her and had learned to develop the art of not showing my love, almost denying it. What a tiresome art it was, what a weird artist I had become. Did that harden my soul and silence my honest speech?

She would disappear and I didn't know for many, many days anything about Pia. She would come back with a poem and a kiss. Something was burning within me, I could hear little explosions inside, but the major part of my art consisted in keeping the surface motionless. After some time that surface became—a stranger. I would look at the surface in a mirror and the mirror was absolutely indifferent, almost hostile ... Still, sometimes in that mirror I could grasp some fragments of me or of my late Dad's, there were some hints of Dean's words or gestures, some of Bobby's anger and lots of Pia's unspoken emotions hidden underneath, which aroused an unknown melody in my soul.

Love!

Did Pia love me without wording it? Is love a person? Is it an attitude? Could it be an orientation of character to the world as a whole, not just toward one person? Whom did Pia love?

Does *'love'* mean the absolute absence of a conflict?

I said that I never feared anything.

But I did.

I feared confrontations with Pia. Feared her leaving.

I said that it was the way we both liked it.

But it wasn't.

Underneath my outsized pride I knew Pia was never *'mine'*. I found myself to be completely under her spell, but kept silent, *'disinterested and distant'*, believing that only *'disinterested and distant'* I could keep her with me.

She kept on writing and winning and I resigned myself to the idea that we would always divide ourselves between poetry and silence, and between the little cracks among those two—a little bit of love.

Pia was hardly ever happy. Happiness is a state of mind, nothing else. But she was predominantly in a state of mind which asked for absolute surrender to it.

The day dawned full of clouds. Pia called almost in a hurry wanting to see me. While we were walking down Appolonia Road, Pia said:

"Today at 11 o'clock I'm departing."

"Where to?"

"To Australia."

"Yep."

I said nothing.

Nothing to her.

To Dean I said that I didn't mind.

But I did.

I cried inside.

Mother faintly smiled. She heard that the Poetess was going away. Far away, indeed. She heard it from Bobby's friend who still used to come and visit as if he hoped that Bobby might have magically appeared out of thin air. That friend of Bobby's, whose name I don't remember any more, never liked women of few words, the moody ones. I remember him, not particularly but only because he said that he never liked Pia's poetry, in his words she was *'worse than Sylvia Plath'*. He said that she was *'suicidal material'*, and that he hated such whims. I hated him; hence I have forgotten his name. I assume when you deliberately forget someone's name, you show utter disrespect or hidden hatred.

Mum said that it was about time that I got a new car.

There, on Appolonia Road, Pia said that she wanted to go to the airport alone. She never liked a *'public display of affection'*. I said to her that I was not an affectionate guy, anyway. She kissed me and went away. I felt so alone on that day looking at Pia's back getting smaller down Appolonia Road.

I got a new car. I told you I was happy because of it, but I wasn't. It was just a car, after all.

When she left, for days I read Plath's poetry.

I never read Pia's poetry again.

There was only one poem of Pia's which I truly liked and loved. It was *'Meryl's Poem'*.

The rest were just self-torturing expressions of the wounded soul.

I never asked her if she planned to come back or was she going for good. No difference.

Dean left. Why did he leave?

Amsterdam.

I said to myself that I would never go to Amsterdam, neither to Australia.

There I was: all alone with mother and our antique furniture. I had a new car. How happy was I supposed to be? I had everything.

My new car was a fancy one. Its bonnet was adorned with a little black horse propped up on its hind legs.

It is needless to say that she never called and never wrote a letter.

She didn't and I said I had forgotten her.

Anyway, she had a neurotic nature and her thoughts were like some dark river threatening to flood my sanity. I was drowning in love and despair, losing ground, losing self-respect and identity. I breathed Pia, recited Pia, imitated Pia, waited for her, bled for her, I almost exhausted my desire to go on living while she was absent writing her poetry.

It was August 30, the day was warmish and I was driving along a riverbank. Suddenly, a man waved his hand and hoarsely called my name. I slowed down.

It was Marcus.

He said that he came back home for holidays.

"Where do you live?"

He said, *"Sydney."* I never knew he lived over there.

He said he saw Pia several times.

He said she had lost lots of weight.

I put my dark sunglasses back on.

Pia!

I said:

"It was a long time ago. I barely remember her."

It was a lie.

I did remember her every day.

He said:

"Lucky you," pointing his hand towards a little black horse propped up on its hind legs *"... you've always had everything. Even as a child you had everything ..."*

"Yeah, I was pretty lucky."

"Even with the girls. You always snatched the best-looking ones. I remember that Italian girl. Good Lord, she had a piece of arse!!!"

Her brother beat the crap out of me!

Physical pain! You can touch it, locate it and eventually heal it.

I came back home and, as always, Mother kissed me.

There was a pleasant smell of quinces on the table. I closed my eyes to invite memories with the smell of yellow quinces.

I opened my eyes and looked at the quinces again. A letter was there—resting against a vase full of flowers. It was addressed to me.

It was Pia's letter.

It said:

"I want you to know that I used to love you. But you couldn't save me from myself. That unbearable emptiness of Australia inspires only a death wish. I hate it here, that's why I've come to this nothingness—only to torture myself.

It is done:

- The woman is perfected.

Her dead

Body wears the smile of accomplishment. —"

What was the name of that friend of my dear Bobby who said that she was like Sylvia Plath? Suicidal. I hate that man, I always did!

I couldn't even cry, I remember her asking me:

"A lasting friendship ... even when I go?"

Doctor's Daughter

The most unusual name she had. It was Hortensia. I mean, it was unusual for this part of the world, maybe somewhere else it would have been perfectly—common. Maybe somewhere else, where people didn't care as much about words and their meaning as they cared in this very perfect place. She was a doctor. A good doctor, it was said. Not a specialist, just a general practitioner (curing common colds and writing prescriptions). But this is a doctor, too, I'd say. Hortensia was, or shall I say, used to be - my mother. The only mother I ever had. When she used to be my mother, back then, when life looked real and almost meaningful, she was distant to everyone including me, as if she never knew any kind of empathy towards other humans. How then, I am asking, could she have been a doctor, for goodness' sake? And a good one, as they said?

She simply left when I was seven. I painfully thought that she had left because of me. Because I had done, or I hadn't done something I was or wasn't supposed to do. It had created some sort of split within my thoughts, actions and desires. My hidden desires. Those which were often buried so deep that even the owner rarely could have been aware of their existence. Especially a young soul.

She left in a hurry.

It was an ordinary day, except that the sun didn't come out on that day. To me it looked as if it was still night. To me it looked as if it was going to be one long, long cold night.

I heard a rooster's cry somewhere between the dawn and my careful anticipation which was growing day by day. The rooster, I'd say, indifferently announced her departure:

"The doctor, the general practitioner was about to leave."

I had covered my head with a duvet pretending that I had never heard the rooster's cry, and that I really never knew Hortensia, the doctor.

Since then I had cut all the flowers around every house I lived in. Counting even those built in my imagination as shelters from daily storms which consequently followed in abundance as a by-product of a simple selfish decision.

Someone once told me that hortensia was the name of a beautiful flower.

I needed no flowers in my childhood.

I had my father. He was rather a - thorn.

When the General Practitioner had left, his thorns quickly multiplied and grew thicker around his previously thin patience. Those thorns had pierced throughout everything: through our days, our conversations, our daily bread and our excuses and accusations. Thorns.

Nobody knew where she had silently gone. I suppose there were many places, anywhere in this world where a general practitioner could be needed. Maybe there were other kids or some other families who needed Hortensia more than we did. Maybe even God does things he regrets later.

She would say that we were a *'dysfunctional family'*. I didn't know exactly what that meant, but this two-word family description brought sadness into some of my games. This sadness manifested in the way I would play with my dolls without sufficient imagination, hence one of them I named *'Naughty Hortie'*. One day I pushed two little needles through her heart … two little thorns avenging my dad's bitterness towards me. That unusual bravery really didn't bring any sweetness or ease to me, but somehow it spoke to that broken part of me. I swear I heard it.

I never wanted to be a child.

Never a doctor's child. Particularly a child of a general practitioner.

***

Seven stale and hollow years had passed. The sky was reddish and I was, sort of, puzzled what good or bad that redness was going to bring with its shades.

It brought nothing in particular, but I bumped into a woman.

"I am sorry", that was what I said.

She nodded her head which resembled an unusual flower. It had petals instead of hair. The head had feathers, not hair. She smelled of something which I couldn't dare to name. I decided to follow that woman with a feathery head. As I followed her, those petals on her head were leaving a fragrance behind, giving me a perfect opportunity to follow her with my closed eyes, as if I was almost walking through an old dream. The unfinished one.

I would always close my eyes when I was faced with uncertainty or when challenged by a strange event.

That habit of closing my eyes I had inherited on that day when I buried my head under the duvet. Since then my eyelids were my mini duvets. Puffy little cushions.

I could follow her easily – firstly, because of the fragrance the petals were releasing, and secondly, because while she was walking, her heels were playing music when touching the pavement. Very fine music.

For me, it was almost as if I was walking through a filmed fairytale. I knew who I was in the filmed fairytale, but wasn't sure who was the object of my keen interest.

There was a bench and she, most elegantly, sat there with all her petals, her feathers, her fragrances and her musical heels; she sat there looking up into the sky as if the sky was about to bring some delicious surprise.

I stood frozen.

(I was always frozen when anticipating a delicious surprise.)

A man came and sat next to her.

He had long, long fingers.

His name was Leon.

When I saw Leon with the feathery creature, I was neutral. No feelings. But this is how it was for me often, more often then not. It was always like that, since the day the woman who used to be my mother had left, on that deaf morning broken in half by the rooster's cry. On that morning, everything was broken in half, including myself and my thorny father.

Leon was my music teacher. Yes, I was seven when he left.

Father said in his thorny voice:

"We can't afford Leon."

I never understood how one person couldn't afford the other ... but silently I accepted it.

We could not afford a general practitioner, a smile, any feelings or Leon.

We stood in a bare house stripped of emotions and of music which Leon would play every second day in our living room. We had a grand piano there and above it was our great-grandfather's portrait. In our house there were never any portraits of the General Practitioner's family but only of my father's. They were *'better people'*, very noble, and they always regretted that my father had married a plain general practitioner. What a waste! He could have married Princess Anne or someone in that line. But it didn't happen. Princess Anne had never met my father, even if she had, she would never have thought of him as a potential suitor. He was plainly an arrogant thorny man. Prickly. Like a prick.

Leon used to bring us chocolate boxes.

One for me and one for my cat. Yes, for my cat. He would leave the other box on top of the piano and say:

"This one's for kitty."

Kitty never ate the chocolates. I tried to feed it with the marzipan ones and the sweetest I could find, but it would smirk and walk away. With its tail up, up, up … touching the chandelier.

Once Leon told me if I played long enough, my fingers would be able to touch any key I desired. I thought, back then, that they would grow longer.

Leon had long, long fingers.

I liked Leon's fingers the way one can like the fingers of the teacher who brings two boxes of chocolates.

One was for me and the other one was for our cat.

Ungrateful cat. It would only smirk and walk away with its furry tail up, up, up … touching the ceiling.

When the rooster counted our days with his cry, and when I finally reappeared underneath my duvet, I looked around for Leon.

No more sweetness.

Just father and me.

He said, *"Don't ask."* In families like father's one never asks. My grandmother talked to him and her eyebrows were nearly touching. She looked like an old angry model wearing too much make-up. She always tried to cover her anger with excessive make-up. The predominant source of her anger came from the fact that my father had married a general practitioner with an unpronounceable name. My grandmother never liked her name, so she called my mother *General Practitioner*.

She called me *Child* and she called my father *Sunshine*.

We had strange names in our family, so I can say now, that Hortensia wasn't, after all, such a strange name.

I even used to like it when I was little. Very, very little.

I used to laugh at its sound. I used to struggle to pronounce it. She told me to call her *Hortie*, to make it easier. So, I called her *Hortie*.

My father called her—*Tensia*.

Like—tension.

There was always tension in his voice when calling her name.

Leon would play loudly and my father would call even louder with tension in his voice:

"Tensia, Tensia!"

I hid myself under the grand piano eating my chocolates given to me by Leon's long, long fingers.

***

I always suffered period pains. I felt as if someone cut me through, intentionally, with the sharpest knife. On such occasions, I could imagine that lots of dark sticky blood was coming out of my tummy. I felt as if I was going to bleed out and to pass out.

That was exactly how I felt on that day: as if someone cut me through with the sharpest knife, intentionally. I didn't bleed; I just stood there looking at Leon's long, long fingers playing with the feathers on the woman's head. He was arranging and rearranging them. They secreted a fragrance which held me trapped in my step and made my blood dark, like some dark, unforgiving river.

I was fourteen and it was my third period.

After imagining that scene of a bleeding, dark, unforgiving river long enough, I started to bleed heavily and then fainted.

Someone cried:

"Doctor, call a doctor!"

And the doctor didn't come.

She stood up and walked away slowly holding Leon's long, long fingers the way a grateful child would hold an unexpected box of chocolates.

She was a doctor with little empathy.

***

I remember that a man came, a young man, and offered me a bottle of water. I was looking at it wondering if anyone had drunk from it before. I was paranoid about germs.

I was taught to wash my hands countless times and never to drink from the bottle someone else drank from before.

After all, I used to be a doctor's daughter.

Nicholas Walks
a Silent Road

One of those days I met Nicholas on the sandy beach of Cadiz.

The wind blew off my scarf and I did not even bother to stand up and get involved with the *levante's* cheeky dance and chase my scarf around the beach. But I sat minding my numerous sheets of paper which would turn into letters as the day approached towards more tiresome hours for me.

He approached from behind, I never heard his footsteps, for the sand was a silent road, nor had I caught his very distinguished odour of strong spirits, for the wind was blowing it away from us. He said:

"Your scarf."

I grabbed my sheets of paper as if I was guarding them with my life and did not know whether he came as a rescuer of my scarf or whether he was an intruder keen to interfere with my tidied-up sentences. I had had enough of the *levante's* interference, for with it my sentences were somehow less obedient to my mind; but I did not need any interference, either from any other natural source or from a man who came as a rescuer, who caught a freed bird I tied below my suspicious chin. Honestly, I did not know what to say, or to take the scarf he was holding, for I was holding my letters tightly to my chest and both hands were full of my conversations with my men and I was very hesitant for if I wanted my scarf, I needed to let go of my letters and it would be more of a disaster to lose my pages than the silken scarf I had bought at the bazaar down in Cadiz town. He read my dilemma in my trembling hands and as he came closer he simply asked if he might tie it around my head.

I did not say *"Yes,"* I did not say *"No"*, but he came closer and tied it around my head and tied a little bow on the back of my neck. I said *"Gracias,"* I said *"Thank you,"* and was looking at my feet which were keen to go; but he said that we could speak English for he was an Irishman who came here, and just like me, was trapped by the wind and delicious food and he never went back to Ireland since, and he never finished his novel, but he said, *"What's the hurry?"*

I said to Nicholas that I was not the easiest person to talk to, and not the best company for the rest of the day, for I was quite a troubled soul who was most comfortable when I was alone with the wind. He said he would never trouble me, for his troubles were numerous but quite well hidden behind a friendly façade and cultured attitude. He said he saw me writing every day and expressed his envy for my passion and dedication, for he said his pages were blank for a number of days, which altogether already leaked into a year.

For this or that reason we humans open up more easily to people we know we are not going to see again, so Nicholas sat next to me and I told him about the broken pieces of my troubled heart and told him about the two men I was writing love letters to every day.

Nicholas was a gifted listener; he kept his eyes on the little shells and his ears on each one of my words, nodding his head speechlessly. He suggested I keep a copy of my letters, for I might need them one day, but I told him that one of the men did not read the letters, that they came back returned unopened, for he did not care about my words any more. I told him I had all my letters, they were still in a sealed envelope, tired of the long trip around the world, twice.

Nicholas asked me which one of the two I loved better, and I told him that I did not know, for both of them were wrong, as I had the gift of choosing the wrong, sometimes troubled man, but I said as long as I could write my letters I loved them both and Nicholas nodded his head as if in agreement, saying, *"I see, I see ... "*, from which it appeared to me that Nicholas understood exactly what I wanted to say, as if he had grasped the real meaning.

The sun was getting down, looked as if it was pouring ochre paint into the ocean; the shadows grew longer and darker, then I turned my head to Nicholas and saw his face for the first time, and he looked so young and sinless and I told him he looked so young and sinless and he laughed heartily and said that no Irishman looked sinless for they were all troublemakers, even though, he said, it sounded like a worn-out cliché, in clichés always a good part of truth was held. I asked him about his sins and he said that he knew all the sins humans invented or were tempted into, for his learning consisted of one after another episode of extravagant choices. He said that he looked young because there was a needy little boy still caught inside of him, but he was often in bitter dispute with a domineering master who asked that his will and wants were instantly satisfied. Nicholas asked me if I thought that it was easy to make peace and live a trouble-free life among the two of them. I said that I assumed we all had a little needy child locked in our subconscious mind and we all had a tyrant that asked for instant perfection and gratification. Then I told him not to take what I said too seriously, for I was not really competent in the field of psychology but where I was at my best was writing love letters, even though it might appear that they were not appreciated, at least from one of their recipients.

Nicholas asked me out that evening or any other to get drunk together, but I told him that I couldn't for several good reasons and did not feel obliged to list to him all my reasons. Instead I took one which looked the most appropriate and told him that I did not drink, for then I did not know who I was and this could be a very frightening experience. He said that he never knew and never would know who he was, but when he drank he thought he didn't really care.

I said I had to go to the post office to send my letters and Nicholas asked why I didn't send my letters by wind, for it would be the same, but without any cost.

Brontë Sisters

First Story:
Briana
(Sydney, 1994-2000)

My name is Briana. My mother, when I was very little, used to call me Brianabell; somehow out of it came the nickname Bella. In Italian *'bella'* means—pretty girl. I was not born pretty. My mother was a very tiny woman but I took after my father's strong family build and was born weighing four and a half kilograms. My poor mother almost died on that absolutely odd day giving birth to her firstborn. She didn't die, but as I was too big, I was later told doctors tried to *'suck me out'* and when I finally came out with a screech and a cry, something went horribly wrong which caused a lot of damage to my eyes and sight, my ears and hearing and, as it would be very obvious later—my speech. I was only eight months old when I underwent a rather long operation in order to fix my eyes that were unfocused, uneven; each eye followed its own policy and searched for different objects of amusement. Mum used to blame my father and his family, for she said they were all, *'Australian weirdos and alcoholics'*. And, they were! She was right. My childhood wasn't a happy one because my mum, as a proper British woman would, had never been ready to show any emotion or affection, believing that it was a sign of belonging to the upper class. Dad was never home—thank God, for when he was, it was a home of tension and bitterness. I was a lonely child trying to figure out, *'Why do I have to put up with such people?'*

After three operations my eyes didn't improve nor did my sight, nor did they look less odd.

When I started to talk, it was obvious that I would have a speech defect, probably to such an extent that it could never be fixed.

All of that brought a lot of sadness and insecurity to my existence and I often felt like an unwanted child, and a misfit: I was an overweight, odd-looking child. Early in my life, I learned how to hide emotions: my mother was the perfect role model, the queen of cool, never showing any emotions, but on the other hand, I was well aware that I would not impress people and ignite softness and kindness in their hearts. I would look at a mirror full of astonishment: who's that chubby, cross-eyed girl adorned by the biggest ears, which were poking out of her curly blond hair? Yes, it was I, and that image never made me feel proud or happy. Then I got glasses with a patch on one side—that brought only more anger, which I stored neatly under my hat.

Mum was often ill, poor soul, she would just be groaning all day long without saying a word; dad, whilst often drunk, went out on his *'walka-bouts'*, somewhere in the bush, somewhere where he thought he would find peace: far from mum's groaning and from the critical look of his five year old cross-eyed child.

Mum was often tired and never had any time to tidy up, thus I grew up in, I'd say, a pretty messy house; everything was allowed, I could get away with anything, for I had a fierce temper and if I was asked to tidy up or to put my things where they belonged, I would get mad: ripping and destroying everything in my vicinity, choosing the most venomous words and shooting the most poisonous arrows towards my groaning, powerless mother.

Oh, no! I could never obey! Never, and no one! From early childhood I decided to be disobedient. It wasn't even a decision; it was some powerful force within me telling me to obey only its wish. I thought that it was the real me, and I let that force do and act as it pleased. When I understood that this force was so powerful, I was unstoppable. I bit my father a number of times and never feared his beatings. I was sorry for my mum because he took it out on her.

Mum had several girlfriends. All of them were very kind to my mum in times of need. They would listen on the phone when she would talk about 'Him'. They never said much; they only listened but never stayed longer than necessary, especially if my mum started to talk about her pain (she was in a lot of pain due to her illness).

The oddest friend my mother had was Emily. I have to admit that she was a clever woman but—she had an opinion on everything. Even literature. She was tidy and always nicely dressed. She smelled nicely and showed her emotions. I wasn't comfortable in her company, for she wanted to hug me or mess up my hair. She never hid her emotions and opinions and would passionately comment, *'If I were you, I would have left him long ago. How can you stand him any longer?'*

I held the same emotions towards him but I didn't like hearing such words from others, especially from Emily. She held herself as if she figured it all out, as if she was the cleverest and the prettiest woman in the whole wide world.

I have to admit, even though it is so obvious by now—I didn't like Emily, but my mother did.

Teya. She was Emily's daughter. She was two years older and when I saw her for the very first time, I still remember it, as if it was yesterday, I thought, *'I have never seen a more beautiful and more sophisticated girl.'*

She was so pretty that when we went out together people would come to her and comment on her grace and beauty. When I met her I was four, she was six, and everybody thought that she was not only a beautiful young girl but also graceful and full of kindness. She was tall too, and very lean, she used a knife and fork with such ease as if she was an adult. I had never seen her spilling her tea, or seen crumbs on the plate after she had eaten her cake. She ate slowly and used her napkin after each and every bite, occasionally looking at Emily. Now and then, when she leant her elbows onto the table, or bent her back slightly, Emily would comment, *'Keep your back straight, Sweet Pumpkin.'* And she would obey! She would obey all instructions Emily gave her: *'Cover your mouth when you yawn, please!', 'Please, do not kick your legs under the table!', 'Use a handkerchief!', 'Say, thank you!', 'Fix your hair, it is messy!'*

All sorts of instructions and warnings! And she would obey with a gentle smile. She would say, *'Ok, Mummy!'*

My mum and I would secretly laugh.

They even showed emotions publicly, demonstrated their love in front of other people: *'Give Mummy a hug, Bubbzie.', 'I missed you, Bubbie.', 'That's for my Sweetie.'*

She was happy hearing this rubbish! My mother never talked to me in that manner. I would drink and eat and create the biggest mess on the table and underneath it, and Mum wouldn't object. Emily would; she would tell Mum, *'You have to tell her; you have to teach her. That's what mothers do!'*

Mum would shrug her shoulders, *'She is hopeless. She was born like that. She is just like her father.'*

I hated being compared to him. I was never like him. But that force within me would wildly react to Emily's words and I would knock off the table whatever happened to be there - cups or plates, even Teya's book or her fancy sunglasses. She would come with a book. That made me even more angry; the fact that she had such peace inside of her, sitting at the table with her back straight, like the most beautiful porcelain doll, smiling while reading her book and occasionally glancing at Emily, or saying, *May I have a hug, Mummy?'*

Everyone said there was complete harmony between Emily and Teya, and I thought it just a cheap show. Fake love and tenderness. No one loves like that; no one shows emotions like that!

Emily often invited us out to the cafés or restaurants. I don't know if they were wealthy, but Emily did everything with such ease: she paid the bills, she bought toys and clothes without considering the price of anything, and she liked and wore only designer's clothes. When Teya grew out of some clothes, Emily gave them to me. That practice didn't last too long as in one year I doubled in size and couldn't wear her pretty dresses any longer. I hated them anyway, for when she wore them she looked like a girl from a TV commercial, whereas in her clothes, I looked like a pumpkin covered with some sort of rag.

I bit her on one occasion.

For no apparent reason.

We were sitting in a café; my father was always restless in Emily's company, so he stood up and went *'walkabout'*; my mother rolled her eyes, Emily rolled her eyes, while Teya sat peacefully, with her back straight, kept on reading her book and smiling, unaware of any changes that took place around the table.

I went down on my knees, and bit her thigh. All three of them jumped up: Teya looked at me with tears in her eyes, my mother screeched, *'What did you just do! You wicked, wicked child?'* and Emily rushed to Teya saying, *'Does it hurt, my love?'*

There is *your love*—holding back her tears!

Your perfect creature - learning the lesson of staying composed in a dire situation.

Mum and Emily, each held one of my arms asking the same question: *"Why did you do it, Briana?"*

I knew that both of them were very angry, for they called me *Briana*. I hated when people called me Bella. Emily used to call Teya, *'Bellina.'* In their house they spoke a different language.

I stood there quietly celebrating my victory.

My mum asked Emily, as if she was a queen ready to pardon, *'Will you pardon her? She is a plain nuisance.'*

Emily said, *'You got to teach her what's right and what's wrong.'*

As if I didn't know it!

I knew it, but the force inside me, just showed me how I could be superior. Teya hugged me after I was forced to apologise. *'I am sorry.'* But I wasn't. I triumphed as Emily said, *'I shall cancel her piano lesson; she is too upset to attend.'*

Teya said, *'Thank you, Mummy'*, and buried her face in Emily's dress.

Emily never hid her thoughts. She said to my mum:

"Look, I am upset now more than Teya is. For today I've had enough of Briana."

My silly mother apologised again.

Emily behaved as if she was a queen, someone who knows everything, someone who has to give advice; she said:

"Mae, you've got to teach her now, don't postpone it; it could be too late."

She walked off with her *'perfect Teya'* hand in hand as if in harmony.

My mother dragged me all the way to the bus stop. She didn't say anything but I knew she was angry. Maybe even disappointed.

I hated Emily even more, for the next time we came to their place she told me to *'eat properly'* to *'use the knife and fork'* and not to *'spill a drop on the table or on the floor'*, for I was old enough to implement those manners. My mother didn't defend me; she didn't say anything. I ate *'properly'*, but when we went to Teya's room, I let loose my rage and revenge: I broke two keys on Teya's piano and that deed hit the right key on Emily's inner instrument.

Teya fought back tears again; Emily didn't fight her emotions, she told my mother that I was completely wild and out of control, and that she feared what the future held for me if no one taught me how to behave in social situations. My mother had tears in her eyes and I just hated Emily with all my heart.

We left, but before we crossed the threshold, Emily hugged my mum and said:

"I know that you don't have sufficient energy for that child, but you've got to do something."

Teya said:

"Bella, don't do that next time."

"Ok. I won't", I said, but I laughed internally.

I didn't feel sorry for anyone, not even for my mother.

I didn't feel sorry for her even the next week when she said that we had to go.

Where? I wondered.

"Unfortunately, back to the UK."

My father went *'walkabout'* and met a woman on his lonely trips, an artist, just like him, a drunkard, just like him, so he left the mortgage behind which Mother couldn't pay any longer.

I never figured out what I did really feel on that occasion. I never figured out why Mum was upset leaving that country, and was never able to answer if I was going to miss Teya. I was happy to accept that I would probably never cross paths with Emily. Ever again.

Second Story:
Teya
(Sydney, 1994-2000)

Everyone calls me Teya but my real name is Dorotea. Everybody called me Teya except my mother: every day, she christened me with numerous new names: *Sweet Pumpkin, Miss Muffet, Stellina,* which is a little star, *Bubbzie* or *Bubbz,* but her favourite, I would say, was—*Cookie* (sometimes, *Sweet Cookie*). She made me laugh a lot. Because she was so funny. In her body, she looked like an adult woman, like a proper mother; but her heart showed a little girl, just about my own age. We laughed a lot; oh, I said that before. She was a very structured person though, and exposed me to *'all the rules that, one day, would make my life easier'*. I think, I always liked structured days: breakfast had to be eaten before going out; washing hands, combing hair, straightening a dress, again washing hands, lunch exactly at noon, piano lessons on late afternoons and drama classes on Wednesday and Friday evening. She used to drive me there, and whilst waiting, she read a book. She always read books, and I often wondered if there was any book in this whole wide world that she hadn't read.

That was the first lesson she taught me: *In the right books you'll find wisdom and answers!*

I was a little bit annoyed by her kisses, as she always kissed me, countless times. I have never told her that because of two simple reasons: I never wanted to hurt her, and I wouldn't be happy either if she stopped it altogether.

After a bath and a dinner she made for me, Mum would tuck me in my bed, sit on the little settee and open a book: oh, my favourite time! She had a wide array of languages and expressions, accents and characters hidden up her sleeve, and on most nights I would fall asleep laughing.

She checked if I was asleep, walked out on tiptoes, and then she would sit at her desk.

As if coming from a faraway distance, I would hear - *'click-clack click-clack'*, the sound of her instrument, her keyboard.

My mother is a writer, a novelist, even though, at that age, I did not fully grasp what she really did. She explained, *'I am creating, arranging and selling words.'*

When I was about five years old, my mother told me that she was *'fif-teen'* when I asked her how old she was. Mother's friend Mae asked, *"Can you repeat that, sweetie?'* I said proudly:

"My mum is fifteen."

Mae stated, looking somehow sternly into Mum's eyes, *'Well, that makes me only thirteen, doesn't it?'*

Mum just nodded her head, and it took me another several years to discover that my mum was, actually thirty plus, but refused to accept it on most days. Especially, when we were alone.

I loved Mae, and Mae loved me I would say.

I had a little problem with Briana—she was that small but burning ball of energy and every time she saw me, she charged into me like a little ram, almost knocking me down. Everyone would say, *'Bella, calm down, Bella.'* Once Mae said, *'Hold your horses!'* and we laughed at that expression, repeating it several times. I never said to Mum that Bella used to pinch me, because my mum liked to correct people on the spot. There were days when I really liked Bella, but sometimes she wouldn't let me read my book, or she would spill her juice onto it. I knew how to talk to her and how to calm her down. When I would say something she couldn't take her eyes off me. Quite often she would simply repeat what I had said, nodding her head. She wasn't really a child that one would label as *'pretty'*, but I thought she was cute in her own way. Mostly, I felt sorry, for she couldn't express her-self clearly and it created a lot of frustration for her. No one really under-stood that she was plainly frustrated because she couldn't focus her eyes or keep her attention on something with ease, or the way any other kid would. When we were alone, she listened to what I would tell her, but when my mum said something or corrected her, I noticed the level of her frustration or anger lifted higher on the barometer of her tolerance. I would opt out in such instances: reading a book or playing the right keys in my head. I often played piano in my head or sang songs, like it served as some neat rehearsals for the future grand concerts in which I, actually, never performed. Even though I loved music so much, I knew I was not going to choose music as my future profession. I never liked being in the centre of attention. Still, I can remember the trembling of my hands and voice when I decided to announce to my mother the decision not to enroll in the Conservatorium at early age. But she said, *'You choose what makes you happy, whatever makes you happy, makes me happy, too.'* Then she added, *'... but, a university degree is expected without a doubt ... it is not optional.'*

I would never question that myself; all I wanted at that age is to *'acquire a lot of knowledge'*, whatever that meant to me back then.

Briana's nickname was Bella, and I liked it because it brought some balance to her little persona. This sentence might appear as awkward, but I know exactly what I wanted to express with such a sentence. She needed balance and screamed for it, but it simply wasn't there.

We had our ups and downs as any other kids, but what made me very sad, and in a way distanced me from her, was that famous bite I got from her. She simply went down on her knees and bit my thigh. I still remember the sting, for days there was a visible sign of her teeth and a dark red circle on the inner and outer side of the teeth mark. She bit me as a rabid dog would. No one ever knew why. She refused to tell us why she did it, and with absolute effort she muttered, *'Sorry, Teya!'* when our mothers insisted on such words that never brought relief to my pain, imprinted on my thigh with her small but sharp teeth.

Mum was very upset; more upset than I was. What I really felt was pain and sadness, which came out of understanding that some people can't control themselves from behaving badly.

Some time later, I reproached my mother for trying to build around me the illusion of this *'perfect world'*.

"Are we going to see them again, Mum?"

"We have to learn tolerance, but she bit you like a little wild animal. This is not acceptable."

"Please, Mum."

"Sure, we'll see them again. Mae's my good friend."

"And Bella is mine. You've always said—we have to tolerate people and accept them the way they are."

I remember the day when Mum and Mae were talking in a very quiet voice. Mae cried, I remember that. Mum hugged her, I remember Mum telling her, *'You got to learn to look after yourself first.'*

Mum kissed Bella and she smiled. I have never figured out if she liked my mum, or if she disliked her, for Mum always asked her to tidy up after her or not to create a mess while eating.

On that day both of them had tears in their eyes: Mum and Mae.

When they left, I asked Mum what was wrong.

She said:

"They are going back to the UK."

"Are we going to see them again?"

"Not for a while."

I knew I was going to miss my little friend, that uncontrollable ball of energy which refused to listen to anybody, just to me, occasionally, or in a dire situation when she feared that I'd stay indifferent.

People used to say that she was a *'naughty child'* or a *'wicked one'*.

I never saw that; all I saw in Briana Bella was the frustration and some strange sadness.

We inherit physical characteristics from our ancestors that are obvious at first glance; I knew deep, deep down she buried that sadness she inherited from the man who couldn't pass onto her much more.

"I'll miss them, Mum" I said, then went into the music room to play the piano. Music was the answer to all my troubles.

Third Story:
Briana
(Sydney, July 2014)

I am in a plane, why am I thinking about him right now? How can I let go of that anger stored over many years when everything reminds me of him? He always told me that I was *'inadequate'*, *'fat and ugly'*. And he was a drunkard.

Mum showed tears at the airport, so strange! Unnecessary.

I wonder: do Teya and her mother still express their emotions so easily? It is so unpleasant; it used to make me feel uncomfortable.

New thoughts, please!

Cambridge, Oxford or Durham?

All professors at Cambridge were so keen except one. What did he want from me? Since the sixth grade they talked about me as a *'genius'*, all competitions and awards fell in my lap so easily. Well, he was a drunkard and a weirdo, but he used to be the most talented artist. He won numerous awards and I was never invited to any of the ceremonies. His *'new kids'* were invited, but not me, *'clumsy, embarrassing Brie'*, as he calls me. Someone gave me a dirty look. Oh, I was talking again to myself loudly—oops!

Teya's mum read my story and said, *'I am stunned!'* Yes, that is what she said to my mum and me; I was flattered. I used to think that she never liked me; that she was vain and opinionated. Ah, foreigners! We, Brits, don't show emotions and do not get excited so easily. I hope that I painted her character wrong only because I was a little insecure girl. Teya had always been kind. I used to be jealous because all attention went her way, everybody commented on her *'beauty and grace'*, but I don't care about that any more. I am an adult, a girl who is going to enroll in one of the most prestigious universities.

After all, that was very generous of them to invite me, I'd say.

There are some boys on the plane wanting to talk to me. I never talk to boys. I don't have many friends; I am not a so-called *'popular girl'*. I bit geeky, the happiest when I read books and I am left alone. I don't get along with my mother because she wants to control me and tell me what to do. I don't listen to anyone. My favourite way of life is sitting on the sofa and reading books. I finish two books in a day. Seriously, don't I?

Oh, people; stop turning heads! Yes, I speak to myself, what's so strange? Everybody does? I just, sometimes, forget to keep it quiet, internal.

I hate being told what to do or being corrected! I hate when people look at me. I am the happiest when I am left alone: reading, writing or painting. In whichever creative avenue I express myself, professors claim that I am a *'genius'*. Funny, though, it has never strengthened my self-esteem. I still hear his voice in my head!

Oh, Briana, change your thoughts! The man turned his head, I smiled at him; he smiled back. I muttered, *'I am sorry'*; he just smiled. I always apologise.

I had butterflies in my stomach when the plane touched down.

That tall brunette with a wide smile can only be Teya. She has grown, she is tall and slim and she has the same face as she had fifteen years ago. She hugged me and I couldn't bear it, but managed not to tell her that I am petrified by physical contact. I hope they won't keep that habit of hugging and touching hands.

Emily was waiting in the car. She walked out and gave me a hug. My arms just hung down, I couldn't wait that she ended those unnecessary outpourings of fake kindness.

What crossed my mind was—thank God she is a vegan, otherwise she would give me a hard time. I am vegan but it wasn't my choice. I didn't have any choice. Mum has been ill for ages and her doctor recommended organic, vegan and gluten free diet. Since then, way back, we eat only what is prescribed as vegan diet. It is often hard to articulate that because people don't accept differences easily. Kids often laugh at me; at my choice of food.

Anyway, Emily is vegan and I hope it'll make my stay easier. She said she was gluten intolerant just like mum and me.

Teya's laughter is spontaneous and sounds like numerous bells ringing. She said:

"No way! I love my prosciutto, camembert, lamb chops and fine rosé."

"So, you eat everything?"

Emily said:

"To be vegan was my choice. I didn't have the right to impose onto her something that even I don't know if it is good for a young child. I found it good for me, but when I was young I grew up on, let's call it, a normal diet: lots of fish, meat, dairy products … In my opinion, kids have to have animal protein."

They have a big house. Too big for two. A bay and mansions around, I wondered—how come?

I couldn't believe—she, Emily, still called Teya *'Bubz'*. And, Teya was OK with it. She still called her *'Sweetie'*, *'Cookie'* and *'Bunny'*. So weird!

She still messed her hair and asked her, *'Did you wash your hands?'*

Unbelievable!

After dinner they sat on the sofa and hugged. I just didn't know in which direction to look. Emily tickled her when Teya said something silly. I found it so weird.

I muttered:

"So weird!"

Emily asked:

"What is weird, little Bella?"

"I am not little any more. I have finished high school and am about to enroll in Cambridge."

"Oh, pardon me, your highness!" said Emily and laughed. I felt uncomfortable; she said:

"Laugh, Bella, laugh! It was a funny remark, wasn't it? You got to learn now that we laugh in this house a lot."

Laugh at what?

Nothing was funny!

She, Emily, was funny. After twenty-four hours of flight she forced me to take a shower. I refused and she gave up! I wanted to tell her, *Mind your bloody business, leave me alone!"*

She bought me a pair of pyjamas and slippers and I told her that it wasn't necessary; I never wear pyjamas or slippers. But the funny thing was, and it was obvious that everything had to be *'proper'*. That middle-class properness! I hate that! I hate being told what to do and how to do it!

I shall certainly tell her off next time when she suggests something like, *'Girls, wash your hands and come to the table.'*

Mind your own business!

I'll just pray that I see her as little as possible and enjoy this beautiful house where I can read books and relax. I have to admit she has an envious library.

If only she goes somewhere for several weeks and me and Teya can have fun together.

The next day I had the house all to myself. They went out; Teya to University and Emily mentioned some interview.

Everything was in order, even Teya's room. They brought a sofa into the so-called music room and it was going to be my room: several guitars and a piano, some other furniture and some paintings. Several photos of them—together.

I read Emily's books and recognised Teya in them. Ah, unconditional motherly love, what a load of crap! Public display of emotions!

I never let anyone hug me or caress me, I feel uncomfortable. I never had a boyfriend nor will I have one, they are all liars, cheaters and horrible human beings.

Teya has many friends: friends from old school, friends from Uni, friends from the neighbourhood and friends from a little café where she works twice a week. Oh, yeah, and her *'tennis friends'*. When I asked her what it meant, she explained that they are all boys from some prestigious religious school in Sydney that she met through tennis games and tournaments. She said:

"Don't worry, you'll meet them all."

While I was alone some un-named anger started to rise out of nowhere, or out of that unbearable tidiness of the house. As often an uncontrollable urge takes over my rational mind, this time I started to add character to that almost *'perfect order'* of things. I knocked down the bottles which were so perfectly lined up in the bathroom, on the ledge of the window, that were obviously never opened. The opposite window was opened and this one served to display her collection of organic shampoos, conditioners and shower gels. They were lined up in correct order: from the tallest to the smallest, a few centimeters apart from each other. Even they looked like obedient soldiers, full of fear of the mistress who arranged them and demanded servility and order. When I knocked them down, they flew into different directions: two of them fell on the floor, the other two in the shower cubicle, one in the sink. As if that wasn't enough, that strong energy I had within me told me to open a bottle of shampoo and to spill it onto the floor, which I did.

I sincerely, but naively, thought that Emily would be more cultured and would not conduct an investigation and interrogation as to what happened to her soldiers. My mum would never treat a guest in that manner. She would simply put up with it until the guest left and comment later. But no! When Emily witnessed disorder among her soldiers, she came into the living room and said:

"*Teya, did you have a shower?*"

"*No, I just came back.*"

"*Bella, did you have a shower?*"

"*No, not yet.*"

"*Ok. So, what happened to the bottles of shampoo in the bathroom?*"

"*What happened?*" Teya repeated, but Emily's eyes were pointing at me. I shrugged my shoulders and thought that this boring and pointless conversation had ended, but this woman wasn't backing off. She said:

"*You spent your day today alone in the house. You should know what happened. The bathroom floor is soaked with shampoo, I slipped and almost fell down.*"

"*I don't know why you are asking me!*" the anger raised my temperature and my voice.

"*Fine!*" said Emily and walked into the kitchen.

She was always in charge.

Her next question was:

"*OK, girls. What are we going to have for dinner? I'll make curry and rice for me, Teya is going to have her Wiener schnitzel with prosciutto, Bella what about you? Do you want to share some curry with me?*"

"*No thanks. I am not hungry.*"

I just ate an hour ago. I was hungry and opened the fridge. I found that famous *'prosciutto'*, as she calls it. It was wrapped in nice paper, finely sliced and it smelled so nice. I tried a slice and I loved it! I hadn't had meat for years and it tasted so good. I put it on the table, cut some cheese with it, cut some bread (I used to love sourdough bread before mum added it to her *'no list'*), and I ate it all. It was so good and filling and simply delicious.

Emily asked:

"Teya, where did you put your prosciutto?"

"In the fridge."

"Yes, but where?"

Teya searched but she couldn't find it. Even the wrapping they wouldn't be able to find, for I hadn't thrown it into the bin but took it out and shoved it into the bush. They talked in the kitchen in a low voice and Teya asked:

"Did you have some prosciutto today?"

"No, don't you remember, I am vegan?"

"Sure!" said Teya and invited me to play a video game until dinner was ready.

I won!

They didn't notice the cheese and the bread, and I kept on eating in secret Teya's food and refusing to eat dinners with them.

She ate quite a lot, yet she was so slim and tall, and when I glanced at the mirror I didn't like what I saw in it.

Emily was slim but petite, and why on earth would a woman of fifty wear the same fashionable clothes as her daughter? Something was so wrong with her! She was so vain! We used to buy our clothes at second-hand shops or St. Vincent's, mum liked modesty, plus the money mum earned mainly went to the mortgage.

Teya took me out. I don't have male friends; so I felt extremely anxious when she told me that we were going out with six boys. They drank cocktails. I wanted to try one and fought a horrible battle to resist. Then one of the boys brought me one and I tried it after several attempts to resist. Teya asked:

"What did you just say?"

I wasn't even aware that I was talking aloud again. When I experience anxiety I talk to myself aloud.

"Oh, never mind. It is lovely."

And it was.

The most peculiar thing was that even when she was out with her friends, Teya was controlled by her mother and she didn't even care! How bizarre! She received a text message and said to the boys:

"My mum said 'hello' guys."

They all said:

"Say 'hello' to Emily."

They all knew her; they all liked her, how strange!

Teya kept on texting her back several times telling her where we were and what we were drinking. What crazy control!

I said:

"Why do you have to report everything to your mother? She isn't your owner!"

"I don't have to! I choose to. I love when she knows that all is good. She knows all of my friends and they like her. I find it cool."

"I find it bizarre! I never tell my mother where I go and with whom. It is not her business. You have to teach your mother to stay out of your business."

"You are weird, my little Bella."

"No, you are weird."

"OK, have another cocktail and world will appear more pinkish to you."

The next day Teya told her about the evening, about drinks and venues … they discussed her friends and Emily knew their private stuff, how disgusting!

A few days later, I felt a little bit more at ease because the weather was beautiful and Teya took me around the city. In the evening there was an interrogation again. She dared to enter my room and open the windows, as she said the room needed airing. She said that I was so messy, without a second thought. She just said, *'You've got to tidy up the room, there's such a mess there.'*

She really hit my nerve and I said:

"Why would you care?"

Her face got a curious expression. When Emily left the room, Teya said:

'My mum likes order. That's the way she is. I'll help you to tidy up. We don't take our shoes into the bedroom. We leave them outside."

"But why? Why so many rules? You are like an obedient puppy to your mother."

"Let's tidy it up and just leave it at that."

They watched television, and I sneaked into the kitchen, opened the fridge door and ate some food. Emily said:

"If you are hungry, help yourself freely."

"No, I am not hungry, thanks."

A whole week has passed and I still feel very strange among the two of them. Teya is so intelligent and quick-minded yet she takes into consideration everything what this woman is telling her. She even invites her out with us. She asks:

"Bubbie, do you wanna go with us?"

After ten days I broke down and cried; I called my mum telling her what a horrible treatment I got from this woman.

She walked into my room and told me to tidy up. Then she told me to take the sheets off and gave me a set of fresh sheets. I refused to take the sheets off. She insisted, and I refused, as I knew that she would find out my secret.

Well, at night my legs and back would get so itchy. Without any awareness of what I was doing, I would scratch my legs and back, and in the morning I would find deep wounds like deep burrows cut into my legs and back. They were bleeding and the sheets were stained with blood. I didn't want this nosy woman to know my secret. None of her bloody business!

I called mum and cried after many years. I told her that she was a horrible woman who wanted to control me all the time. Mum was puzzled, for she said that she never remembered Emily in this light.

She just left two sheets and pillowcases in my bedroom and went into the garden.

The next day, early in the morning, I took the sheets off, put the new ones and walked out of the house. I found a container where I shoved the sheets and came back into the house. I found her on the sofa writing on her laptop. She said:

"Good morning, Pumpkin. Where have you been this early?"

I am not her Pumpkin! And why doesn't she mind her own business. I told her:

"I went for a walk."

"Oh, that's nice. Make yourself a nice breakfast now."

Finally she let me do something instead of saying, *I'll fix something nice for you.'*

Teya got up, and the first thing she did she kissed her. Like, coming to the altar of a Goddess! Pathetic! Even more pathetic conversation. Emily asked:

"Did you sleep well? What did you dream about?"

She had to know everything; she even wanted to own Teya's dreams. Teya said:

"Oh, I got to tell you. Crazy, I had that dream that I was navigating a plane …"

She kept on retelling her dream while Emily smiled and nodded her head.

I counted their perfumes: there were exactly fifty-six. Why on earth does someone need that many perfumes? One would pass unnoticed anyway, unless she counted everything—let's test her.

Two days later she still didn't mention the perfume. Strange! I thought she'd notice it.

Everybody liked Teya. I couldn't figure out, was it because she was pretty or because she had that aura of a *'good girl'* around her? She had so many friends and her life appeared to be easy. I wasn't jealous, but just comparing her life to mine was like comparing a hard working ant with a beautiful carefree butterfly. Though, I have to say—she was her mother's daughter! She was touched by vanity herself as she went to the hairdresser regularly, put make up when going out and wore the finest clothes. When she was in company of male friends, she was chatty and flirty and asked them to do things for her—a similar attitude that I had recognised long ago in her mother.

More weirdness I witnessed when the Redhead came over.

Teya said:

"Lex is coming. She'll take us to Palm Beach."

When Lex came, they hugged and kissed each other several times. Lex hugged even me, not knowing that I disliked hugs from any person. My mum never hugged me as both of us found it a very strange habit.

Lex was chatty and didn't stop talking. She was pretty, too. Apparently funny, but I never found their sense of humour genuine or amusing. They talked about other people and had an opinion about everything. So annoying. Brits are the only cultured people. We don't talk about others and we do not express our opinion.

When we came back after almost the entire day, there was Lady Emily at home. Lex ran to her and hugged her. Emily kissed her saying:

"Oh, I haven't seen this baby for a long time. Where have you been? Studying hard?"

And to my astonishment, Lex started to tell her where she had been for the last two weeks, what she had done and how many exams were left. Then she asked Emily about her novel and Emily said:

"I finished it. I just started editing."

"Congratulations!

Teya said:

"Emily, would you be so kind and make us your famous pizza? Please, Emily."

Lex said with the biggest smile on her face:

"Please, Emily."

I couldn't believe my ears! From bossy woman she turned into a tyrant as she said:

"Yeah, but you are going to pay for that. You are going to prepare everything, and when you've eaten - clean the kitchen and lick the floors."

They laughed! It sounded so offensive! Derogatory! Would anyone do that just for a *pizza*? She treated Lex as she was her private slave. She told her:

"Lex, bring me some water from the fridge. There is half a lemon on a little plate, bring that over too."

And the poor girl did it.

"Child labor ..." I muttered and rolled my eyes, but no one really paid attention to what I said; Lex sat next to Emily and told her trivial stories about her sister and father and some other people. Emily pretended to care

and gave unnecessary comments. I was playing games on my mobile, as I couldn't bear to listen to a petty conversation.

When they finished eating, they started to wash up and tidy up. I was sitting and playing on my mobile. Emily was going through her sheets of papers when she asked:

"Aren't you going to join them?"

I had enough of her telling me what to do so I snapped:

"Do I have to?"

"No, you don't have to, but that would be nice to help them to tidy up after dinner."

"I haven't eaten your pizza. As I said before, I don't eat meat and I don't eat gluten, which the pizza base contains …"

She cut me in the middle of the sentence:

"Oh, I thought that you do eat bread, unless we have a little mouse."

"Teya eats bread."

"She does. But a loaf of bread lasts Teya one week, nowadays a loaf of bread lasts one day. Obviously some little mouse chews on it. Same with the prosciutto - half a kilo in one day. Usually, it lasts a week or two."

"Emily looks like you are not happy that I am here."

"That's not true. I am not happy if you don't tidy up! That's all."

"But I am not your slave. It is your house; you have to do that. When we have guests, it is in our culture to tidy up after them. We never tell our guests they are messy. It is so rude."

"Oh, really? Is it rude? What then do you tell your guests if they create a mess?"

"Nothing! In our culture we are always polite, we say nothing and put up with the situation, only when the guests go away can we comment within our four walls."

"Oh, give me a break, child!"

"I am not a child, stop treating me like one."

She kept on reading, the girls kept on tidying up the kitchen, and I went into my room and sat on my pile of clothes that I never wanted to put in order just out of spite. I cried, again. Why are people treating me like that? My father treats me like that every time I visit; my granddad's wife treats me like that. Why does no one like me?

I just decided to do something quite memorable before I left this house.

But I hadn't yet had a clear idea what would hurt the most.

I liked Teya, though she could be annoying at times, but still, she was mainly nice and agreeable; but Emily was all about control. And I couldn't stand any kind of control; I was disobedient, free and spiteful.

She was going to learn that lesson well!

It was early morning and pangs of hunger woke me up. I walked into the kitchen, took out some *'prosciutto'*, some cheese, several olives and some olive bread. While I was eating, quietly, like a ghost Emily walked into the kitchen in her silken gown.

"Good morning, sweetie. How come so early?"

I quickly tried to hide my banquet food but she looked at it and said:

"Oh, you do eat prosciutto and cheese … even bread. What a relief, we don't have a little mouse in the house who chews our food at odd hours."

"I am really sorry …" I started to apologise, but she said:

"I am joking with you. You have to learn to joke. And you have to understand that I say what I think. I am not a bad person, I just say what I think. I always opt for the obvious or for the truth. But, truth doesn't harm. It liberates."

"I want to apologise if I was a pain …"

"Not need for it. You were not a pain. It is just that you need to relax and go with a flow. Laugh more. Enjoy life more. Trust life and people."

"OK. How come you got up so early?"

"I do get up early in the morning. Time for my creativity. My Muse is calling."

"Have you finished your novel?"

"I have."

"Would I be able to have a look at it? I am curious and keen."

"Yes. I am going through the first draft. You can read it and give me feedback, you are so well read."

I started to read the manuscript and give her some feedback, my impressions.

After the third week I had to go to visit my uncle whom I never met before. I never had much contact with Dad's family, especially since he left. I knew Granddad, for he visited several times, but Uncle Malachi I never met. Mum told me to give him a call but I refused. If he were anything like Dad, I would never want to meet him. Mum said that I had to visit and stay with them those two remaining weeks. I didn't wanna go anywhere: I liked Teya; I liked the house, the food, Teya's friends and that cool atmosphere. I didn't wanna leave even though I disliked Emily. I wanted to stay another two weeks.

When we came back from the city one late evening, Emily was still awake, sitting on her sofa, reading her papers. Teya kissed her and recounted where we went; she listed each and every bar we visited; she listed each and every person we met and talked to, then I commented, *'Gestapo got its report!'*. Emily asked:

"What did you just say?"

"Oh, nothing."

"What did you just say, Briana?"

"Stop asking me questions!"

I stormed into my room and called my mother telling her about the horrible habits of that nosey woman. I couldn't stand her interrogations.

She followed me and then said:

"Leave those boots out of the room."

"Why?"

"Because this is what we do!"

"But who are you to tell me what to do?"

"I am the owner of this house."

"So?"

"So, you've got to obey my rules."

"And if I don't want to?"

"Well, then you've got to pack your bag a day earlier and go to your uncle's place."

"I don't wanna go there."

"Are you going home then?"

"No! My holiday finishes in two weeks?"

"And where are you planning to stay?"

"At Teya's."

She left the room with a very funny expression. Obviously no one had ever taught her a lesson to keep her nose out of other people's business. She thought she was some sort of ... special person ... or something.

I cried myself to sleep and my shins bled heavily that night. I screamed several times because my dreams are always populated with strange but dangerous creatures that have been chasing me for years.

If I wanted to stay, I had to apologise. I hated apologising to people, especially to her. But I did it. First thing in the morning. But there was no kindness in her eyes. She drank her coffee and read the paper.

"Emily, I am sorry. I am not a rude person, not a bad girl. I just get confused at times. I think you are a great writer and a nice person. I just sometimes can't control my temper."

She just nodded her head without a word. She looked angry. Yes, that was a new expression on her face, but I would say it was anger.

I went out and waited for Teya to finish Uni. After Uni we had lunch and I told her I wanted to stay. She didn't say much, but after a while she asked:

"Wasn't your holiday meant to be a family reunion?"

"*No.*"

"*But?*"

"*Mum talked to Emily and she said I can stay with you two as long as I like.*"

"*Probably, she didn't mean it literally, we knew that you were planning to visit your family after a short stay at our house.*"

"*What I understood was that I could stay.*"

"*You did. You stayed three weeks, now you've got another two with your family.*"

"*They are not really my family. I've never met them.*"

"*That was the purpose—to meet them finally.*"

"*Mum said that I could stay at your place as long as I like.*"

She was probably under Emily's influence. Usually, she is much nicer. I had the impression that she wanted me to go, too. I just wanted to stay longer. I wanted to read the manuscript, wanted to go out with them and have dinner in a nice restaurant. Wanted to visit Teya's Aunt Inna again. She was kind. The kindest of all of them. She behaved like a real lady; she kept a proper distance and had a soft voice. She wasn't bossy at all. She looked like a noble woman who would never dare to say what she thought. If only Emily was more like her, I could then possibly extend my stay. I wouldn't in that case be pushed to think hard how to get even.

When we walked in, she said in the most annoying voice, '*Girls, wash your hands there's some pasta Bolognese just ready.*'

"*Mum, Bella doesn't eat pasta or meat.*"

"*Oh, don't you worry, she'll manage. It is fresh and yummy. Get some parmigiano out of the fridge and enjoy it.*"

I refused to eat. I told them that I was vegan and gluten intolerant. She pretended that she didn't know that. I just looked at Teya and shrugged my shoulders, then I took an apple and Emily said:

189

"First thing—wash your hands!"

"Do I have to?"

"Yes!"

"But, why?"

"You haven't come here to me to learn that lesson. You should have learnt it seventeen years ago. Now go, wash your hands and come back."

Later that evening Emily put her papers in a plastic folder, next to the sofa. She said:

"Did you call your uncle?"

"I will, tomorrow."

"Can you call him today?"

"Why today?"

"Because you said that yesterday. Please, call him now and make arrangements with him."

"Do I have to?"

"Yes, Bella. Please call him now."

"But I don't even know him."

She insisted, so I called him. He knew I was in Sydney because Mum had e-mailed him. He said that he wasn't prepared to take me so quickly. He said he needed some time, a few days. Emily talked to him. She said:

"I have to travel tomorrow late afternoon. Please organise something otherwise the girl has to go back earlier."

"I don't wanna go! It is my well earned holiday and I paid a lot of money for the plane ticket!"

After a while he agreed I could come. He said that my mother told him I might visit for a day or two. I knew that but said nothing.

It looked to me that this woman didn't do anything else but sit on her sofa and write or read her writings. We couldn't get rid of her. I couldn't stand seeing her sitting there any longer.

Early in the morning she was already there as if she had never left.

Teya made pancakes. I ate with her.

"Aren't you gluten intolerant?"

"Oh, stop it!" said I, and she said, *'You don't have to be rude'*, to which I replied:

"Your mother put me under so much stress now. I have to go to some people that I have never met. And judging by my dad, they aren't the brightest bunch."

Emily made me call my uncle on that day and ask what time he was coming to pick me up. She gave him the address. Then she said:

"OK, now you get ready."

"Do I have to, like, right now?"

"Yes, please."

"Can't I do it in half an hour?"

"Yes, you can Bella, but be ready by two o'clock."

"Yes, commander!"

Teya hung her head and said nothing.

It was Saturday; she said she was travelling somewhere. I never believed her story. She just wanted to get rid of me, toss me as if I were hot coal into the unwelcoming hands of my uncle.

Reluctantly, I packed my bags, took some things that belonged to Teya, anyway she had more than one person would need in her entire life: why would someone need four pairs of sunglasses? Or six or seven purses? She would never even need it, let alone notice some were missing.

When I packed up and *'tidied up'*, as she would say, I came to the lounge room. There was no one. Her famous leather sofa was bare. Only her famous manuscript in the red plastic folder was next to the sofa.

I walked there, collected it and put it into my bag.

When I walked out of the house, they were sitting in the sun. At the little marble table, in the middle of the garden, they were talking in the language I didn't understand—how rude!

I said I wouldn't wait in the house but on the road. Teya said she'd keep me company here in the garden and Emily went into the house. Shortly after that she called me in.

She is notorious for interrogations. She asked:

"Bella, did you see my manuscript?"

"No!"

"Are you sure?"

I felt panic in her voice and silky amenity in my pit.

"I am sure!"

"Teya! Come here!" She continued with her interrogation:

"Did you see … did you move my manuscript? It was next to the sofa."

"No, Mum, why?"

"It isn't there!"

"Can't be!"

"Well, can't be, but it isn't there. Listen, Bella, I'll ask you once again, think carefully—have you taken my manuscript?"

"No! Why would I?"

"I have no answer to that question! All I know is that the manuscript is missing and this is not an Agatha Christy plot. It can't be any simpler: we were three in the house. I haven't moved it, my daughter never, listen to me: never lies, so when she said that she didn't move it, I believe her. The only person that remains is you. Have you taken it?"

"No!" I said angrily, but she locked the entrance door. She said:

"Do you understand that this would be a crime if I prove you have taken it. I can't force you to admit it, nor do I have the authority to do that. But I shall not let you out of the house until you hand it back. Or, we can call police and they will search through your bags, who knows what else we might find there that doesn't belong to you."

Instead of the police, she rang her auntie saying:

"Please, Inna, come over here. I have here a very tricky situation and I'd like someone to witness it."

Then I broke and started to cry.

This woman wouldn't let go, she was like a police interrogator, she kept me locked until her aunt came and told her the story, and then in her sternest voice she said:

"Call your mother now! Right now! Call her!"

And I did.

Fourth Story:
Teya
(Sydney, July 2014)

One can't just take and take without giving anything in return. Simple gifts are only signs of kindness and a warm heart.

Bella screams and argues at night, I rush into my music room where Mum brought a sofa for her. But she is fast asleep. In deep slumber. She talks and gesticulates vigorously. When I ask her in the morning if she had a nightmare, she says *'probably'* and she also says that she never remembers what the dream was about, the only thing she remembers is the constant presence of a faceless man who chases her. I am worried. I am also worried because she harms herself. Mum said that she is worried, too. Mum worries that she might harm me in her sleep, as she keeps on repeating how she bitterly bit me when she was a child.

Lex is like my sister. We met when we were little girls and formed a bond which only grew stronger each passing year. She has that mellow heart and laughter like a trillion harps playing. She sees only the good in people. She noticed Bella's sudden mood changes.

Mum is nervous. I rarely see my mother nervous. She is often in good spirits, even when she writes disturbing stories. She always comments, *'It is just a story.'* I don't like seeing her nervous or upset, so I said to Bella:

"All Mum wants from us is to tidy up our rooms, clothes or the table after we eat."

Lex needs not to be told. She knows what would be right, but Bella said:

"You are not her slave, neither am I."

When I said that to Lex she was so angry she wanted to confront her. I said, *'Don't!'*

Bella thinks that everyone is impressed with her accent; she said:

"Wherever I go everyone asks 'Are you British?'. You Australians have such a funny accent. Everyone tells me 'You sound so posh'. Yes, we are posh."

I said, *'Whatever."*

One day, Mum went out and was looking for her shawl. It was her favourite; Aunt Lily gave it to her. Aunt Lily always gave best gifts. It was a Louis Vuitton shawl made of the softest cashmere. After unsuccessful attempts to find it, she stormed out saying:

"It couldn't simply disappear into thin air, it was on my side chair yesterday evening."

When I told Bella that Mum couldn't find her shawl, she said:

"Why is she making so much fuss about it? It is just a shawl."

I got worn out. My friends are polite but I see that they struggle to put up with her remarks, especially when she is so proud to be *British*.

Actually, I do that because of Mum. But on the other hand we all struggle. She doesn't wanna give anything, like her good will to help about little things like Lex does, who feels as part of the family. Bella always shrugs her shoulders or makes remarks that I can't fully understand as she talks quietly to herself.

I want my bedroom and my music room back. I want my quiet life back. She doesn't wanna call her uncle. She told me she doesn't want to see him.

Mum has to go to Melbourne for a couple of days. She told me she doesn't want Bella to stay in the house whilst she is away. Mum doesn't feel comfortable any longer: things have been displaced, some items are missing and she talks back to Mum.

Mae asked Mum if she could stay with us for a week, and Mum said, *'She is more then welcome to stay as long as she likes.'* We knew she was coming to visit her uncle for five weeks, which by this time was questionable. When Mum uttered that phrase, *'as long as she likes'*, what she really meant was, *'Yes, a week, and even two if she wanted to extend her stay.'*

Mum said, *'I am leaving for a few days, you'd better call your uncle and make arrangements.'*

"I'll stay with Teya."

A firm, *'No!'* was Mum's response.

Mum is kind, a very kind woman, but when she has enough she has enough. I knew she would express her thoughts; she would take a stand.

When Bella packed her bags and waited for her uncle to come, Mum called me:

"Teya! Did you see or move my manuscript?"

There were always just the two of us—my mother and me.

There were only two things that she would give her life for: me, and her books. I felt as if a big storm was approaching and I wanted to hide in

195

the basement. I knew that expression on my mother's face: saw it only a few times but knew that she was shattered!

It was different to discover that the manuscript was missing than the Louis Vuitton shawl. My knees trembled. I didn't want to believe such an assumption!

Mum called Aunt Inna. She just said:

"Come over, right now. My manuscript is missing."

Our Aunt Inna is full of grace: she walks slowly and talks always lucidly. When Bella started to cry I ran out into garden. I couldn't believe it; I refused to believe it.

When Bella took the manuscript out and handed it to Aunt Inna, Mum fell on the chair and buried her head into her hands. I came and hugged her. Bella cried and Aunt Inna was comforting her:

"Everyone makes mistakes!"

"I am not a bad girl! I am not a bad person!" Bella kept on repeating.

"Why did you do that?" asked Mum when she calmed down a bit.

"I don't know, but I am not a bad person!" she kept on repeating and sobbing. Aunt Inna brought her a glass of water and kept on talking kindly to her. I mostly worried about Mum, I know, particularly in this novel she poured out her heart and soul. It took a lot out of her and I witnessed how exhausted she was on particular days whilst trying to finish it.

"Call your mother! Right now!"

Mum talked to Mae.

Mae said:

"I can't believe this story, Emily. Why would she do that?"

"You ask her, I don't have a clue. Ask her!"

"That's your part of the story, Emily. Every story has to be told from the perspective of the other protagonist. I have to hear Bella's story as I don't believe it to be true."

196

Aunt Inna stayed at ours until Bella's uncle called. He came two hours later than he promised to come.

Aunt Inna accompanied her to the street.

She looked at me and asked:

"Teya, are we going to stay friends?"

I just smiled gently.

"Teya, you are my best friend, say we'll stay friends."

I said:

"I hope, Bella, that this would be a good lesson for you. I wish you all the best!"

On the top step to the street, she turned her head once again and said:

"I am so sorry!"

I went back into our house to hug my mother and tell her that all is over. She was crying but managed to say:

"Sit next to me, Sunshine."

Dining with Felix Farenheith

Well, it isn't easy for me to talk about it. Come to think of it, it isn't easy for any woman to begin a discussion on this topic.

But to make myself clear right away—I've turned forty. Yes indeed, slowly and cautiously and without crumpling.

This is the tentative period in life when you think you can successfully hide your wrinkles, if possible with make-up or, better yet, with diffused lighting, with the play of shadows. Dimmed rooms are good, desirable; twilight is pleasant, full of support and understanding.

The lines impressed around my mouth give me an austere expression and this upsets me. The crow's feet around my eyes can still be hidden if I don't smile or if I fix my gaze on one object only. I wear dark glasses. Strong light wrinkles my forehead and nose. No, no, I can't bear the idea of a plastic doll.

There is this Kikki, and it's simply nauseous to look at her eyes or mouth. True, she is much older than I am and certainly far more superficial. To get the picture, I am well read and well educated, while she married a rich man. Her look is as cold as the eyes of the dead fish on her painter's canvas. Her mouth looks like a sewed-on tiny sausage, a hotdog; when she talks, words awkwardly fall from her glossy lips. It is obvious that this mouth is not a part of her, and she lacks the skill to use it.

However, one thing was beneficial: In light of the impression of inept use of the mouth, the truth of actually not knowing how to use words was concealed. But the sausage inadequately hides that truth; her eyes are unfurled wide like an open umbrella. Full of astonishment! You know, the kind of inner astonishment that even manages to peep through such wide-open eyes: *What am I doing?*

Now that's a question I've always been afraid of. You know, those are years when one draws a line. That line can be a thin one, even though it harshly severs the desire of youth and the reality written in the corners of our lips.

I don't like the wrinkles around my mouth. In fact they are astringent and there is no way to hide them. As if the truth that was never uttered left its trace around my lips, like punishment for *that* silence ... yes, yes, years ago ...

Oh, change the subject!

***

I didn't want to have children.

The phone is ringing, just a moment.

Ah, Felix Farenheith.

He wants me to have lunch with him tomorrow.

I have already rejected him three times. *Why did I?* I no longer go out to lunches. Especially not during the summer. Only suppers in some dim ambiance.

A child destroys one's figure, makes the breasts flabby.

Or, is there some other reason?

My master's degree!

Frankly, I was torn between my intellect and ambitions that were in conflict with my interest in maintaining a gorgeous appearance.

And was I pretty!

I was exceedingly beautiful.

You know, when I walked out into the streets, I'd cause traffic jams. Cars honked, wolf whistles came from all sides, now and then a sassy comment ... but I would just toss back my lion-like mane of blond hair, lifted my head and nose high into the air and went on, disregarding the commotion. It was as if it was not I. Yes, in fact I've always had two personas living in me, though not in utter harmony.

It often happens that I see my own name in newspapers, that I drink coffee with colleagues, my tastes satisfied with literary themes, European classics of the eighteenth and nineteenth centuries, and I quote Shakespeare with ease, or in a jocular or mocking tone serve Machiavelli to colleagues *'wiser'* than myself.

This alter ego is able to share with me the pleasure of the above mentioned; yes, she is the persona that brings a stop to traffic in the street; that throws back her *'superfluous brain'* together with her lion-like mane. Sometimes I feel that the one with the lion-like mane is precisely the one who discredits me in my own eyes, yet on the other hand I feel quite the contrary, that without her things would be exceedingly boring, certainly there'd be a lack of fun … and I wonder, with the disappearance of fun, do these lines become impressed too deep?

I don't know, but the process of aging can't be stopped and intellect is useless in this respect! What good do I have from all the books I've read in the domains of philosophy, medicine, Zen Buddhism! *Does this knowledge free me?*

I see myself in the mirror and know that it is no longer the image that makes me happy!

Don't get me wrong; I am not superficial. Therefore, take what I say as my most intimate admission. Something that hardly anyone is ready to admit.

I've written several books. I defend myself by saying that they are my children. But my books do not belong to me, save that they still carry my name. They sold like hot cookies and were dissected, analysed, some of them adopted; my thoughts were dispersed to all four sides of the world, placed into libraries to gather dust, sent off into history. I realise that they no longer belong to me, but are a common good. And when I do happen to see my name on them, I wonder why it is there.

I never wanted a pet, dog or a cat; I don't have many friends and in some kind of egoistic way I am a self-satisfied and self-sufficient person. I can tolerate somebody an hour a day or somewhat longer by phone, since when I talk over the phone, I'm totally absent and toy with my own thoughts.

Lately, I've really become disgusted with the two vertical lines and sharp wrinkles at the corners of my lips that have endowed me with a wholly new physiognomy.

It isn't me any more!

They even changed my thoughts, so much so that I've begun to believe that thoughts have an absolute connection with my physiognomy. And my style of writing, like my wrinkles, is becoming sharp and cynical.

Hold on, I have to answer the phone. I don't suppose it is Felix Farenheith.

It is!

He is now calling me out to supper.

I agreed under the condition that it does not take more than an hour.

He tells me that I am a woman of principle who is disinclined to compromise. Even though he actually thinks I am the perfect woman. He always admired my intelligence and my physical appearance saying that I was a masterpiece. He is utterly unaware of my numerous shortcomings. He is unaware of my insecurity. So I am at a loss, indeed, when he tells me that in my forties I am more attractive and interesting than ever. Or could it simply be his ungainly way of comforting me?

You see, only recently have I grasped that I am susceptible to erosion and corrosion. That I am, indeed, mortal. That my clock is ticking away as it leaps towards old age.

I would like to write several more essays or novels, even though I am aware that that will not defend me from old age and deterioration. It will only give my envious critics more material to mutilate my thoughts by giving them totally contrary meanings. They love to interpret ideas of others, persuading readers that they are quite assured in what authors want to say, how they feel and how they compose their characters.

They have a regular need to play down the values of others since that is the only way to highlight their own.

But let's return to the lesson on tolerance.

A woman who has read the books with my name on them tells me, *"I fully understand you when you write about freedom of the individual, for instance, take me, I have to go to Frankfurt to wear jeans and tennis shoes, you see, because I am a totally free person there"*, and then with a conspiratorial glance of one that knows her *'importance'* she adds under her breath, *"But nevertheless, in this town I can't allow myself such a liberty!"* Oh, give me a break! She claimed to be a psychologist! Or … could it be that she was in need of one? I might have mixed the facts.

After her brilliant statement I dozed off in the armchair. Dreams detach me from realities in which I don't want to participate, and because of the assertions of such intellectuals, one is prepared to move to another city, country, continent. Open a new chapter of different substance where tolerance spans further than the hackneyed and hollow sentence in which the freedom of the individual is measured by the tightness of jeans.

But what shall *I* wear this evening?

No idea. Felix Farenheith is so solemn, a pure classic. Conversations with him can be quite interesting and pleasant, providing he does not delve into the past.

He proposed to me once when he plucked up the courage. That was a long time ago. Yes, I rejected him. And so down the line, I rejected all of them.

At the time I had just enrolled for my master's degree, and I was doing a lot of writing …

The time and circumstances were wrong.

A few wrong names … but I'd rather not go into the past.

That is why I limit meetings with him to one hour, enough time to order the meal, to ask one another about one's work, family and health.

When he starts to pay me compliments, I know that his time has expired, so I wave to the waiter as I open my purse, or the like.

He sometimes pushes me under the table with his foot, to which I retort by giving him the most repellent face in my arsenal.

This makes Felix Farenheith choke or cough.

Others would narrate this story in a different way.

In the labyrinth of the story it would take other passages.

And as I narrate this, I myself know not whether I am mixing my so-called reality with literary fiction, thus giving myself, and Felix to boot, completely different attributes. Is what I have said simply my own understanding of Felix's perception of me, and is Felix's understanding of me entirely different than my own perception of myself through Felix's perspective?

If we do not believe one another, as was the case, how can one then find the closest answer to this question?

When I deeply and comfortably recline in reminiscences and analyse them, I can imagine, act out, or live through a night out with Felix Farenheith in the same way as I live through every situation in my fiction, and I can take the liberty of identifying myself with any of the characters of my novel and end the evening right here, in my living room, without Felix Farenheith having even an inkling of it.

When he phones tomorrow and asks me what had happened, I will be able to give him countless replies.

For instance:

"Felix, I've already seen that movie", or *"We've already played that"* (even better *"I've already heard that music"*).

Felix Farenheith is regularly befuddled by such replies.

He sometimes musters up the courage and asks, *"Who is speaking from you?"*, and I adore that question, it stimulates my intellect, ignites my imagination, urges me to explore, *"Who is speaking from me?"*

But before I act out the scene of my supper with Felix Farenheith, I must take one more look at myself in the mirror, reproduce my own image, reproduce the wrinkles around my mouth in the mirror, as it absolutely reflects the movement of my lips when they utter, *"Good evening Felix Farenheith ..."* This evening the mirror will reproduce my image, my wrinkles, and perhaps even my sentences.

NB. I've always been in conflict with the mediocrity of the so-called reality and the unreal world of a bizarre romance on whose black and white surface I moved about with ease, like a queen in all permissible directions.

Tartaglia's Bride

When Linda Purcell got married, present guests raised their glasses, raised their voices and cheers came from all directions except from the ceiling. Intimately, she hoped that the voice would come from above to whisper something in her ear. It could have easily been the case that she had already heard this voice, regardless of discarding and burying it a few months ago deep down in the earth, several meters under her feet, but she still believed that it could come a second time around. But it never comes—a second time.

She wore a white dress. A laced dress that her future mother-in-law picked and bought for her. That happened three weeks prior to her wedding; it was still at the time she used to hear the voice in her ear. It was faint but still present.

She wore ivory sandals with a discrete golden buckle. The heels were high, so high that it made her see the top of the head of her future husband. She saw the bald patch which his hairdresser tried to cover up by combing some hair over the patch, but somehow she managed to see it on the day of her wedding, and seeing it almost provoked the voice in her ear to be louder than the organ filling the church with excitement and anticipation.

She wore a golden tiara on top of her head. Her hair hung lose; dark, yet it had a golden glow reflecting the shine of the tiara down to her waist.

Three days before her wedding her future husband knocked on her door and opened a very expensive box. There was that golden tiara and Linda's jaw dropped, she was lost for words but he just simply smiled. His big dark eyes glowed. There was not even the slightest hint of mystery in Carmine's eyes, just a pleasant glow.

On the day of Linda Purcell's wedding a distracted or weary-looking woman came closer and said:

"*Say—'No! and run away'!*"

Preceded by the woman, another, chubby, woman came holding a crucifix in her left hand. She brought the crucifix to Linda's forehead and said:

"*May God help you, child!*"

As if they were apparitions, they disappeared and were never seen again. Linda thought it could have been the stuffiness that filled the church, the incense or a light fever she experienced the whole day that formed visible beings which never belonged to this world.

When congratulating Linda on her fair day some said plainly, *'Good luck!'*, while others said, *'Good luck!'* with some emphasising the word *'good'*, others emphasising the word *'luck'*.

He returned from his native country in 1985. A year after Linda Purcell was born. There was nothing in her childhood that would differentiate her from the others. She wasn't the brightest child, just an average young girl to whom the simple things had to be explained twice. Her mother used to say if she inherited Aunty Leah's looks, life would be a little bit more generous to her. At least, she would marry a wealthy man, if her temperament never matched her father's. She was a quiet and obedient girl until she hit fifteen. At that time she had enough of her mother's remarks, of her father's anger and of her unambitious friends.

She hadn't had much of an ambition herself but she knew one thing— *If one wanted to succeed in anything, one had to go to New York.* I might correct myself and say, she didn't really know it, she rather heard it phrased in third-rate movies that she watched on lazy Sunday afternoons and engrained several sentences into her brain.

On the day of her wedding Linda Purcell had a feeling that she had lived this moment before. That sudden moment of fatigue, she read somewhere, or rather overheard; some psychologist said that fatigue formed in the pit of the stomach when one has such a premonition.

Standing on her high heels, Linda felt as if she was going to fall onto the church floor and then break down into thousand pieces (as if she was made of glass) which would scatter all over the church, and some might run into the darkest corners of the church to gather dust and the dark secrets that the church had concealed for centuries.

Carmine tightened his grip, he looked at her; he winked. Linda smiled.

There were more awkward moments which were going to occur apart from those brought by the two unknown women who talked to Linda on that day.

When she walked down the aisle, the loud music of the organ carried her to the bench where she left her flowers on the night she met Carmine for the first time. She carried the flowers in a basket on that day offering them to the passers-by; no one bought anything; her feet inflamed, all she got that evening were a few compliments and some, almost vulgar, comments.

She felt like crying that evening. Then a car stopped and the headlight revealed the face of a man standing next to her. He said:

"Give me those flowers."

"Just a bunch?"

"Give me, give me all of it."

"All of it?" she asked in disbelief.

He took the flowers and left, believe it or not, two notes of a hundred dollars. Linda never saw two bills of hundred dollars together.

She got almost drunk that evening. She could buy whatever she wanted.

After that accidental encounter Linda's life took a rather speedy transformation of her dreams.

Two days later the same car stopped and the same man came out of the car. He asked Linda what her name was. Full of anticipation she asked if he wanted to buy flowers. He said, *'Yes'*, gave her, this time, three bills of hundred dollars and left without taking the flowers.

She waited only several hours to see the car again, and the man who walked out wasn't the same man. He said:

"Carmine wants to invite you for dinner."

Without any further explanation he held her by the upper arm and walked bewildered Linda into a limousine.

She felt an almost physical sense of humiliation as she sat there without a word.

Even though Linda Purcell wasn't the brightest child, she could always rely on her intuition which led her to often non-regrettable decisions. She could hear that voice which led her into the direction she wanted to be led. After a while she only relied on the voice and never questioned it.

When she came to New York the voice got weaker, but it still was present when she needed it the most. New York was a noisy place where she felt quite comfortable only when tipsy. When tipsy she could do anything: several times she stole some unimportant items, for she never had the guts to steal something that might land her in jail. She stole cosmetics, fine hosiery on a few occasions, chocolate bars regularly and on another occasion she stole a book that she never managed to read.

When he said his name was Carmine, Linda repeated, *"Carmine?"*

"Yeah, an Italian name."

"Italian?"

"Yes, I was born in Italy, but grew up in New York."

"You were born in Italy?"

"Why? What is so strange? People pop out in any place in the world. It just so happened that I popped out in some Italian village. Actually it isn't a village, it is a small town, but there is exactly the same number of people there as in this street tonight."

When Linda met Carmine's mother, she said:

"Ma perché una Americana?"

Linda smiled not knowing what to say. Carmine said:

"Ma, you got to accept it if you wanna see me. I love you, Ma, but this is the right girl for me."

Carmine never even proposed properly. He just kept on buying presents. Expensive, luxurious presents. Everything: jewels, clothes, even a car.

That was a life Linda's mother was hoping she might have when she said *'If she were lucky to fetch a wealthy man due to her resemblance to Aunty Leah'.*

He didn't even ask her if she wanted to move in. He paid the last rent and that was the last time Linda saw her belongings which were later taken by the owner or given to the poor. There was everything that she might need in the house waiting for her.

Was that a dream? Linda wondered often.

There were several more events that I perhaps should record but at the time of such happenings Linda had chosen not to see or hear any fragments of such stories.

***

On the day of her wedding, Linda Purcell heard Carmine's surname for the first time. That was going to be her surname too.

209

It was a surname too difficult to pronounce for a simple American woman: Tartaglia.

Carmine Tartaglia.

It didn't sound familiar at all. Not to Linda Purcell. She was going to be Linda Tartaglia. She struggled to pronounce it, *Tartaglia*, in her head when the priest voiced it in this sentence:

"We are gathered here today in the face of this company, to join together Carmine Giancarlo Tartaglia and Linda Margaret Purcell ..."

It was a hazy moment.

When the priest asked:

"Linda Margaret Purcell, do you take Carmine Giancarlo Tartaglia to be your lawful husband to live in the holy estate of matrimony? Will you love, honour, comfort and cherish him from this day forward forsaking all others, keeping only onto him for as long as you both shall live?"

"I do."

Someone behind Linda said:

"She looks like his youngest daughter."

"Late youngest daughter."

"No!"

"Yes! God bless! Last year when she went all by herself to pick up her parcel."

"Was it in the parcel?"

"Shush now, I'll tell you later."

After that Linda Tartaglia couldn't hear the rumours any more; on the day of her wedding, after they said, *'I do'*, everyone spoke Italian.

She was luckier than Aunty Leah.

She just turned eighteen and she had it all.

Who Whispers
Wisdom to Beatrix C

We bought the tickets on a rainy day. I saw the reflection of Papa's face in the bigger raindrops; I heard his gentle words bouncing back when the raindrops hit the roof. Papa passed away but we still talked to him as if he was still seated in his favourite armchair. We talked about regular things, nothing special as if one would in honour of such a dignified man. We just informed him of usual happenings, even when it was about food he liked the best. For instance, Mamma would say: *"You know, Papa, your favourite soup was a bit too salty today, I just couldn't stop retelling you the story about Maggy's new mischief, I was carried away, then simply put in too much salt."*

Terence would say:

"Papa, the stock market has fallen today and I've lost a substantial sum of money." He would frown, he only talked to Papa when distressed or about negative topics, perhaps hoping that Papa could fix it somehow.

I talked to Papa quietly and no one knew I conversed with him except on the rare occasions when I really needed him so badly and couldn't care less if I was going to be heard or judged.

But when he passed away, a miracle happened to Bea and her writing. I am going to talk about that. Bea was the one who warned us, *"Do not get your tickets on a rainy day."* It was just a pure coincidence (or was it?) that she named her story exactly with such a title:

We Bought the Tickets on a Rainy Day.

There were three children in our household: I was the first-born: rather quiet, rather obedient, tidy and organised child and Papa believed that I might, or certainly should, make a good lawyer one day, thus some years latter I graduated from a Law School.

Then two years later, Terence was born. He was such a beautiful baby-boy that the *'birds stopped singing out of astonishment and of sweet pain when they saw his face'*, as Bea put it into words many years after. He was tall and athletic as a youngster and was keen to make lots of money. Many of his ideas Papa often disliked, especially when he expressed an interest in the stock market, Papa said, *"It is equal to gambling. That would be dishonestly earned money."* It was expected more from Terence than from me to become a lawyer so that he could take over Papa's practice. Even though he made himself a career and name in the world of law and order, his heart firmly stayed in the stock market, therefore he would gamble, make money, lose money and never talk about it with Papa. Only when Papa passed away, Terence started to tell him about his passion and obsession, assuming somewhere, deep down, that there was no need to hide the affairs of the world to the deceased.

When Bea was born (I clearly remember the day when they brought her home as I was five years old and disliked her at once!), that day wasn't marked with anything special. Mamma only said: *"Thomas Hardy was born on this day in 1840".* Thomas Hardy was Mamma's favourite author, and when I tried to read his stories I wondered why Mamma liked him that much: *Was it because of his stories, or was she, later, in some silly way proud that her youngest daughter was born on the same day as such a distinguished man?*

No one had any plans for Bea. She was as free as a bird. She was, indeed, a spoilt little brat, doing things that I was never allowed to do. She could stay late at a much younger age than I ever could when I was in the last year of university; she could have a small glass of Papa's favourite red wine at the age of seven—incredible! Papa would laugh and say, *"Let her taste it!"*

Taste it!

Bea effortlessly wore fancy short dresses and skirts, extravagant stockings, hats and make up and Papa would say, *"Bea knows how to enjoy her life."*

I would never even try any of those things as Papa always believed I was a responsible, clever and serious young woman. I was considered to be a woman at the age of fifteen while Bea was considered to be a child still in her early thirties.

But, I loved free-spirited Bea in my own way! I can't say that I understood Bea, but I loved her even though it was not apparent from our unusual relationship.

Bea changed several university courses but never completed the task; she never held a job longer than a few months, she never wanted a *'serious relationship'*, ran away from men that could potentially love her, and crumpled their hearts so easily as if they were cut out of soft cardboard.

The thing is: We think we know people we grow up with in the same house, but we rarely do.

When Bea was twenty she published a book. No one knew that. I came into a bookshop and found a book written by an author with the same surname as mine. Curiosity took the better of me - I took it in my hands and learned that the author's name was the same as my little sister's.

There was no author's biography, so I wondered who the author might be. I bought it and brought it home. The next day I couldn't find it. I asked Bea had she found the book I purchased yesterday, but she shook her head right and left. I asked Mamma, I asked Terence; they knew nothing about it. I asked Papa and he said with a little peculiar smile on his face, *"Come in"* and I entered his study. In his velvety and quiet voice he asked:

"Can you keep a secret?"

That was how I learned that my little sister was an author. I learned a year after that she had won some major literary award when she was only seventeen. She went under a pen name and lied about her age.

After she published a few more books by the age of twenty-five, I had to take care of her, for she attracted a lot of envy not only from her peers, but random people would say all sorts of things out of pure malice and jealousy. She could put up with lies and all; unnecessarily but carefully targeted, poisonous arrows shot into her direction. The most hurtful, at that stage, for her was the deliberate undermining of her work. She didn't win the awards because of *'her Papa'*, nor because she was *'pretty'*, nor because she was *'pushy or rude'*.

I stepped in; Terence would have too, but was too preoccupied with making money. Later we had learned the real reason behind his obsession with money. He met a woman and temporarily lost his mind. Her disease of craving for material things infected him, as she really never knew what was it that mattered in a life of a good, honest human being. She took after her mother Lelia, who was known to be a monstrous chaser after other people's money. Not that they were poor, but she had two daughters she wanted to marry into *'wealth and prestige'*, dreaming some dreams that were not relevant any more; acting some roles that were pure science fiction.

When Papa passed away, on the second day Bea stopped crying. Some never-seen-before smile started permanently to twinkle in the corner of her lips. Unearthly peace came over her and she appeared as if she couldn't care less about the visible world.

Her writing took a different course. Her words began to radiate a fragrance. It smelled of frankincense or of roses; it resembled the words which were carried from faraway shores where people still believed in reincarnation, in a multitude of gods and goddesses; where more value was placed on human life than on money; where they believed that the human soul was a real, permanent and ever-present force. She was the only one who really talked to Papa, as he would come into her dreams from where he advised and governed all of us. He told Terence to let go of Lelia's tricks and give money to charity: we were all astonished by the ease of Terence's letting go. Who would ever have said that Terence would give money to charities; who would ever have guessed that Terence would face the truth about the emptiness of materialism? He gave some of his belongings to the poorest and walked out of Lelia's daughter's cell, tailored to suffocate the life force out of him.

Papa would appear on Bea's pages talking to Mamma, telling stories that were forgotten before he dusted them out and brought them into the light of her consciousness, the stories which contained wisdom and strengthened Mamma's soul.

One day Bea wrote the story, *We Bought the Tickets on a Rainy Day.*

It was a day after we bought the tickets. It was a rainy, cold day. That day never resembled anything that would awake memories about Papa. It was as if the day was taken out of some story which never belonged to our family, just a random page that would not have a happy ending. I felt uncomfortable believing that such a feeling came from the dampness of the day itself. Mamma was restless but she started packing the bags and organising the house. Terence telephoned and offered help but Mamma said she had so much time on her hands, wanting him to concentrate on his work.

No one heard from Bea for three days.

Then she delivered the story.

When Mamma read the story, she called me. We stopped regarding Bea's stories as *'plain weirdness'* even when they appeared to be weird reading. There were layers in her stories that one had to discover going each time deeper into the story.

Mamma said when I finished reading:

"What does it mean - 'Do not get your tickets on a rainy day.'?"

"I think we have to take it literally."

"We have purchased the tickets already ... I think she is still grieving ... it is nothing else but pure grief."

"But, Mamma, we learned that lesson. It might be a grief partly, but there is a strong warning coming across. Let's see what Terence has to say."

Terence said:

"Cancel the flight!"

"That would be more than five thousand dollars ..."

"... or three saved lives ..."

"What about Aunt Nadine?"

No one answered that question.

The flight wasn't cancelled. I slept at Mama's place. Everything reminded me of Papa; it still brought tears to the edges of my eyelashes. After she delivered the story we didn't hear from Bea. No one knew where she was. Mamma worried, she never knew how to handle her, as that was Papa's delightful and successful duty.

I woke up from a dreamless sleep. The house was full of light. The sun was high up. Strange, I never wake up that late.

Terence's messages on my mobile.

Mamma's still asleep.

Unusual morning.

Flight!

Did we miss our flight!?

I ran into Mamma's room. Next to her bed I found Bea kneeling. She was singing quietly and rocking her body. Mamma looked like a chubby child fast asleep after a fairytale was read to her. Chills froze my body. Bea was crying quietly, not singing.

"Mamma! Mamma!" I cried out.

Bea turned her serene face and smiled.

Mamma opened her eyes and said:

"Bea, when did you come?"

"Last evening."

"Where is Terence?"

He just entered Mamma's bedroom in haste, and said:

"Why no one answered? Hurry up! We'll miss the flight!"

"You already have." Said Bea still smiling.

That afternoon we heard on the evening news that the plane was shot down. Why did the plane fly over the war zone? No one had the answer.

Maybe only Papa and Bea did.

Bea said nothing; collected, mysterious and serene, she kept on writing her stories. And we kept on reading each and every one of them: once, twice and three times, always trying to apply the wisdom of Bea's whispers in our daily life.

Milan Cubrilo's Smile

When my dear father passed away, it was the saddest day. I had all sorts of conflicting emotions, but deep sadness sat at the core of my soul and started to spill its aroma in and around my being as if it couldn't wait any longer to get a hold of me.

If I set aside the strongest emotion, utter sadness, which set in determined to settle for many years to come, the second strongest emotion was pride. I was proud to be his daughter.

My mother inconsolably cried and my, older, only seemingly stronger sister cried, even my brother, who was never seen publicly crying, cried *'like a little lost boy'*, as my daughter put it, running away into the garden urged to escape the reality and the heaviness of his tears. She has always been fond of my brother; he was a father figure for her: a tall, strong minded man who knew the answer to many questions.

But the irreparable pain in my Mum's soul was obvious when she said, *'Now days will be colder and nights longer; food will be tasteless and words will lose their real meaning."*

I'll talk about pride a little bit later as I am aiming, for the sake of my own soul, to narrate the story from some sort of beginning, or aiming for some sort of closure or just, purely, indulging myself egotistically in my pain.

That morning, a very unusual dream awakened me, which I am not willing to retell right now as it is something I consider to belong only to me. But, the flavour of the dream stayed with me whilst I was preparing my breakfast, while eating it and driving to work a little bit later. I was preparing the morning news, looking for some other interesting feature-stories and often my mind went back to review the dream I had. I said it was an unusual dream, but dreams are often more than usual... Somehow, I thought that there should be some meaning attached to it; something that would change my day … for the better, for sure.

I live with my daughter, a beautiful dark-haired young girl that, as a rule, everyone at first glance assumes is my sisters' child. My sister has dark hair and big dark eyes and I always wanted her almond-shaped warm eyes, whilst she thought that I was blessed with our mum's fair, soft looks. My daughter took after my sister instead, and that made me, some years ago, truly happy, for in some way my wish was granted. My daughter never calls when I am in the studio running the program, no matter what.

I came home and found her with moist eyes, sitting with her guitar. She said:

"Sit next to me, mummy, I want to tell you something."

I sat attentively assuming that she might have had one of those little things to share… like, someone who told her would ring has forgotten it, or she was again anxious to go to live in Switzerland for an entire year… or, something else. She hugged me and said:

"Mummy, your daddy passed away."

I just felt a terrible, terrible, unfriendly, violent and inevitable pain grabbed me somewhere … or everywhere: by my shoulders, by my head and hair, pulled me down and inward, pushed me into different directions, the sky grew dark, my heart grew dark and weak, and my eyes stopped seeing light, and my throat started to squeeze the life out of me. She held me tight, I don't remember for how long. Once again, she held—me.

He was gone without warning. He said nothing; had a shower before dinner and sat in his favourite armchair waiting to be called when dinner was ready. But he never made it to the dining room.

Was there anyone to blame? For I wanted to blame someone … like, poor government or disinterested doctors, or some sort of entity who was so malevolent, on the constant lookout to harm.

But there was no one to blame. We have our days given in the right order and numbered on each and every page. His book was due to be closed.

It was a beautifully, neatly written book. With elegance and grace, with the right amount of laughter and the strong sense of justice.

I wanted to tell him that my latest novel was dedicated to him and the famous scientist Nikola Tesla, to their origins and shared family background. I wanted to tell him that he was a good man, the father I wanted to have… I wanted to thank him for all the right things he taught me, or showed me, and I wanted him to know how proud of him I was.

Above all I wanted to tell him how much I loved him.

But I couldn't.

Awareness grew: I would never be able to express it any more.

In the chorus of crying people I started to reflect on those days and emotions that made me smile, which made me proud.

Many people came and sent cards, flowers and words via different avenues. Each and every word was exactly the same as if they were tailored in the same beautiful-word-factory. Words can't bring him back, neither change my memories, but they confirmed what I knew all my life: he was a kind, cultured, good-hearted and just man.

I was wondering, *'Is it ever possible to fill the void?'*

Why did I think he was immortal? Or, that his life would be extended to suit my needs? Mum told me that he was *'very quiet last week'*. He was a quiet man, but ever present. Mum said *'his quietness required solitude.'*

I still didn't grasp the meaning of such a need. Am I to blame? If I had only understood those little signs! What would have happened then?

While everyone cried, my train of thought went down the lane and we walked all the paths we walked before, once again: I saw myself as a six-year-old holding his hand, walking down to the beach, carrying a little back-pack and a rubber toy, my golden locks bouncing while I was skipping and asking him questions to which he would comment, *'How on earth do you come up with such questions?'*

"*Because I am clever.*"

That would make him laugh. Holding hands, we walked right to the moment when he accompanied me, last time, to the airport. I hugged him and said:

"*Look after yourself and see you next year.*"

He shrugged his shoulders saying:

"*Hopefully. One year is a long time at my age.*"

"*What are you talking about?!*"

"*Just being realistic.*"

"*Being a pain, now that I'm leaving.*"

He hugged me and said:

"*I am being silly. See you next year... but hurry up.*"

When I cried again, I cried because *'why he couldn't wait another three months.'*

What am I going to do in those three months?

Age has nothing to do with it; we grieve the absence of someone we deeply loved. The void: the hole which swallows everything as it is hungry for feelings, yet it cannot be satisfied.

Time: the biggest healer. The reorganising of the family. New roles. A stronger bond.

On the morning my father passed away, I didn't know that I was going to feel like a little lost girl for a while. I had that peculiar dream, the symbolism that I could not figure out what it might represent.

He bought me a brand new car and I wrecked it. Once, twice, then the third time, in my dream.

Once he told me:

"To lead a good life the best driver is needed. Take that steering wheel and own it, take the curves with caution, leave enough space between, don't break suddenly or when it isn't needed."

When everyone sobbed I looked at my daughter. That was the first time I saw him in her colours, in her fine jaw-line and those smooth movements.

And this is the circle. It could be that my daughter's wish for *'mummy's blue eyes'* will be granted when her daughter sees the world and opens her eyes for the first time. I will live through my granddaughter as my dad's life goes on together with ours: pictures and stories, gestures and colours, unique wording and expressions, a certain way of doing things…

On the day when my dear father passed away, something invisibly but drastically changed. That book was closed, but I opened a new chapter.

When I dedicate my latest novel to my father, together with the protagonists on its pages, it will give him some sort of immortality.

I just wanted to say again how much I loved him, and that conflicting emotions can go hand in hand. While deep sadness is nestling in my chest, pride is pushing it gently away, taking more and more room in the silent but determined attempt to rule this kingdom wisely.

... and there, in the near distance, I see him with the Mona Lisa smile on his gentle face ... approving my story.

Visit us at: www.speakingvolumes.us

Visit us at: www.speakingvolumes.us